Louis J. Dupré

**Fagots from the Camp Fire**

Louis J. Dupré

**Fagots from the Camp Fire**

ISBN/EAN: 9783337255329

Printed in Europe, USA, Canada, Australia, Japan

Cover: Foto ©Andreas Hilbeck / pixelio.de

More available books at **www.hansebooks.com**

# FAGOTS

FROM THE

# CAMP FIRE.

---

BY "THE NEWSPAPER MAN."

---

WASHINGTON, D. C.:
EMILY THORNTON CHARLES & CO., PUBLISHERS.
1881.

# INTRODUCTION.

## EMILY THORNTON CHARLES.

*(Emily Hawthorne.)*

In presenting a new book to the public, it is not necessary that the reasons therefor should be set forth in a long introduction or a tedious explanation. It is appropriate, however, that as the publisher of this unique volume, I point out its strangely original features, which impelled me to take an interest in its success and commend it to the rank and file of our army of brave defenders, as well as to those who wore the gray. Many books have been written since the war, illustrative of battles, teeming with glowing descriptions, and claiming glorious victories won by mighty generals, as in the history of the campaigns written of or given by Grant, Sherman, Johnston, and others. Most of these volumes have been biographical, rather than historical. Of those last emanating from the South, that of Hon. Alex. H. Stephens is, perhaps, the most just and unprejudiced. It gives expression to the views of a statesman, thinker, and scholar. It is therefore on a high plane, and may not, as it should, be thoroughly understood by the masses.

"Fagots from the Camp Fire" is exceptional in its style and scope. Its graphic delineation of the coarsest phases of every-day life; its portrayal of most thrilling incidents within the experience of soldiers and people of the South; how they loved and hated, starved and died; and the tender pathos which marks many pages, although told in the rude language of the uneducated, yet bear that "wondrous touch of nature which makes the whole world kin."

While leaders of opposing armies may not acquiesce in all theories propounded in "Fagots from the Camp Fire," the common people, and especially soldiers who participated in these campaigns, will agree that these extraordinary narratives are as nearly literally true as it is possible to make them, after the lapse of fifteen years.

That "truth is stranger than fiction," is often illustrated in these pages. The chief of scouts, who figures so conspicuously, holds a paper signed by General J. B. Hill, Provost Marshal-General of the Confederate Army, and endorsed "Approved" by General Joseph E. Johnston, now a Member of Congress from Virginia, which states that Captain *** * ******, of Company B, 7th Texas Regiment, Granberry's Brigade, served as a scout in the campaign of Georgia, and that he acquitted himself with great skill, courage, and adroitness. Thus the absolute accuracy of the "Captain's" statements is attested. The distinctive features, therefore, of this publication, are that it gives an insight into modes of life in the Gulf States and in Tennessee, which have never before been portrayed; that the wild adventures and desperate deeds of Southern scouts are authentic incidents and true to the life; and that it is the only book published which, while reciting such adventures, and depicting such scenes, is written. from a Union standpoint. If the author at times advances theories which may not be approved, it must be remembered that these are one man's opinions in relation to subjects about which so few think alike. It must not be forgotten that a truthful and just picture of the country, people, and times could not have been given if the rudest, most ludicrous stories told had been omitted.

Having, as the editor of the *World and Soldier*, at Washington, been the recipient of thousands of letters within the past few months, from veteran soldiers of the Union; knowing how eagerly the "boys in blue" read every scrap of war history, and having received, also, many tributes from Confederate ex-soldiers in praise of the soldier's paper, although it advocates the interests and tells of the deeds of their former foes, I earnestly believe that the time has come when dissension should be buried in the grave of oblivion, and that those who wore the blue should clasp hands with those who wore the gray—

> For both have suffered and both have lost,
> And victory won was at fearful cost.

Therefore, commending this book to the public, we shall follow it, in a few weeks, with "The Soldier's Scrap-Book," a volume of campaign stories for the rank and file, in which many of the war incidents related by common soldiers will appear, with a collection of battle, decoration, and memorial poems. No one can conscientiously conduct a newspaper in the interest of soldiers without a desire to benefit and immortalize those who so bravely endured danger and privation, suffering and death. Such, at least, has been my experience; and—

> My thought keeps guard with funeral tread,
> O'er silent bivouacs of the dead;
> O'er fields where friends and foes have bled;
> O'er hospital and prison bed;
> O'er plains where death his phalanx led;
> My mind is as a lettered tome,
> In which is writ, *they ne'er came home.*

# PREFACE.

I do not tell of great battles, or Generals, or Presidents, or Kings, and therefore, do not write history. I only define the woes, triumphs, modes of thinking, living, fighting, and dying of scouts and common soldiers. I tell of wild adventures, hideous deaths, and marvelous escapes. I recite terrible incidents, others ludicrous, and others most pitiful; and if a narrative be rude in expression, significance, or morals, it is because, if more tasteful, it would not be truthful.

Mankind recks more of Thermopylæ, with its handful of heroes, than of all the fields of filthy carnage on which Persians fell and Greeks triumphed. The Alamo, with its one hundred and sixty-five immortal defenders, leaving no survivors, will be the subject of song and story when Arbela, Cannæ, and Austerlitz are forgotten.

I cannot help thinking, therefore, that with such themes, and when I tell, too, of the woes of women, and of vices that sprang from war, and then of the negro and his relations to victors and vanquished, that this book will excite interest. This will hardly be lessened when, because of my apprehension of his virtues and character, I have chosen, without his consent, to dedicate this modest volume to Colonel W. W. Dudley, the maimed veteran whose devotion to the interests and fame of Union soldiers is only equaled by his generous estimate of the virtues of those who starved and fought for the hapless Confederacy.

THE AUTHOR.

# CONTENTS.

## CHAPTER XXIII.

## CHAPTER XXIV.

## CHAPTER XXV.

## CHAPTER XXVI.

## CHAPTER XXVII.

## CHAPTER XXVIII.

## CHAPTER XXIX.

# CHAPTER I.

After Grant's victory and Bragg's defeat, at Missionary Ridge, in
November, 1863, and after the repulse of Hooker's Corps at Ringgold
Gap by Cleburne's Division, Federal and Confederate armies went
into winter quarters—the former at Chattanooga; the latter, at
Dalton, Georgia. Detachments of Federal forces occupied positions,
at short intervals, from Knoxville to Chattanooga, and thence to
Bridgeport on the Tennessee River. Small bodies of Union soldiers
held each railway station between Bridgeport and Nashville. Over
this road supplies and re-enforcements for Sherman's army of invasion
were drawn, and an army was required for its protection. General
Joseph E. Johnston, commanding the Confederate forces, had his
headquarters at Dalton, thirty-eight miles from Chattanooga, drawing
supplies over the railway from Atlanta. General Pat Cleburne's Division was encamped along the brow of Tunnel Hill, eight or ten miles
north of Dalton. In February, this cantonment was transferred to a
point east of Dalton on the Spring Place Road. Our cavalry held the
line from Kinton's Farm, nine miles, to Varnell's station, on the
railway from Dalton to Cleveland, and thence along the hills to the
Stone Church, just south of Ringgold Gap, thence to Villanow
and to the boundary line of Alabama. The railway distance from
Dalton to Chattanooga is thirty-eight miles. Between these points
occurred many of the strange and extraordinary incidents and adventures of which subsequent pages will tell.

The area of country between the two armies within which scouts
operated, having the average width of fifteen miles, extended from
Knoxville, in East Tennessee, about one hundred and eighty miles,
to Huntsville, Alabama. Generals Sherman and Johnston both
employed large numbers of scouts, but collisions between these were

neither as frequent nor dangerous as between Southern scouts and citizens of the country, the greater number of whom were devoted to the cause for which Sherman fought. The domestic enemies of the South were the more dangerous, not only because more blood-thirsty and murderous than soldiers, but because it was quite impossible to distinguish these bushwhackers, as they were termed in the partisan jargon of the period, from unoffending country clodhoppers.

We contemplated the most innocent-looking and rudely clad country bumpkins with keen suspicion. They recognized us at a glance, and hied away, as soon as our backs were turned, to tell our enemies of the course we had taken and of our probable resting place for the night. After asking directions from such persons, which we never followed, we were accustomed to listen for the firing of signal guns, of which we comprehended the import as well as they to whose ears they were addressed. With the armed bushwhacker we knew how to deal, but were helpless in the presence of those who seemed wholly intent upon the perfection of crops and cultivation of fields and gardens. We soon learned that most innocent-looking farmers underwent sudden and violent transformations of conduct and character. Rustiest, most illiterate and rudely clad plowmen became even demoniacal in blood-thirstiness, and in this were wholly unlike our Northern public enemies. From hollow trees, or from beneath ledges of stones on mountain-sides hard-by the farm-house, concealed breech-loaders were drawn, and assassins' bullets sent many Confederate soldiers to untimely graves.

Women and children were as false to the South and as true to the Union as fathers, brothers, and sons, and woe to the Confederate soldier, recognized as such, who followed paths into which he was guided by these loyalists. Many an unnamed grave tells where unknown and forgotten scouts heedlessly confided in statements made by matronly dames or blushing maidens. Often were brave men lured into modest cottages by proffered food temptingly spread before the weary and hungry. The feast was one of death. While hunger and thirst were appeased, and repose cunningly invited, an unseen member of the household sped away to mountain fastnesses to carry tidings of the scout's folly to the bushwhackers' strong-hold. The messenger returned with enough resolute men to render escape impossible. Matron, maid, or boy hastened from every mountaineer's home to tell bushwhackers the route of every body of Confederate scouts that traversed the so-called neutral ground between the two great armies of the North and South. Such was the condition of affairs and such the conduct of the masses of the people, especially in Eastern Tennessee. The people were poor. They read the Bible and Brownlow's *Whig*. They listened to Andrew Johnson, if Democrats; to Brownlow and Nelson, if Whigs; and thus, as political thinkers, were led, almost *en masse*, into thorough Unionism. The strongest passion of these illiterate descendents of heroes of King's Mountain and Cowpens impelled them to kill. "Death to enemies of the Union!" was the legend inscribed upon their hearts and memories. The bushwhackers' definition of war was written accurately in tears and blood, and flame and famine by General Sherman. It was simple destructiveness. It meant to kill.

At this period President Lincoln had won little popular sympathy or affection among Southern loyalists. His potency came later and was greatest after his death. Then Eastern Tennessee and Northern Georgia celebrated his apotheosis, awarding to his name and memory profounder respect and more honest reverence than was conceded by those who were near enough the veritable demi-god to discover human frailties.

These facts are defined that Northern people may confess some inadequate appreciation of the sturdy, honest devotion of those men and women whose sacrifices in behalf of the Union were a thousand-fold greater than of men who bought substitutes, paid taxes, speculated in shoddy and bonds, and celebrated the Fourth of July and Black Friday.

East Tennessee loyalists believed that the enemies of the Union deserved death, and death it was, and this internecine war, waged by one against another household, or by members of the same family, arrayed against one another, was the most relentless, bloody, and ruinous that ever desolated hearths and homes.

Rarely, very rarely, was it a "rebel's" good fortune to encounter in this region devotees at the shrine of "Confederatism." Now and then, as these pages will show, this "Switzerland of America" produced a secessionist, as earnest, devout, and active as were Union men like Crutchfield and Brownlow. It may not be improper to suggest that the first blood spilled in the great conflict was not, as is commonly supposed, at Alexandria, Virginia, when the zouave fell, but in Chattanooga, when "Bill" Crutchfield, afterwards, when Reconstruction progressed, a Member of Congress, was stricken down in his own hotel in Chattanooga. Mr. Jefferson Davis, having resigned his seat in the United States Senate, was on his way to Jackson, Mississippi. His first speech in behalf of the "new nation" was made at Bristol; his second, at Chattanooga, and in the bar-room of the old hotel, of which "Bill" Crutchfield was proprietor. Davis was defining numberless wrongs inflicted upon the South, and woes that had befallen the country in the election of Lincoln, when Crutchfield, intolerant as Davis, pronounced Davis' statements false. One John W. Vaughn, sheriff of Monroe County, afterwards made a brigadier by Davis, instantly, in defence of Davis' wounded honor, broke a black bottle, snatched from the shelf of the bar-room, over Crutchfield's head. The bleeding, stunned Crutchfield was borne helpless and senseless from the scene of conflict, shedding the first blood spilled in the war. It trickled out of East Tennessee into the mighty torrent that soon afterward flowed, steadily and sluggishly, along the course of Sherman's march to the sea.

The neutral ground contained few inhabitants entertaining the feelings or convictions of Vaughn, and Northern, encountered no such dangers as Southern, scouts surmounted or evaded at every step in Eastern Tennessee and Northern Georgia. Now and then a woman was loyal to the cause of the South, and the bravest and truest of our race, whether adhering to the Union or to the Confederacy, were fearless women of the mountains and valleys between the two armies. When England and Scotland were at war, the Border produced no more illustrious examples of splendid heroism or of nobility of character, or of fidelity to a cause espoused, than this mountainous, rugged district in which incidents occurred of which these pages tell. Some Walter Scott will yet make posterity remember, when traversing Northern Alabama, Northern Georgia, Western North Carolina, and Eastern Tennessee, that a sort of sanctity overshadows this region, and that it is holy ground, baptized in the blood of a border war more deadly than that waged with the rude weapons of a rude age in glens and mountain fastnesses of Scotland. For such a story-teller this modest volume contains facts on which fiction might build a pantheon peopled with gods of heroism and patriotism.

# CHAPTER II.

What follows in this narrative is nothing more than a plain recital of facts drawn from memoranda made at the time. Written with a pencil eighteen years ago these are not always perfectly legible, but enough can be deciphered to recall vividly the minutest details of incidents strongly impressed upon the memory of one only eighteen years of age when he became a chief of scouts in the army of Joseph E. Johnston.

On the day abvoe mentioned Major-General Pat Cleburne, of the most skillful and bravest of General Johnston's subordinates, selected six men, of whom I was given charge, instructing us to make the circuit of Sherman's army. We were to fix the location of each command, define the force at each point and the strength of each fortified position. We were to go first to Charleston on the Hiwassee River and learn what progress was making in rebuilding the railway bridge burned there by the retreating Confederates.

After a toilsome march of thirty miles, avoiding public highways, we rested for the night at Red Clay, a little village on the boundary line of Tennessee. We dared not make a fire. Armed with Henry rifles and Colt's repeaters and having forty rounds of ammunition and rations for five days, our journeying had been toilsome and fatiguing. Our conversations were conducted in an undertone. We moved even cautiously in the thicket in which we were concealed, fearing that the slightest unusual noise would attract the attention of some drowsy Federal sentinel.

Surely one who has never occupied such a position or confronted such dangers can never comprehend the emotions excited by our

2

suddenly changed condition.  For months and years we had constituted inseparable parts of a great mass of armed men.  We were
never conscious of personal danger.  The possibility of capture or
death, save in battle, never occurred to us.  We had never a thought
for ourselves.  Parts of a vast machine, we lived and moved as such
until personal identity was almost unrecognized.  But here were six
men—a seventh, a newspaper man, joined us at Charleston—giving
only voluntary obedience to one of their number.  We were not only
removed from the mass of which we had become an inseparable part,
but thrown, in the midst of extraordinary dangers, wholly upon our
own resources as men and as individuals.  We could not sleep.  We
were in the enemy's lines, and when fatigue wooed repose and fitfully
closed our eyes, we dreamed of spies dangling at ropes' ends beneath
shadows of great oaks that stretched mighty arms above our resting-
place.

Wherever we slept one or two men always stood as sentinels until
we resumed our march.  We will never forget the feeling of unutterable solitariness and hopeless helplessness that possessed nerves and
soul, and almost paralyzed us when we lay down on the frozen hillside
to rest on the night of December 14, 1863.  We could hear the dull
roar of innumerable human voices and footsteps about the camp fires
of Sherman's countless legions.

We stood guard in turn, each serving four hours.  After daylight
we dared to have fire enough to prepare strong coffee, most grateful
to men who had passed a bitterly cold December night upon the bare
earth, each covered by a single blanket.

At daylight we resumed our march, moving in indian file along the
verge of the mountain range's summit.  At noon we approached the
Big Blue Spring.  One of our number ascended a tree with a field
glass, whence he scanned hills and valleys on every hand.  We made
coffee, rested an hour, and marched towards Cleveland where, at
nightfall, we bivouacked.

We could hear the drum-beat of the Federal garrison and ourselves
next morning were aroused by reveille.  We loitered two days gathering information from the people of the place in reference to the
strength of the garrison and examining for ourselves the earthworks,
and marched to the Hiwassee River just below the village of Charleston.  Here, as details hereafter given will show, our small force of
six men was recruited by the accession of a seventh, a newspaper man,
who had escaped from Knoxville when the place was captured by
General Burnside.

We wanted other edibles in substitution for hard-tack and bacon.
It was agreed that Spratling, a fearless, gigantic young soldier, and I
should apply at a farm-house fifteen miles away, said to have a well-
stocked larder, to buy such provisions as were required.  We had
learned that the farmer we proposed to visit was a peaceful Union
man, but were advised to be watchful.  "He might betray us."  We
reached his pretty cottage late in the afternoon, and ate at his table,

paying for the privilege. We were not his invited guests, and as such, owed him nothing. Spratling said that this reflection, ever afterward, gave him great satisfaction. The farmer and his wife agreed at table that they would send a well-freighted market wagon next morning to our camp. The wife was especially demonstrative, suggesting that we might have a fire and occupy a small house a few rods away in a corner of the yard. We expressed a proper sense of gratitude and soon sought this resting place. We built a fire, talked cheerily half an hour to our kindly host, spread blankets before the blazing faggots, smoked our pipes, and then, bidding him good night, with repeated assertions of gratitude, rested on the floor.

But neither Spratling nor I slept. As soon as the sound of Mr. McMath's footsteps was inaudible, Spratling whispered :

"I mean to watch that old coon. I think he is playing falsely, and if he seek to betray us, he won't find Spratling stupidly sleeping."

I concurred in this, and we covered the blazing faggots in the fire-place with ashes. When the flames were extinct, Spratling and I, lying on our faces, crept out of the hut. One stood as sentinel while the other slept just outside the enclosure about the buildings. An hour had hardly passed when Spratling, then on watch, saw McMath issue from his doorway with his wife. She even followed him to the stable, urging him to ride "hard and fast" to the bushwhackers' camp, not more, as we learned afterward, than five miles away.

We now knew what was coming. We discussed the propriety of leaving ; but Spratling insisted that he must await the issue.

"I would never forgive myself," he said, "if I fled without punishing that old scoundrel's treason to pretended friendship and hospitalty. If he return alone, we will capture and send him south. If he come with five or a dozen bushwhackers, we will stampede or seize their horses, kill as many of the enemy as possible, and take refuge in the creek bottom which we examined this afternoon."

Spratling and I had slept two hours each, when we heard the clatter of coming hoofs. We counted the bushwhackers as they entered the gate, near which they left their horses. The mistress of the cottage met them at the door. She had been keeping watch, and would have discovered our "change of base" if we had not crawled noiselessly, lying on our faces, out of the cabin.

It was nearly five o'clock in the morning when we could see that some one of the eight persons in the house always watched the cabin door. McMath's wife was now actively engaged going in and out of the kitchen, and soon breakfast was spread. It is needless to suggest that Spratling and I were not asked to share this early matutinal meal. We saw the good, fat dame convey a significant brown jug, soon eloquent, as through all the ages of the world's history, of devilish deeds, into the hallway occupied by the six bushwhackers. They drank. It was the last draught of alcohol that ever went hissing down the throats of more than one of those terrible men, who thus nerved themselves for bloody, murderous deeds.

Spratling and I had gone to the rear of the house, nearer the woods, and were at a point whence we could see distinctly every person in the hallway.   In this, as stated, the breakfast-table was spread.   We were now protected by the palings, shrubbery, and peavines in the garden between us and the house.   The sun had hardly lighted up with earliest rays the tree-tops on the highest hills when the bush-whackers, McMath watching the door of the cabin we had vacated, sat about the breakfast-table.   Their guns were ranged, leaning against the wall, on either side of the broad, open hall.

Our opportunity had come.   We were about to avenge, in advance, our own contemplated deaths.

Three bushwhackers sat on either side of the table.   We crawled along the palings till we reached a point from which only two of the enemy and Mrs. McMath, who sat at the head of the table with her back towards us, were visible.   Three men in the line of each of our shots, we leveled our rifles.   I gave the word "fire," in a hoarse whisper.   I abhorred the necessity.   A cold tremor ran along my nerves.   I shuddered.

We would have repeated the shots, but feared that we might kill the woman.   Such were her screams when her guests fell dead or wounded, that her more timid, treacherous husband was wholly help-less.   While he was wringing his hands and running from one fallen friend to another and then to the relief of his suffering wife, we crossed the enclosure, and selecting two of the best horses and lead-ing two each, rode away towards our encampment.

We were not apprehensive of pursuit.   McMath had asked and we had spoken falsely as to the distance and direction of our camp and knew that some hours must elapse before he could summon a force that would dare to follow us.   He supposed we had straggled from a command only seven or eight miles distant, not less than five hun-dred strong.   While we apprehended little danger at the hands of the bushwhackers, the facts would be noised abroad and we could not remain in safety about Charleston.   We congratulated ourselves on the acquisition of just horses enough, fresh and strong, to mount my footsore and weary men.

We had ridden three or four miles before we began to talk of what had happened and of what we had done.   It was the first killing that either Spratling or I had had ever perpetrated, except in an open field and fair fight, and both confessed qualms of conscience.

"How could we help it?" asked Spratling.   "If we had not killed them, they came armed to kill us.   If we had fought them openly, we would have fallen, and certainly by suicidal hands.   To fight is to kill, and this is our business, and there was no escaping the necessity for methods we adopted.   If our numbers had equalled theirs, we should have resorted, and properly, to the same stratagems.   General Sherman is right.   War means murder, desolation, destruction, and death.   We are warriors," said Spratling.   "We are murderers and horse-thieves, I greatly fear," was my earnest answer.

Spratling confessed that he did not like it, that his conscience was troubled, and that he was almost sorry, though we had six horses, that he had not assented when I proposed to leave the bushwhacker's place before his coadjutors came.   Hurrying events and impending dangers made us forget everything but the fact that our speedy departure from Charleston was a matter of urgent necessity.

We had already spent two days at Charleston on the Hiwassee watching the process of rebuilding the railway bridge.   Thence we rode to Pikeville, in the valley between Walden's Ridge and the Cumberland Mountains.   Late in the afternoon we · came to the Tennessee River five miles below the little village, Decatur.   A skiff, or dug-out, was soon discovered.   But while a comrade and I had been searching for such a means of crossing, others discovered a whiskey distillery.   They and their canteens, in the absence of the proprietor of the gum-tree pipe through which the alcohol flowed, were soon well filled.   We crossed the river, concealed the dug-out in a thicket for possible future use, and a mile farther west, near a country road and the river shore, rested in a dense wood.   Our sentinel stood near the highway.   Unhappily, · his canteen was bursting with raw, corn whiskey.   He drank too deeply, and when a wagon with a dozen country girls and boys occupying it came rattling over the stony roadway, echoing songs and laughter burdening the cold night wind with the delicious music of women's voices, our sentinel could not restrain himself.   He knew that the party of revellers came from a farm-house we had passed during the day, and were celebrating a country wedding.   Brandishing his musket, he confronted the roysterers, demanding instant surrender.   The women were frightened beyond measure.   Their screams drew us to the spot.   Our sentinel was holding the rein of one of the horses attached to the vehicle, and insisting that its occupants must come down and surrender.   He brandished his repeater, and when we appeared, the young men, seeing that resistance would be worse than idle, descended from the wagon.   They were assured that no harm was intended, and that this intoxicated sentinel and others like him need only be appeased.

What a vision of beauty I beheld in the perfect face and form of one of those mountain lassies!   The luminous splendor of her great, lustrous black eyes lighted up her pale, beautiful features, as I first beheld her beneath the clear moonlight gilding hills and valleys, with matchless radiance that fascinated me.   Why, I could not tell, but frightened as she was,—perhaps because I was only a year or two her senior,—she ran to my side and seized the hand that clasped my rifle. I looked into her pale, beautiful face, amazed and startled by her charms.   I had never imagined that a woman's figure, eyes, pleading face, limitless confidence, and silent appeal for protection could be so eloquent.   The hot blood, when I pressed her hand, rushed to my face.   I said to her, "You shall not be harmed," and then added, with much hesitation, "Won't you tell me your name, and where do you live?"

"O, yes," she answered, "my name is Mamie Hughes. I am here visiting relatives. My home is on the other side of the Union army in Georgia, and I can't get there now."

Here Mamie was suddenly silent. She suspected, I thought, that I was a "rebel," but was doubtful. I was conscious that I could trust her. Her wonderful face and eloquent eyes had won my confidence, if not my heart, and I said to her, in a whisper, "I am a Southerner. Say nothing. If you utter a word, we seven will be hanged as spies."

At this moment our boisterous, half-drunken sentinel was insisting that the fiddler should organize cotillions and that we should dance by moonlight. Thinking to humor the fancy of my intoxicated men and let the merry-makers go in good humor, I said :

"Yes ; we will dance by moonlight, and these gentlemen here shall drink with us and we will part friends, regretting that we frightened these beautiful young ladies."

This apology exasperated the drunken sentinel, who drawled out, "Friends ! did you say, Captain ? These people are d——d Yanks."

"The rest of them are, but I am not," whispered Mamie, pressing closely to my side.

It was needless to attempt further concealment of our character or purposes. I stated to the oldest of the East Tennesseeans that we were Kentuckians on our way to join the Southern army and were going out by way of Cleveland. I said further that our comrade was only impelled by too much whiskey when he arrested them and that I regretted the fact as did my associates.

There was no response. The young men were sullen and silent and only the pretty Mamie beside me pressed my hand very gently. Another girl, more fearless than the rest, said, laughing :

"Oh ! it makes no difference. Let us make a night of it and dance with these soldiers. What a jolly story it will be to tell. We are prisoners of war and can't help ourselves. Let us dance."

"Surely," I answered, "no harm is intended, and I would gladly have those gentlemen there join us. Such opportunities do not often present themselves, and we soldiers must take advantage of them."

I whispered to Spratling, when the young East Tennesseeans made no reply to my proposition, to see that neither of them left while we danced. He stalked out, a very giant, into the roadway and stood like a massive statue of granite, his presence a significant menace.

The fiddler, half-drunken, began his task. I led in the dance with Mamie Hughes. She soon entered into the spirit animating us and forgot that we were strangers. I was lapped in the joys of Elysium. I forgot the lapse and value of time. I told in whispered. earnest words the story of my love, and surely the pretty, blushing, silent girl was not displeased.

Spratling came at last, while I was looking into Mamie's fathomless eyes and dreaming I knew not what, and said to me :

"Captain, it is time we were off. This place won't be safe for us after daylight. These prisoners of mine are furious and most impatient. They have been plotting our destruction. One of them there, I am sure, loves madly that pretty black-eyed girl you have been dancing with. He would murder you now if he dared. Our presence here will be reported to Yankee scouts within an hour and we must be off. Escape even now is hardly possible.''

While the rest of Mamie's friends were clambering into the wagon she told me where her parents lived. I said to her:

"You must not forget me, Mamie. I will surely see you again. You will not forget me will you?''

"Come and see me,'' she answered. " I will tell them at home how good, and brave, and true you are.''

She was in the act of clambering over the wagon wheel into the body, where her friends were already seated, when I caught her arm and whispered, as I raised her into the vehicle, a reassertion of my deathless love. I detected a tremor passing over Mamie's frame. She turned to look, as I lifted my cap, into my sunburnt face. The wagon moved rapidly away.

Kissing her hand she tossed the breath that passed her rosy lips, as if it had been a sparkling gem dissolved in morning mists, towards the spot where I stood entranced, motionless, and oblivious of everything except the wondrous charms of the departing divinity.

I don't know how long I might have stared in the direction Mamie had gone if Spratling, the bravest and truest of men and scouts, had not said :

"Captain, it is time, if you don't propose to follow that pretty girl, that we were getting out of this country. Within two hours a squad of cavalry will be here looking for us.''

Within ten minutes we resumed our march, but not in the direction of the towns I mentioned to Mamie's friends. On the contrary, we moved westwardly towards Walden's Ridge. We had not proceeded five miles when we heard signal guns in many directions and the sound of horns used for like purposes by the native Unionists or bushwhackers. We ascended the ridge to its summit. Day was dawning when we looked down into the long, deep valley below. Signal fires still blazed at different points, and a rocket, making lights of different colors, climbed through the air far above the ridge and exploding fifteen or twenty miles away, recited the story told at headquarters of the Union army by Mamie's friends. It stated, "There are seven spies within our lines.'' In any event this was the translation we gave to this sign in the heavens, as significant of capture and death as was that of victory and empire which appeared to Constantine.

Throughout the weary day, when we peered forth from our hiding place, we could discover bodies of horsemen moving in the valley below, in all directions, in search of the Confederates known to be within the Federal lines. Using a powerful field glass we defined during the day the route we were to pursue during the night that we might cross the valley in safety between Walden's Ridge and Cumberland Mountains.

We descended, with darkness, into the valley and moved rapidly across it. We reached the mountain's summit before day dawned. After this toilsome march, occupying the whole night, we were without food, fatigued beyond measure, hungry as famished wolves, and in the midst of relentless enemies. We had neither food, tobacco, nor coffee.

Our condition was becoming desperate. At two o'clock in the afternoon we found in this sparsely populated district a modest little log farm-house. Stationing my men about it to prevent the escape of its inmates, I applied for food. The mistress of the cabin refused to sell anything. There was no help for it. We entered the cabin, and telling the good dame that we were starving and desperate and that she must give us bread or her home would be destroyed, she sullenly prepared dinner of the coarsest food. Two men, that we might not be poisoned, watched the process of cooking it, and we ate ravenously. The timid nominal head of the household begged his wife to give us all we demanded, and soon intimated privately that he was a devout "rebel." We knew he was lying, but accepted his assertions as if we deemed them true. We stated that we were of Morgan's cavalry, and *en route* to Kentucky to bring out recruits. We made minute inquiries about roads leading north to McMinaville. He answered truthfully, as we happened to know.

Late in the afternoon, when about to depart, we almost made a rebel of his red-haired, hideously ugly wife by presenting her five dollars in United States currency. She grinned so gleefully when Spratling gave her the money, and drew so near to express her amazed gratitude, that Spratling, dreading a kiss from the ignorant, vulgar, frightful creature, leaped from the doorway. He told me he was never "scared before in all his life." She was very thin and her back was bowed, as Spratling described her, like that of a "razor-back hog." Her frowzy, red hair, unkempt for twenty years, was powdered with ashes. She wore two garments. The outer, made of four yards of dingy gray calico, was tucked up at the waist, exposing her red, rusty, sinewy limbs almost to the knees.

She was offended by Spratling's sudden terror and retreat, and we knew that this Medusa of the mountains, if possible, would avenge the indignity. She began to denounce us. Her eloquence was absolutely wonderful. Daniel O'Connell's traditional fish woman could never have been more voluble or coarse than this frightful hungry-looking, red-faced, red-headed, and red-mouthed angular creature. She leaped violently around the great barrel-churn in the yard and kicked at each of a dozen lazy, cowardly, yelping hounds that lay about the great receptacle of sour milk. She made and sold butter to Federal soldiers encamped in the valley, and in neighboring villages.

Spratling was noted for his tremendous strength. Like most physically powerful men, he was exceedingly good natured. But it was wholly impossible to withstand shocks to one's temper administered by this voluble termagant. Spratling was first amazed, and when she finally stood facing him, her arms akimbo and legs extended as far apart as the contracted calico would admit, and poured forth a volley of disgusting epithets, Spratling could no longer contain himself.

He suddenly seized the scrawny, bony creature, and inverting her, high in the air, as suddenly thrust her, head foremost into the barrel-churn half full of milk. The woman's stockingless legs were twirled about piteously above the top of the churn. I was paralyzed for a moment. The scene was painfully ludicrous. But the woman was drowning. Convulsive movements of her red legs showed that she was in a death struggle. Even the dozen dogs stood up and looked on in mute astonishment. To spare the woman's life I suddenly tipped the churn over. Her clothing was rudely displaced and as the milk spread over the lower side of the little enclosure, and her head and shoulders were uncovered, she crawled out backwards.

Evidently those dogs had never witnessed such an exhibition. As the good dame backed out of the barrel on all fours, the dogs stood transfixed with astonishment, staring a moment at the unusual spectacle, and then, howling piteously, each turned and fled in abject terror. Convulsed with laughter, I ordered my men to fall into line and march. Spratling was holding his sides and rolling over and over on the ground. The mountain groaned beneath roars of laughter.

It was horrible and cruel, but no incident half so ludicrous was ever witnessed by a squad of veterans. The good dame's senses were hardly restored when we began at last to move rapidly away. She finally rubbed the grease out of her eyes and began to comprehend the ridiculous aspect she had presented. She gathered up her consciousness, and pulled down her petticoat and began to gesticulate wildly, and pour forth an interminable vocabulary of coarse epithets. She pursued us to curse poor Spratling who ran down the declivity roaring like the bull of Bashan.

We traveled rapidly perhaps five miles along the road we had been directed to take leading to McMinaville. The moon had not risen and total darkness enveloped us. Leaving the highway we entered the woods going directly back towards the scene of buttermilk baptism. We moved as silently as possible and had not reversed our course half an hour till we heard the red-headed woman's sharp, clear voice ringing out on the cold night air. She was urging a dozen bushwhackers to keep pace with her in pursuit of "infernal pimps of hell and Jeff Davis." Her wild fury and shocking imprecations made us, rude soldiers as we were, shudder. The winds stood still that they might not bear on their weary wings the insufferable burden of her horrible oaths. We were even sickened by the woman's mad depravity and infernal fury. When the echoes of her harsh, sharp voice were no longer audible, I said to Spratling: "Hell hath no fury like a woman—baptised in buttermilk." Spratling's suppressed laughter shook the tree against which he rested his sturdy body, and we resumed our toilsome journey over shapeless stones and through mountain thickets, never resting through that livelong. weary night.

We marched by night and rested during daytime until we reached Stevenson near the Tennnessee River on the Nashville, Chattanooga and Memphis roads.

# CHAPTER III.

---

A devoted rebel family at Stevenson furnished supplies while we were encamped in a secluded spot near the village. We mixed occasionally with passengers on railway trains, from Memphis and from Nashville, meeting at this place. Spratling was a capital farmer, and I, a plow-boy. We wore the rude "butternut" or homespun goods of the country and only a pistol and knife, never visible. We received northern newspapers from every quarter and carefully filed away every paragraph that might be of value to Generals Bragg and Johnston. Wounded and sick soldiers, in endless trains, now and then moved northwardly, and interminable supply trains, day and night, went south. We noted everything. From sick-leave officers awaiting transportation, and from quartermasters' and commissaries' agents we learned how many they fed or transported in many divisions and corps. We made contracts to supply an Ohio brigade with eggs , and potatoes which were never executed, perhaps because "bread and butter" brigades, and divisions, and corps, alone, came then, as now, out of Ohio.

Early on the morning of December 30, 1863, the good dame who had furnished our simple meals came to our resting place to say that a little child of a bushwhacking neighbor had said that the rebel camp on the mountain-side would be attacked that night and its occupants shot or hanged. I proffered the woman fifty dollars in greenbacks. She refused to accept it; but when I said, "You are poor, and I am paid by the government and given this money that I may give it to such as you," she said, "I did not know how I could live when you went away, yet I came to urge your immediate departure. With this fifty dollars and what I have saved I can feed and clothe myself and children almost a year." She kissed my hard, sunburnt hand, and with tearful eyes turned away. I never saw her afterward, but no braver or truer woman lives than Mrs. M———y, of Stevenson.

How bitterly cold were the last days of December, 1863, and the first of January, 1864, surviving soldiers serving under Rosecranz, and Sherman, and Johnston, and Bragg will never forget. Early in the morning of the 30th of December we strapped our blankets on our backs and with three days' rations traversed the distance between Stevenson and Bridgeport. We reached the river just after nightfall. Fiercely cold as were winds and waves there was no help for it. We must cross. There was no security save in placing the river between ourselves and the relentless bushwhackers. We could find no boat, and the swollen river, divided in its midst by a long, narrow island, was then, perhaps, two miles wide. It seemed, when we looked out, wistfully and anxiously enough, that bitterly cold night, upon its moaning, starlit waters, certainly ten miles in width.

Of a wrecked boat on the shore we constructed a raft capable of conveying our blankets, clothing and weapons. We swam beside it down the river to the island. Almost frozen when we reached the sandy bank, we lifted the raft out of the water, bore it across the island, launched it again, and again drifting down and across the river, landed safely, but paralyzed by cold, on the southern bank. Icicles clung to my hair and beard. My teeth chattered and I felt that numbness and drowsiness slowly overcoming me which immediately precedes death. We rubbed, one another violently with blankets and when thoroughly dry and re-clad in woollen I never enjoyed so keenly the sense of perfect youthful vigor and vitality. I was aglow with ecstatic physical blessedness. We soon ascended and followed the ridge that connects Bridgeport with Lookout Mountain. We stood upon the summit of the precipice that overhangs the railway and the Tennessee. The railway track rests upon the verge of the stream and enormous, rugged stones superimposed on one another like those of some mediæval ruin rise precipitously hundreds of feet, and are projected beyond the railway and overhang the water's edge. At day-dawn we looked down from this dizzy height. A railway train going to Chattanooga came roaring and shrieking from Bridgeport. It seemed as we contemplated it, moving with tremendous velocity constantly accelerated into the river. We shuddered involuntarily when it went down out of sight under the cliff, and seemingly headlong into the broad, boisterous bosom of the Tennessee. Then ensued the silence of death. Great, projecting stones cut off sounds and vision, and the sudden stillness that pervaded mountains, valleys, and river was painful to the last degree.

With a wild shriek of seemingly ineffable delight the locomotive, its great, black pennon of smoke curved backward, rushed from cavernous depths below to greet from the hill-top it ascended, the splendors of the sun just rising on the brightest and coldest morning that ever dawned upon the South.

In re-writing these memoranda I omitted a page to which I now recur. While we were at the railway bridge which Federal soldiers were rebuilding across the Hiwassee River at Charleston we encountered a gentleman who had been now and then in the Confederate States' service as a staff officer, but for several preceding months editing a paper at Knoxville. He was well known to us and and at his own suggestion became, temporarily, one of our number. He withstood hardships uncomplainingly and whiled away tedious hours of compulsory idleness with stories he had gathered while war raged. His purpose was to reach Atlanta, whither his newspaper, when Burnside, with snowy locks, and side whiskers, and smooth towering occiput came down upon Knoxville, had been removed. On the night of December 31, 1863, colder if possible than the preceding night, we climbed the summit of Lookout Mountain. If the one hundred and fifty thousand soldiers then within fifty miles of Chattanooga were reading at the same instant, the above sentence, they would each whistle and shudder, and perhaps one hundred thousand would exclaim, *una voce*, clapping their sinewy hands, " It was —— cold ! " It's a pity, but old soldiers will use frightful exclamations. But none have forgotten the terrors of the night which witnessed the death of 1863 and the birth of 1864. Seven of us, with a blanket each, not daring to build a fire and hungry as famished wolves, spent that fearful night on the topmost summit of Lookout Mountain whereon some ancient fable tells that Hooker fought a battle even among the clouds.

In the starlight, while looking for a place protected against Northern blasts, a shallow cavern was discovered. We gathered dry leaves and made a resting place within. And yet such was the insufferable cold that we could not sleep. We smoked our pipes and "spun yarns" through the tedious hours of the weary night.

"Gentlemen," said Bowles, one of our number, "I have seen and shared in several battles, and a big battle is only a rapidly alternating succession of d——d big scares; but I never witnessed such an infernally big scare as the red-headed milk-maid of the mountains inflicted on them d——d dogs."

Then followed such shouts of laughter that I absolutely feared the echoing peals would be borne by cold blustering winds down into Federal headquarters just below in Chattanooga.

" If the dogs have got back," said Spratling, " and I'm going there to see about it, I'll bet ten to one that every time she stoops, 'she stoops to conquer' and them d——d dogs go flying and howling down the deep jungles of Sequatchie Valley."

" I can never forget the scene," interposed Blake. "When she stood on her head in the churn, her little, starveling legs dancing an inverted hornpipe, the picture was sublime in its very uniqueness. But when the captain here overturned the churn and the dogs all stood up and looked on with growing interest, licking their chops and crying over much spilled milk, and then, when their attention was gradually arrested by the old woman backing out of that churn wholly uncovered and on all fours, it was entirely too much for the dogs. It was more than I could stand. I turned away only to see and hear the dogs frightened, shrieking, and flying in all directions."

"Do you know," continued Blake, "that the woman's husband was delighted? He sneaked off. I saw him behind the chicken house, throwing himself back and forth like a cross-cut saw, and holding his sides with both hands, his cheeks swollen and his eyes bursting from their sockets. It was keen enjoyment of fun struggling against the terror in which he held his red-headed, dreadful wife. We made a good rebel of him. Don't you remember that we heard not a word from him when the wife led our pursuers so noisily and vengefully on our track. We have won him, and if ever I go on another expedition in that direction I would not hesitate to trust that man. His gratitude to us is boundless, and his devotion will be admirable."

# CHAPTER IV.

The Newspaper Man Tells of His Escape from Burnside.—Compulsory Sermon-izing.—"Tristram Shandy."—A Solemn and Terrible Indictment.—The Good that Came of It.—Descent of the Mountain.—Hunger and Roast Hog.—Plans for the Future.

There was silence and an unavailing purpose to sleep when the newspaper man said that he had told us how he escaped from Knoxville, going out on one side of the then little city when General Burnside entered on the other.

"It was impossible to go directly south. The railway leading to Chattanooga was held at every bridge and station by Federal pickets. Therefore I went towards Nashville. I spent a day at Kingston, an ancient town of twenty-five hundred inhabitants on Clinch River at the base of the Cumberland Mountains. Thence I journeyed slowly southeast, pretending to be a Kentuckian on my way to Chattanooga where my brother was dying in the hospital.

"I had, as a Whig and Unionist, traversed this district, and now from the home of one friend I was directed to another. I traveled at night, and was accompanied, on horseback or in a farm wagon, by the political and partisan friend with whom I had spent the preceding night. I was educated, before I entered the university and afterward the law-school, at a theological college, and learned how to prepare very acceptable sermons, perhaps for the reason that I could memorize readily and recite *ore rotundo* what I had written. When I first encountered you, and when Blake recognized me, I had been forced, most unwillingly, to enact the role of chaplain and missionary sent down from Cincinnati by the Young Men's Christian Association. Of course I sought the acquaintance of the best people of the place, and was at last forced to deliver, much against my will, two sermons while traversing the country from Kingston to the Hiwassee at Charleston. The last was pronounced, the day before we met, with infinite zeal and fervor. In my audience were many grim, but devout, Union soldiers. On this occasion I delivered the sermon which you read in Tristram Shandy. Of course I had amended, modernized, and localized it. Those most familiar with Sterne would hardly have recognized the pretty homily. I used this charming discourse because I had mastered it perfectly and was sure I would go through with the day's work never incurring a suspicion or exciting a doubt as to genuineness of the character I assumed. If I had not played Beecher, on the rostrum, to perfection, I would have performed as a spy under the gallows most awkwardly. But I was no spy. I only sought to escape into the Gulf States and was overjoyed when I recognized my learned friend Blake here in the rude garb of an East Tennessee clodhopper at Charleston.

"So much by way of prelude to a recital of incidents of the previous Sunday. There was a Methodist conference in session in the village of Kingston. I had just reached the place, and, Sunday morning as it was, found idlers about the tavern eyeing me suspiciously. When any two persons saw me approaching they parted at once and each went his way. The somewhat aged landlord was studiously polite and reserved. Seeing many people coming into the village I learned that the Methodist conference of the district was to sit and resolved, rather than be captured by these bushwhackers and shot or sent a prisoner of war beyond the Ohio, to become a Northern missionary. I took a conspicuous seat in the church soon filled to overflowing.

"Near me sat a bright-eyed, slender, sallow little preacher. He wore a threadbare broadcloth coat of the Methodist regulation pattern. There were constant nervous twitchings of the corners of his mouth and laughing devils in his merry eyes. His name, as I learned afterward, was Weaver, a famous practical joker as well as eloquent evangelist. A song was sung. The venerable Bishop of the district occupied a raised seat in front of the pulpit and bending in the presence of God uttered a fervent prayer for peace and for the 'restoration of harmony and good government.' Though there was nothing in the prayer pronounced by the devout old man to offend a 'rebel,' he was evidently loyal to the 'Stars and Stripes' as were nine-tenths of his hearers.

"Silence, when the Bishop resumed his seat, pervaded the assembly. At length a youthful, graceful preacher addressed as 'Brother Williams,' evidently much excited, and pale and tremulous, rose in the midst of the congregation, and, hesitating and stammering, said:

"'Brethren, Brother Jones and I came to town early this morning with Brother Weaver.'

"I turned and looked at Weaver. There were a thousand merry devils lurking in his bright, mischievous eyes. The corners of his mouth were drawn down and lips suddenly compressed. Seeing that the eyes of the assembly were turned upon him, he modestly bowed his head and sat in moody silence and perfect stillness gazing at his feet.

"Brother Williams proceeded:

" 'While we were crossing the main street of the town awhile ago, brother Weaver, looking up at the windows of the hotel, remarked, in very sad, solemn tones, to Brother Jones and myself, that the last time that he slept in that hotel the landlord's wife occupied his apartment. Of course I was startled, not to say shocked. Brother Jones, too, was much excited, and both of us listened intently to Brother Weaver's reply when I asked him if it were possible that I heard aright. He answered, "Yes, my brethren, it is my duty to tell the truth and whatever you may think, and whatever the consequences, I must repeat that what I have stated is true. The last time I occupied an apartment in that hotel the landlord's youthful wife was my companion."

" 'Brother Weaver's face, while this speech was uttered by him, was expressive of profoundest melancholy.'

" 'And I am persuaded,' continued Brother Williams, 'that he was moved to make this painful confession because the face of the Lord was never more patent in His goodness and heavenly benefactions than when it shone upon us this morning in the gorgeous sunlight that suddenly flooded plains, hills, and mountains. It rolled and fell like a brilliant Niagara of jewels and gold from the summit of the mountains yonder into this deep, beautiful valley. Clinch River, my brethren, shone lustrously as burnished silver, and the very splendors of the morning and pearly brightness and purity of skies overhanging this matchless land of beauty and blessedness were eloquent of God's goodness and suggestive of man's penitence. Brother Weaver, I am sure, could not withstand the force of nature's persuasive eloquence; and coming, as he was, to God's temple, he was moved to make this painful confession of his heinous crime.

" 'I appeal to Brother Jones, who accompanied us, to attest the truthfulness of my statements.'

"Williams sat down and Jones, an illiterate circuit-rider, rising, slowly and timorously said:

" 'Brethren, all that you have hearn is only too true.' and his eyes filling with tears, he used his handkerchief, and hesitating, stammering and weeping, was at last enabled to drawl out in broken accents, 'I hope, my brethering you will deal leaniently with Brother Weaver. The flesh you know is weak and Brother Weaver has repented. I know he has because he has confessed.'

"A torrent of tears swept down Jones' rugged features and with an audible groan he dropped, like a dead man, on his seat, utterly crushed by the weight of this unspeakable sorrow.

"Profoundest silence reigned, broken by sobs and groans of miserable and sympathetic Brother Jones. No assembly, christian or heathen, was ever more profoundly shocked. Women of the congregation, nervously excited, grew pale and haggard. The face of the Bishop's venerated wife was of ashen hue. Weaver was the flower of the flock of young preachers.

"At last the Bishop rose and said:

3

" 'Brethren, you have heard, with horror and dismay, statements made by our two young brethren. I see Brother Weaver there, his head bowed beneath the weight of shame and penitence. Will he not speak? Has he nothing to say?'

"The Bishop resumed his chair.

"Slowly, most deliberately, and with an irrepressible twinkle in his clear, bright eyes, Brother Weaver, drawing himself up by the back of the seat before him, rose to confront the eager gaze of the excited assembly. He stood some moments looking sorrowfully over the throng gazing intently into his attractive, but saddened, solemn face.

" 'Brethren,' he said at last, 'I did make the confession which my friends heard and have accurately repeated; but it so happens that when I occupied the room mentioned, with the landlord's wife, as stated, I was the landlord, and the woman was my wife.'

"The true state of the case was slowly comprehended by the duped and stupefied multitude. The Bishop and his wife were first to discover the immaculate innocence of the two circuit-riders, Williams and Jones, and a broad smile spread over the kindly face of the godly man. His fat wife began to laugh immoderately. The infection spread, and when it had grown into a great roar the lantern-jawed, solemn, weeping Jones sprang up in evident disgust and exclaimed:

" 'Sold! awfully sold! Weren't we, Brother Williams?'

"This outburst of the mortified Jones, who had wasted bitter tears and sweetest sympathy upon Weaver, perfected the sudden revulsion from profound sadness and solemnity to an apprehension of the absurdity of the facts and their utter incompatibility with the seriousness of the place, day, and occasion. The Bishop's fat wife crammed her handkerchief into her mouth and the Bishop himself, contemplating the vacant look of empty astonishment that overspread Jones' heavy face, who seemed to ask himself, 'How could I have been such an arrant fool?' was wholly overcome. He caught a glance from the tearful eyes of his agonized wife and could contain himself no longer. He threw his head backward, clapped his hands to his sides, and roared with laughter. I never saw a religious assembly, on the Lord's day, in such a deplorable, unseemly condition.

"The incident served to divert attention from myself. I mixed and talked and laughed with busy, garrulous men and women, and each seemed to think the rest had known me always. The Bishop, first mildly chiding Brother Weaver for the innocent fraud practised upon two zealous circuit-riders, pronounced a sermon of singular simplicity and marvellous incisiveness and force. The minds of his auditors were diverted wholly from sinful rebels, and when I returned in the afternoon to the hotel, having passed under the inspection of the multitude, the venerable landlord greeted me most graciously and called forth the good-looking wife that I might see, as he stated the proposition, 'how naterally even a preacher might go wrong in his hotel.' "

Artillery and cavalry bugles and drums at a thousand glowing camp fires blazing along the curves of Moccasin Bend and on the slopes of mountain sides and down the deep valley of the Tennessee, were sounding the reveille when the modest journalist concluded his recital. When, some weeks later, it was written out, I had not learned how to insert the words ["laughter,"] and ["great applause"] in brackets, as since introduced by party leaders; otherwise these pages would show how keenly the story, here imperfectly reproduced, was enjoyed by cold, comfortless, and hungry scouts ensconced in a little cavern on the summit of Lookout Mountain, on the ever memorable night of December 31, 1863, the first anniversary of the battle of Stone River.

The mountain was veneered with sheets of ice. We knew that few were abroad on such a morning, that sentinels and pickets stood near camp fires, and that scouting parties of the enemy sought shelter within cabins of bushwhackers. Avoiding paths and roadways and cabins we began to slide, rather than walk, down the mountain. In a few hours we reached McLemore's Cove and thence, painfully fatigued by sliding over the frozen ground sheeted in ice, we plodded wearily along the ridge, known, I believe, as Taylor's. Night was coming on. We had eaten nothing for twenty-four hours. Made reckless by suffering, one of our number shot a hog. It was hastily skinned, washed, sliced and roasted to a crisp, in thin strips, by a roaring fire made to glow with the farmer's rails whose sustenance we devoured. Without bread or salt, we ate ravenously. I have since dined at the Fifth Avenue, at Morley's, the best *cafes* of Paris, Berlin, and Vienna, but never derived such exquisite pleasure from food as when we half-frozen soldiers sat about the blazing rails, and ate unsalted pork on the heights that look down upon Chattanooga.

Two days later, moving at night, and concealed and resting in densest thickets during daytime, we rested at Tunnel Hill, where General Pat Cleburne was encamped. He congratulated us in most flattering terms on successes achieved, was pleased with the fullness and accuracy of information given as to the numbers, purposes, and positions of the enemy, and made me accompany him to General Granbury's quarters. Here we spent most of the night while I recited, as given in these pages, the story of our adventures. I gave, besides, minute descriptions of the country and relative positions of the forces of the enemy and the strength of each position defined in pencil sketches I had made. That night it was determined by these two Confederate leaders that a permanent body of scouts should be kept constantly employed between the lines of the two armies. I was commended by these officers to General Joseph E. Johnston and soon afterward given charge of a body of scouts and entered upon the execution of hazardous tasks incident to the position. I am glad to state that I never forfeited the personal esteem and unlimited confidence of either of these three great leaders; and that I, a boy not quite eighteen years of age, won and retained under such an ordeal, the unfaltering friendship and confidence of these accomplished gentlemen and soldiers, is the most pleasing reflection incident to my conduct in life.

# CHAPTER V.

After a few days rest, I was given charge of thirteen men and assigned the task of arresting deserters and bushwhackers. We established a rendezvous about midway between the two armies and between Ringgold and La Fayette in Georgia. One man was made cook and commissary, remaining always at our place of encampment, while twelve men were constantly on duty. Six went out each morning, three going east and three going west. When these came back, the other six in turn explored the "neutral ground." Seven men were always ready to defend our stronghold, and the country about us was perfectly patrolled. Within a week we captured and sent back eight deserters to be tried and shot. Returning to camp late one afternoon I was startled by a rapid fusillade in its direction. I was sure the bushwhackers had attacked my little garrison and hurried to its relief. Of course, anticipating an ambuscade, we moved, when within a mile of the scene of conflict, very cautiously. But the firing was suddenly silenced. We feared the worst—even that we would find our comrades dead on the unnamed, unknown field of conflict, or hanging to great trees hard-by. Just then there was an explosion as of a six-pounder field-piece. Then the garrison shouted as if a great victory were won and an enemy put to flight. We moved forward cautiously, full of gravest apprehensions.

There was a prisoner held in our camp, the meanest villain, and murderer, and coward that ever slunk away from an open fight to do assassin's work at night or by the roadside. It was my purpose to send him that night, to be court-martialed and shot, to General

Cleburne's head-quarters.   He had recently waylaid and murdered, as my men knew, two of the bravest soldiers.

By some means, in my absence, the little garrison had been supplied with "mountain dew," that intoxicating beverage which, while war ravaged the South, came trickling down, drop by drop, from green logs upon sheds of poverty in deep glens, first to madden, and then to lull jaded inmates to repose.   While the scouts were half drunken, this wretched murderer and deserter had attempted to escape.   He had been fired upon, and swooning unharmed, in pitiful terror, was brought back to our resting place.   His meanness and cowardice exasperated the drunken soldiers.   One of them climbed a slender hickory tree, forty or fifty feet high, strong, tough, and elastic as whalebone.   The weight of the soldier's body barely bent the top of the tree to the ground.

At the moment I came in view of the spot, the bushwhacker, attached by a cord about his neck to the tree-top, shot upward through the air.   His head was jerked away from his light, sinewy, little body. The neck seemed, as the little villain sped upward and away through the air, quite a yard long.   He was instantly killed, the dead body having been thrown by the slender, elastic tree more than one hundred feet from the point at which it left the earth, describing a semicircle above the tree-top.   The hickory tree almost instantly re-assumed its erect position, and when I stood in the midst of the men, the dead body, almost motionless, swung down among the top-most branches of this extraordinary gallows.   The men, drunken as they were when firing the fusillade of triumph and when they exploded an old musket barrel half full of powder and driven downward in the ground till only the touch-hole was exposed, stood sober and erect, and stared upward in horror at the dead body of the wretched bush-whacker dangling from the tree and swinging helplessly around its top.

I asked no questions.   None were needful.   An ugly, brown jug was overturned on a blanket.   Its open mouth, from which whiskey gurgled, in melancholy accents, recited every incident of the horrible crime.   Its breath was noisome as its deeds are always disgusting and hideous.   Drunken as were my guardsmen and incapable, I was forced, by every consideration of safety, to find at once another rendezvous.   The explosion of the gun barrel invited spies and scouts and bushwhackers from all directions, and assured of their speedy arrival, our safety demanded instant flight.

My whole force had been rapidly drawn together, and within twenty minutes we began to move.   Time was too valuable to devote a half hour to the burial of the ghastly corpse in the tree-top.   We left it, a hideous spectacle, swaying restlessly to and fro as the winds moved the body of the slender tree.   Birds of prey, in unbroken, untraveled forest solitudes, devoured it.   There was no Rizpah to defend it.   Its bones, when stripped of flesh, were restive as before, and still were dancing, when fierce, wintry winds bent the great forest oaks, a ghastly dance of solitude, around the body of the tree of death.

We moved to a point near La Fayette, a village in Walker County, Georgia. There, one of my men learned from a country girl he often visited, that the bushwhackers of the district would meet, in order to effect an organization, the next Saturday night, at an old church in or near McLemore's Cove several miles away. The girl was informed that forty or fifty armed men would be present. We could only be assured of the damsel's truthfulness by going into McLemore's Cove. There was great hazard to be incurred. If assailed and overpowered there was only one way of escape, and our force was too weak to cope with that to be organized by the bushwhackers. We held a council of war, and after due deliberation, condemned the proposed expedition. Five of us persisting in the purpose to capture the bushwhackers, finally arranged it that we would secure the co-operation of a cavalry force at the nearest Confederate outpost, and make a vigorous descent upon the country church. Fortune favored us. We had not gone five miles in the direction of the proposed rendezvous before we discovered a solitary horseman, who proved to be the very man we wanted. He came upon us so suddenly, in an abrupt curve of the densely wooded roadside, that he had no opportunity to escape. Covered instantly by five muskets, he dismounted and surrendered without a murmur. We agreed with the prisoner, who was quite fifty years old, such was our eagerness to obtain information, if we found his statements truthful, and if he would give us information we wanted and no more wage war against the South, that we would release him. He assented, and confirmed the story told by Ralph's sweetheart. We found all his assertions correct, and the bargain then made was afterwards faithfully executed. Two men, with this prisoner, were sent to the nearest cavalry encampment. Fifty men were placed at my disposal ; the church, while the bushwhackers occupied it, was completely invested ; and its occupants, about fifty in number, were captured without firing a gun. They never dreamed of the possible presence, in that remote, inaccessible cove, of a strong body of Confederate cavalry.

Of course, we who participated in the hard march and toils and dangers of this expedition into McLemore's Cove were not a little irritated when, returning to camp, we found that our comrades had done nothing in our absence. They had participated in many country dances. They were telling of the beauty of many maidens, occupants of many cottages and cabins everywhere within ten miles of the village. They had forgotten our existence and inquired most carelessly about the result of the fortunate expedition. We were grievously offended, and proposed, at the earliest opportunity, to punish their timidity and selfishness.

A country dance was organized and appointed for that very evening. We five who had shared in the expedition into McLemore's Cove made no sign, but went quietly to the ball. We danced as vigorously and joyously as the rest till perhaps eleven o'clock. Then, as prearranged, three of the five mentioned went unnoticed to a point near the court-house, half a mile distant, and fired a volley of muskets and pistols. Instantly the music was silenced and dancing suspended. Each soldier hurriedly armed himself. No further demonstration of enemies or friends occurring, two of my recusant scouts, blustering monstrously and asserting much fearlessness, said they would go out and discover the cause of the alarm. Accompanied by a fun-loving Irishman, I followed, pursuing a street parallel with that taken by these mock heroes. They went not farther than two hundred yards, and stopped beneath the dense shadow of a great cedar tree. We fired our muskets into the tree-top above their heads. Each thought the other mortally wounded. Both cried out, "They are coming! They are coming!" and fled precipitately. We fired our pistols to accelerate their flight, and heighten the terror of their dismayed comrades. They rushed into the hall among frightened women and unnerved men, unnerved because dangers environing them were unseen and unmeasured. Rapidly girls and beaux of the immediate vicinity ran away to their homes, and there was such a stampede, as "when Belgium's capital had gathered in her beauty and her chivalry."

My object was accomplished. The men who had refused to go with us into McLemore's Cove were wofully frightened. This Capua in Lombardy which had wrought such fatal paralysis of the soldierly virtues and energies of my scouts, was divested of attractiveness, and next morning, rising before the sun, my men were ready for the execution of any task of toil or feat of daring. I explained the incidents of the night before and stated that soldiers were made worthless by whiskey, dancing, and women, and that, if reform were impossible, I would send them back to the ditches and have others, in their stead, detailed for this free and exciting service.

I should not forget to state that the honest bushwhacker we captured won my confidence to such an extent that I told him how completely my heart had been entrapped by the charms and wiles and graces of pretty, confiding, frank, and fearless Mamie Hughes. To him I entrusted my first letter to Mamie. I retained no copy, but remember that I suggested that she should take advantage of the bushwhacker's thorough knowledge of the country and of his trustworthiness, and accompany him to her own home below Dalton. I confessed to the bushwhacker how thoroughly I was devoted to the charming girl, and promised, if he would conduct her safely to her own home below our lines, I would do him any personal service he might require. I am not sure that my judgment approved the arrangement I made for a meeting with Mamie. If I had loved her less, I would never have proposed her subjection to the dangers and fatigues of such a journey even with such a guardsman. But I had never ceased to think and dream of Mamie's great, lustrous, black eyes and of that limitless confidence I read in them when she looked upon my face and held my hand by the moonlit roadside where the compulsory dance occurred on the cold, bleak hillside not far below the village of Charleston. Every day some soldier, noticing my abstracted manner, said that Mamie Hughes had wrought a marvelous transformation of my conduct and character. When relieved of duties and anxieties incident to my position and to dangers almost always environing us, I stood aloof from my men, no longer participating in their rude sports or occupying a place at some improvised card-table. I was dreaming of Mamie Hughes, and sought solitude, that undisturbed, fancy might reproduce her matchless charms. She had promised never to forget and meet me at her home. From the day on which I transmitted the letter telling her to come, that I must see her again, that I loved her passionately, that I had never been able to dismiss the splendid vision wrought by her presence or repress aspirations excited by the hope that she would love me—from that day I had been a changed man. I was conscious that I had entered upon a new life. I had found one to share it who had already become an inseparable part of my existence.

Wedded life, if marriage be unity, begins before we go to the altar and before the priest utters his meaningless jargon. This is only a ceremony; the fact is accomplished and real wedded oneness begins beneath the moon and stars, as when, on the roadside, Mamie and I met and parted so suddenly that her face and form constituted an imperfect memory, while their effect upon my conduct and emotions wrought such a change in my character and habits that my associates knew that we "twain were one flesh." They had seen how I was dazed by the wonderful fascinations of the little sprite that sprang, a brilliant, startling vision from dreamland, in the midst of the mountains of East Tennessee.

From many sources I had learned the history of Mamie's family. Her brother was a Union soldier serving under Colonel Cliff. Her father, a life-long Whig, was a devout loyalist or Union man, while she and her mother were enthusiastic rebels. It is a strange fact, soon discovered in traversing these mountainous districts of several coterminous States, that while men were commonly "loyal," women, more impulsive and sympathetic, and apt to serve the weak against the strong, were ardent "rebels." Political and partisan considerations involved were never valued by Mamie Hughes. She was born rich and a slaveholder, but never dreamed of the pending conflict as a struggle to maintain or extirpate slavery. She was not of those who went to war because the Union would not suffer southern masters to convey negros in the abstract to an impossible place—Kansas. She would not have given one drop of the blood of those dear to her for the freedom or slavery of all Africans in the South. Fighting was begun, and womanly sympathy impelled Mamie to espouse the cause of the weak and of those she knew and loved. Her father, recognizing, as the daughter and wife did not, ties of partisanship, and listening, as was his wont, to the sturdy, practical, simple eloquence of Andrew Johnson and reading the *National Intelligencer*, a Whig and conservative newspaper that once entered the home of almost every slaveholder, was an unfaltering, earnest Unionist.

I had observed differences between northern and southern women produced by the institution of slavery. If the northern dame were self-reliant, she was also cold, selfish and practical. If southern women were physically helpless, and unused to toil, and knew not how to serve themselves, they were also wholly ignorant of the depravity, as well as selfishness, of men. The hybrid race stood between the maiden of wealth and social vices of which she never dreamed. Chivalry honored and respected virtue because there was no necessity, as society was arranged, for assaults upon its strongholds. But beyond this, the co-existence of two races, the one enslaved and by no means faultless, imbued free-born damsels with a degree of self-respect, and pride of person and race which repelled every approach of degradation and dishonor. Selfish interest concurred with and heightened and ennobled the tenderest sensibilities and truest sympathies of southern women. It was their province to minister to the sick, to clothe the naked, and feed the hungry. Their reward was two-fold: in dollars that glittered in greasy, healthful, shining African faces, and in that higher, holier pleasure derived from the consciousness of doing good, in ministering to the delights of others, and relieving woes of the helpless, dependent and unfortunate. Slavery, therefore, produced the noblest women possible, and I loved Mamie Hughes none the less that she was an hereditary slave-owner. Infinite and numberless as were evils incident to the "peculiar institution," it begat a class of men and women, and a state of society, in many of its aspects, as admirable and delightful as that is degraded and brutal in numerous localities has supplanted African servitude and white mastery. Planters were petty kings, wielding powers almost of life and death. The master's slightest nod was the iron law of the realm. None of God's creatures are so good and great that they are worthy of such autocratic power, and few so ignorant and depraved that they should be subjected to this despotic authority; the right of masters was no more divine than is that of kings. Mamie's father, like my own, reigned unrestrained despot over five hundred human beings, and such a father hardly tolerated the unconquerable fidelity of the mother and daughter to the "treasonable Confederacy." That both might entertain changed or modified opinions, they were separated, and Mamie was sent into East Tennessee to spend a few months with her "loyal" cousins. There I had met her, as already stated, and there I was hopelessly enchained, a helpless victim of the simple wiles and native charms of pretty Mamie Hughes.

Before the deluge of woes, war, poverty, vice, and crime swept over and annihilated it, the hospitality of the "Old South" was traditional as it was matchless. In fact, monumental virtues, as well as vices, were sturdy outgrowths of negro servitude. These were expanded and flourished, until (in its social aspects, as seen from without and as presented in the every-day life of southern households) strangers deemed it paradisical. The characters of the planter and of members of his family were shaped by peculiar influences wrought by peculiar

relations of master and slave, and by consequent peculiar modes of
life.   He trafficked and traded with nobody.   He only gave.   His
cotton or sugar or rice factor, in the nearest commercial mart, sold
his crops and bought his annual home, and plantation, and household
supplies.   His overseers commonly bought mules, and horses, and
bacon, and the planter only rode over his estates, and watched the
growth of crops, and determined questions of right and wrong arising
among "his people" on his broad estates.   Humanity was profitable,
and hospitality, where farms and gardens and orchards produced
everything that hospitality consumed, cost nothing.   Planters were
even willing to pay for agreeable society.   Therefore, their residences
were hotels where no bills were presented.   They had dogs, and
horses, and guns, and wines, and dinners to attract those whose
society they courted.   Having no business or trade relations with
their neighbors, they had no quarrels or law suits, and thus the loftiest
and most admirable personal virtues were cultivated and exercised,
and worthy men, as well as admirable and haughty women, sprang
from the centuries of African servitude.

Mamie Hughes was thoroughly imbued with the feelings, and
instincts, and ineradicable pride of race that distinguised the best and
truest and haughtiest of her sex.   She had been blest, and injured in
nothing, by influences exerted by negro subordination to the white
race.   Rich, never having known a want ungratified, she was self-
willed and arrogant.   Accustomed to the exaction of obedience, she
expected limitless concessions to her demands.   The time was coming
when Mamie must adapt herself to conditions of life wholly subverted.
She was anticipating it and schooling her proud spirit even then, that
she might defy poverty and cheerfully accept its griefs.   The tide of
desolating war had already swept over the homes of her kindred in
East Tennessee.   There she had led the way in executing each
arduous household task suddenly imposed by hard necessities of the
period upon her aunts and cousins.   She encountered every stroke of
poverty with seeming indifference.   She toiled steadily, intelligently,
and skillfully, and such was her patient, smiling heroism, that
misfortunes became sources of pleasure, because of the delight involved
in retrieving them.

And Mamie Hughes was a true representative of her class.   The
richest, and proudest, and noblest of the South when poverty came,
were never heard to utter a lament.   There were no Jeremiads
in which were inserted tedious parenthetical descriptions of gorgeous
splendors and fabulous wealth in the midst of which she had moved
and reigned in unrestricted authority.   Mamie, as subsequent pages
may tell, was true to herself, to her class, and to the nobility of her
race.   She was fearless and confident, encountering calamities and
triumphing over poverty with a determination and steadiness of
purpose that exacted every concession of gratitude and love which
intelligence and truth always award to the loftiest heroism.

Besides a sugar plantation in Louisiana, Mamie's father owned rice fields in South Carolina; but his preferred home was in the broad, rich valley, in ——— County, Georgia, fifty-eight miles from Atlanta. Here Mamie's mother, and grandmother, and great grandmother, were born, and here her fathers had tilled the soil, and gathered wealth, and owned countless slaves, through many generations. Great old oaks, and walnut trees, and Lombardy poplars had been planted one hundred years before in long lines leading through the enclosed forest to the rambling, irregular cluster of apartments, passages, dining, dancing and music halls, and library, and bedchambers that constituted the ancestral home of Mamie Hughes. How I happened to go thither, and what vicissitudes of fortune befell Mamie, her brother, and myself, will appear hereafter.

# CHAPTER VI.

The Fascinating Deserter and Gay Widow.—An Accommodating Negro.—The
Capture.—Unearthing a Deserter.—"Ef this 'ere Umbaril would shoot."—A
Corruptible Juvenile.—A Woman who loved Whiskey, and how it mollified
Her.

We had been pursuing the usual routine of scouts' duties several
days near La Fayette, capturing deserters and bushwhackers, and
incurring at all times unseen and unmeasured dangers, when we
learned, through a woman, of course, that a lieutenant of a Georgia
regiment, Longstreet's Corps, who had escaped as a deserter from our
lines, was harbored by his cousin, so-called, a gay and charming young
widow of the town. We were eager to capture the young gentleman.
Our fair informant, moved by jealousy, said that he had concealed
himself in the forest while we were in La Fayette, but returned when
we left the place. I went about the streets everywhere stating that we
would move south, into our own lines, the next day. With my whole
force, and with baggage packed and rations prepared for a long march,
we moved out of the place. Five miles away we entered a thicket,
remaining there till midnight. Then, with four men I retraced my
steps and reached the widow's house in the suburbs about one o'clock.
In the darkness I stationed my men about the house, supposing that the
gay Lothario, hearing of our departure, would return before day-dawn
to his accustomed and most comfortable quarters. We were only
mistaken in the date of events. We rested, watching intently, but in
vain, for the Lieutenant's approach, till streaks of gray light danced
and flashed and disappeared, and then marked the verge of the
eastern sky. Then it occurred to me that our intended prize might
have entered the house almost as soon as we left the place.

Just then a drowsy negro appeared. He came out of his cabin
hard-by, slowly yawning, and stretching himself, and rubbing his
eyes, to the wood pile behind which I was seated. He was muttering

to himself and cursing the cold weather and "Massa Jones" who had ordered him to kindle fires in the "white folks' house." Silently, and unseen, in the gray mists of early dawn, I leveled my musket. The sleepy negro's nose struck the cold barrel.

"Golly! What's dat?" he exclaimed, starting back, and throwing up his hands.

"Be silent, you black rascal, or I'll blow away the top of your head," was my low response.

Cuffee was now wide awake. His greasy eyes glistened in the pale, thin fog. I said to him that if he obeyed me he should not be harmed. To steady his nerves and confidence I gave him a silver half dollar. He had not seen one since 1860. He grinned when rubbing and looking at it, and then an awfully black pall of gloom settled instantly and fell over his sooty face when he contemplaced the lowered musket, still pointed at him.

"Cuffee," I said.

He started, thrusting the half dollar into his breeches pocket.

"Cuffee," I continued, "I want that Lieutenant who is staying in your mistress' house."

A broad grin slowly spread over and illuminated Cuffee's portentously black physiognomy. He was silent a moment, and then said:

"Go an' cotch him, massa. He's in dar."

"Yes," I responded, "I know that, but he is armed and desperate, and if I open the door he will shoot. You must open it. He knows your voice and will come unarmed to admit you with your load of wood. When he opens the door my musket will make him stand harmless and helpless."

"You is gwine to tuck him wid ye, is ye? An' he aint comin' back enny mo?" Cuffee asked, with a look of anxious inquiry.

I answered him that the deserter would be seen no more in La Fayette.

"All right, massa. Mistis nestils to him moas too much enny how and Cuffee doesn't want any white boss on dis place."

He piled up the wood on his shoulder and moved to the house. He leaned forward and the wood struck the door. He had hardly asked the Lieutenant to open it when the young gentleman appeared in his night clothes. The click of the lock and gleam of the bright gun barrel almost touching his face, paralyzed him. "Walk out," I said. "Cuffee, bring out the gentleman's clothes, and don't forget his pistols and other property. He must go with us, and we have no time to lose. When the sun rises, the bushwhackers, knowing we have left, will take the town."

Pale and trembling, his lips white and eyes starting from their sockets, the young man read his final doom in the facts before him. It was not my musket that frightened him. He saw the gallows just behind me. His knees shook, teeth chattered, his face was of ashen hue.

"Come out," I said. Holding the door-facing, and moving helplessly, he advanced, as I stepped backward. I whistled. My comrades came instantly. Cuffee assisted the deserter in dressing himself, and we were moving away when the vigorous widow, by some means became advised of what was occurring.

She leaped out of the house in her night clothes, and alternately weeping and railing at us, demanded the release of her "husband." She sought to pass me and reach the two men between whom her lover was rapidly moving away.

I caught her arm and asked if she had "reflected what disgrace she was bringing upon her name by this public betrayal of relations subsisting between herself and that deserter? The neighbors are awake. See the lights in that cottage, and how fires blaze this cold, bright morning on many hearths, and yet here you are in your gown howling after that deserter. Your child will be dishonored!"

The woman stopped. She covered her ears with her hands and stared fixedly and wonderingly in my face.

"Go back," I exclaimed, and thrusting her hand violently from me, I left her mute and motionless. I had not gone very far, when, looking back, the hapless widow had disappeared. I never saw her afterwards, and am sorry to tell her, even now, since every wanderer in Northern Georgia will read this book, that her lieutenant was sent under guard to his command which had been transferred to Virginia, and there he was tried, convicted, and shot for desertion. For obvious reasons I have not given his name, once honored everywhere in the South, or that of the fascinating dame who surely loved him very tenderly.

We moved leisurely toward Ringgold. We had heard from a farmers's good wife, from whom we bought eggs for breakfast, that there was a deserter, as she believed, secreted at a designated neighbor's house. We were then about nine miles from La Fayette. She said that the mistress of the place had a child not more than ten or fifteen days old, and that half a dozen women were always there to serve up the gossip of the country for the delectation of the poor mother, still bed-ridden.

"It will happen, therefore, said the good dame, that if you search the loft and inspect the out-houses, you will be beset by the most frightful scolds that ever assailed a soldier. The women that meet there are unlettered wives or daughters of bushwhackers and one or two men would not be safe in attempting to discover the hiding place of a deserter from the southern army.

Very unwillingly did the two females who met us at the doorway, admit us into the house designated. My force was now reduced to six men and our appearance was not very imposing. But when the women saw that we were armed and resolute, we were told by a thin-visaged, long-nosed, angular creature to "search and be derned!" She shook at us an old cotton umbrella and said: "Ef this 'ere umbaril would shoot I'd kill the last derned one of ye! I thot you . was a lot of Jeff Davis' sneaks and spies to cum pokin' about under people's beds and things!"

Here a meek-looking, tearful woman nudged the fierce declaimer with her elbow. I observed the movement and accepted the suggestion in reference to the beds. But the violent old harridan talked and raved only the more violently and volubly until she finally broke down giving way to floods of grief pumped up by impotent rage.

We peered into every nook and corner of the house, and looked under every bed and finally went away, still believing that a deserter lurked about the place. But we abandoned the search and concluded at last the bird had flown. We loitered for a time at the spring under the hill near the house. A barefoot boy, a cunning little rascal, twelve or thirteen years old, was throwing pebbles into the spring. I soon discovered that he knew what were our purposes, and where the deserter was concealed. I offered the urchin a silver half dollar to tell. He yielded at last, unable to withstand a bribe involving the instant delivery of a box of percussion caps. He told me to raise the planks under his sick mother's bed and I would find there a man whom he "didn't love." He said this fellow "had bin thar more'n a year, off and on, and my own dad, he's bin a soldiering sumwhar in Virginney," he believed.

The boy asked what we proposed to "do with Mr. Jobson." I asked why he wished to know.

"Oh! nuffin much," said the youth, "he aint my dad and I'm jest tired of folks axin' me ef he aint."

We returned to the house, encountering at the entrance a fiercer volley of imprecations than before. Even the silent, weeping dame, whose pitiful face and heart-rending sighs had excited our compassion, was now voluble and defiant.

"Here's six pore lone wimmin right 'ere in this 'ere naberhood an' nary a man to take care of us, and look arter us, but one, and you mean Jeff Davisites want to take him away."

She broke down completely, dissolving in a flood of tears, and fell weeping beside Spratling, who, with a cocked pistol in his hand, disappeared under the sick woman's bed. She screamed, the baby shrieked, the women all crying out, danced hysterically about the apartment.

Spratling lifted a plank from the floor and ordered the "d——d ground hog," as he pronounced him, to "crawl out." The cocked pistol nudged him under his ribs. He begged Spratling not to shoot, and came forth submissively enough. I had obtained a pair of hand-cuffs in the jail at La Fayette. Persuaded by Spratling's repeater, the deserter, Jobson, dropped his wrists into the iron bands. I locked them and turning to the petrified, horror-struck virago who had abused me so mercilessly, I said most harshly:

"Hold up your hands! you, too, shall be hanged for harboring deserters."

Her courage gave way. She gasped for breath, grew pale as a corpse and fell backward, her head striking the floor heavily.

The excitement had been too much for her. I was alarmed. It

never had occurred to me that I would kill a woman. Of men slain in an open field and fair fight, or to save my own life when assailed by ambushed enemies, I never recked a moment, but when this ungainly, obstreperous woman fell, I confess I shuddered, and simply because of the sex of the dead. I dashed a bucket of water in her face and when at length she gasped for breath, I thrust a canteen of whiskey down her throat.

It is a solemn fact, incredible as it may seem, and three of my comrades of that day, still living, will attest this statement, that when the fiery liquor began to gurgle, as it trickled and leaped along the rough-ribbed channel of her elongated œsophagus and finally lighted blazing camp fires beneath her diaphragm, she sighed and opened her eyes. Then she looked up into my face very tenderly, and smiled, oh! so lovingly! The fiery draught was

> "Sweet as the desert fountain's wave
> To lips just cooled in time to save."

I rose up exasperated and wished at the moment that death might seize, and the devil fly away with the grateful, whiskey-loving creature. I jerked the canteen from beneath her toothless gums. Her lips collapsed and struck one another as did the sides of the empty Confederacy not very long afterwards. The secret of womanly devotion to the ungainly, cowardly Jobson was disclosed. He was a distiller of "pine top" or "gum log" whiskey in a cavernous valley, and a canteen would have been more effective than a repeater in discovering his hiding place.

Mr. Jobson fettered, I ordered my men to march.

After the annoyances and excitement of the day there was a radiant serenity of light crowning the hills, and glowing at sunset about more distant mountains, that throbbed in its intensity. It was divinely restful, like the passion and peace of love when it has all to adore and nothing to desire. The splendor and beauty of mountains crowned by the glories of the setting sun and contemplated through this transparent atmosphere were matchless. There was a gleam of divine glory in aspects of nature about me and I basked in the sweet invigorating air that was like a breath of Paradise.

Ten days later Jobson was tried, convicted, and shot as a deserter.

# CHAPTER VII.

When my brigade was going into action at Chattanooga, September,
1863, Tom Ellison, a private from Coffeeville, Texas, grew very
sick. Weak nerves caused his fall. He was simply paralyzed and
helpless from insane terror. I have seen brave men, so esteemed at
home, and because of courage illustrated in deadly personal conflicts,
shrink into absolute helplessness when first moving under fire and
advancing upon serried ranks of armed battalions. Again I have seen
those bravest in battle, and then utterly oblivious of themselves, who
shrank timidly from a personal rencontre. Fear is an unaccountable
passion, and I am persuaded, after no little experience in fighting, as
a scout, as a veteran, and as a private citizen, that courage is commonly the fear of being thought a coward. Few are wholly devoid,
like General Forrest, of the passion of fear, and the bravest are
sometimes hopelessly victimized, when they least expect it, by absurd
terror.

But this man Ellison, in the presence of danger so imposing and
sublime that most soldiers, in its face, absolutely forget their own
identity, becoming wholly reckless, shrank down in his place in the
line of battle, and no force or danger or sense of shame could drive
him forward. Afterward, and from that day, he was dangerously
sick. Doctors said his nervous system was wholly shattered by
terror.

When our army retreated from Missionary Ridge, in November,
1863, Ellison was left sick within the Federal lines. His comrades
said he had taken the "iron-clad" oath of fidelity to the Union, gone
north, and died. But soon after we had captured Jobson, a country
dame informed us that a deserter was sojourning at a neighbor's house

4

hard by Jobson's den. We were especially anxious to capture this faithless Confederate, because, assured of encountering and mortally offending one or more of the horrible women who sought so earnestly to prevent the extraction of Jobson from his subterranean hiding place. But greater became our anxiety to secure the deserter when informed that he was a Texan. Our brigade was from that commonwealth and felt itself disgraced that a citizen of Texas proved false to the cause we had espoused.

We surrounded the house designated by our informant before day-dawn, that none who slept within might leave without our assent. At sunrise I knocked at the door. Heavy footsteps of my men and clanking of our arms at once extorted groans from the sick man. I did not, of course, know who he was and only that he pretended to be suffering fearfully, and yet had walked during the week, to Chattanooga and back, quite forty miles, in a single day. I knew these to be absolute facts and am sure that he would have deemed me a heart-less wretch if he had beheld significant smiles overspreading mine and Spratling's faces when we heard his heart-rending groans and pitiful cries for relief.

Sure enough, when a pretty girl admitted us, she asked us to step lightly, saying, "There's a very sick man within. Any noise distresses him. He is very sick and nervously sensitive. Step lightly. I am not sure he will be glad to see you. He is from Texas and must be true to the South."

The bright-eyed, cunning woman smiled, bent her knees, her body went down about four inches, her head was projected slightly, and she pulled gently upward at each side of her homespun, striped dress-skirt. Such was her salutation, as she stepped lightly backward, inviting us to enter. The details show that a veritable queen of fashion, among *hoi aristoi*, could hardly have greeted us in a more approved manner. Then, too, she smiled as blandly and naturally and graciously as if she were even delighted because of our coming.

What social triumphs this cunning, pretty creature, whose form was perfect as her face was fair, features regular, and eyes brilliant, might have achieved if she had not been born and reared in comparative poverty among the mountains and sand-hills and pine-covered straw fields of Northern Georgia.

I could not help discovering in the fascinations of the laughing, youthful, and beautiful woman very potent apologies for the unearthly groans and execrations that proceeded from the apartment of the dying (?) soldier. I whispered to Spratling:

"No wonder he is dying. A true soldier could afford to die for a woman like that. I don't blame the fellow, even though he be a Texan, for desertion."

"I don't see how he could well help it," was Spratling's generous response, and Spratling still stared vacantly at the doorway within which the pretty sprite had disappeared.

Evidently the great, rude soldier was the victim of the winning, merry eyes and sunny smiles of the meteor-like vision of beauty that flashed so suddenly across his pathway.

What was our amazement on entering the sick-room to behold the familiar face of our late "dead" comrade, Ellison. He, too, was startled. He drew his hand across his eyes. He rose up in bed. He shrank back abashed. A death-like pallor overspread his face. He had evidently been dreaming of scenes in which the chief actor sits on his coffin while a dozen soldiers, half of them using muskets charged with blank cartridges, that no one of them may know who does murder, fire upon the deserter. Such executions are very frequent in civil wars. There were northern men in southern, and Southerners by birth in northern armies. To desert a cause which it cost so much to uphold, and abandon an undertaking which seemed hopeless, and more than purposeless to those who revered the Federal Union, was easy. Multitudes were fighting against their original convictions of duty and right, and others encountered dearest friends and kindred on bloody battle-fields. That desertions in such a war were numberless surprised no one, and the very greatness of their numbers rendered severity and certainty of punishment the more necessary.

No wonder Ellison shuddered. He knew that of all men Spratling and I would be most anxious to punish one who had brought disgrace upon our brigade. He groaned in an agony of terror. I could not help pitying him. But the necessities of the case were inexorable. I ordered him to rise and dress himself. He groaned and wept and insisted it was impossible. I drew a gleaming knife and holding his head said that if he did not obey instantly I would cut off both his ears, and if he still refused I would order my men to fire on him. Groaning and weeping like a pitiful baby, he crawled out of bed and with trembling hands and quivering limbs dressed himself and sank upon the floor exhausted by his terror.

"You may rest a moment," I said, "but you shall march thirty miles to-day. Bushwhackers are on our track. We must take the woods. Be cheerful; order breakfast for all of us. We will pay for it in silver, and I think"—the wretch was fumbling with a pair of crutches—"you can leave your crutches. You didn't take them with you when you went to Chattanooga and back, last Tuesday."

Poor Ellison! I was sorry for him. He stared at me a moment, and then fell over backward, shocked and swooning. I baptised his face in whiskey, pouring a little in his open mouth, and his senses returning, he looked vacantly around the room for a moment, and said: "I am ready. Tell me what I must do."

I repeated the suggestion as to the necessity for our immediate departure, and ordering one of my men to hand-cuff and take charge of Ellison, felt that the game was my own.

Spratling had modestly suggested his own willingness to see that we had an early breakfast. In social life he was unique. He talked little and rarely laughed; but if his stories were brief, they were most amusing, and the more, because of his profound solemnity.

He was a fine-looking, blue-eyed, light-haired, good-natured young fellow, six feet four inches high, of infinite pluck, enormous strength, and perfect truthfulness. He was born and reared wholly innocent of contamination by books, in the mountains of Tennessee, had migrated in his early youth to Texas, and came back a soldier, twenty-eight years old, with Granbury's brigade, in 1861, to his old home.

I assented, of course, to Spratling's proposition to have breakfast prepared for us and went out to see that no one approached, and station a sentinel at a proper point of observation. Spratling, I discovered, was in the little kitchen in the yard with the pretty maiden and her mother. He was evidently pointing towards Ellison's bedroom, and telling of the great miracle wrought, and how it was effected, when poor Ellison heroically put aside his crutches and walked before a persuasive musket. Bessie Starnes—I learned the name soon afterward from Spratling—laughed so immoderately and neglected culinary duties so sadly, that, when I drew nearer, her mother was chiding her. Finally the good dame said, "Mr. Spratling, if you want breakfast, you must quit spinnin' them funny yarns. That gal thar allus was a rebel, and I aint mad about it, and now she's clean gone daft because you tell her about the devilment you've done and because she thinks you a game, true soldier, and not one of them thievin' deserters like that hand-cuffed wretch sittin' at the gate thar and aweepin' like his heart would break. I do hate the likes o' him, and Bessie loves a brave feller."

Then the good woman suddenly checked herself and cast a most inquisitive glance at her pretty daughter gazing steadfastly in Spratling's honest, earnest, clear blue eyes.

He began to tell of the fascinations of his wild home-life on cattle-flecked plains of Texas. Bessie listened breathlessly and so intently that the mother's warning was unheeded, and roasting potatoes were utterly forgotten. The mother gazed in her face again, as if to read her inmost thoughts, and sighed. Perhaps it was because she feared her child's fidelity to plighted troth was endangered. Evidently the mother ascribed to the daughter the feelings which I traced and discovered in Spratling's absent-mindedness. He had at least confessed, for the first time, boundless admiration for a woman.

The mother seemed to brood over the facts' before her. She was silent, and talked and smiled no more. What evil in her eyes threatened her winsome child? She devoted herself the more earnestly to accustomed tasks. She kneaded corn meal dough, adding salt, in a poplar tray. When it was of proper consistency she made round, flat "pones," almost an inch and a half in the middle. These were deposited in the midst of the fire on the hot hearthstones, and covered with red hot hickory ashes. The bread was thus roasted. When extracted, piping hot, it was the famous negro "ash-cake," to be eaten with butter and milk. Each of us ate one of these ash-cakes, weighing half a pound, and drank a quart of milk. Broiled spareribs, biscuits, and coffee made the breakfast perfect in a soldier's eyes.

Bessie served us at table and I am sure that Spratling never knew what he ate or whether he ate at all. Bessie always stood, by accident of course, where she could look into Spratling's face, and such a feast of love and luxuries was never spread. Spratling, a very cannibal with his eyes, was devouring the charming girl.

Hebe never moved more daintily or served at Olympic feasts with more graceful decorum than did pretty Bessie Starnes, when gliding noiselessly about the rude table spread for rebel scouts.

Bessie we knew to be a devout rebel. The mother, when we paid for the breakfast, in silver half dollars, was moved to confess her devotion to the Confederacy, and ask us to call whenever it was possible. The head of the household, in Oglethorpe County, below our lines, when our army retreated, found it difficult to secure access to his home. In his behalf we promised Mrs. Starnes to intervene when we returned to the army.

We left Spratling and Bessie at the gate. Spratling was holding her hand.

"Join us," I said, when I passed him, and when going away, "at the 'Big Spring,' at noon to-day."

Bessie gave me an astonished, but as I thought, a grateful look. Spratling's face was slightly flushed. I pressed Bessie's hand, and with Ellison before me, walked away toward Cleburne's encampment.

Conscious of the honest sincerity of Spratling's devotion and of the depth and strength of his affections, I was anxious to be assured that his love was requited. If Bessie rejected his proffered love and fidelity, I believed he would be utterly unmanned. In any event, I so dreaded the result that I could not refrain from asking him, when we were alone at noon, "whether Bessie could be trusted."

He evidently divined the true meaning of this modest inquiry, and answered :

"Of course ; but I must go there again as soon as you can spare me."

Each relying upon the other as confidently as upon himself, and each having often imperiled his life that the other might live ; inseparable as Spratling and I had been from the hour that Jefferson Davis lighted the match at Fort Sumter that set a nation aflame ; made friends by common toils and dangers and by indestructible confidence ; still Spratling never alluded to Mamie Hughes, and the word "Bessie" never passed my lips. I recognized the sanctity that invested the name in Spratling's eyes, and he knew that woman alone may enter the gate-way to that garden of the affections in which the sensitive love-plant blossoms and bears most delicious fruit.

Anticipating somewhat the order of events, it is proper to state that Ellison, our prisoner, was tried by a drum-head court-martial for desertion, and properly acquitted. He had been left sick in bed in the enemy's lines, and was never a deserter. He returned to his place in the ranks, and there was no better soldier from that day forth than Ellison. He lived, it is true, in a sort of trance, was always silent and abstracted, obeying orders mechanically.   Some weeks after his acquittal and after events here recited occurred, Spratling was sitting beside me in our tent, in front of General Granbury's, when Ellison, with his accustomed anxious, feverish look, passed us very hurriedly.

Spratling, pointing towards him, said:

"I am sorry for that poor fellow, and for myself that I aided in arresting and frightening him.   True, we secured testimony that saved his life, but I sometimes think that we caused him to become the silent, nervous hypochondriac that he is, and then, do you know that he loved Bessie Starnes to madness.   He thinks I robbed him of her love.   I will tell him everything, some day."

There was infinite sadness, to be accounted for hereafter, in Spratling's low, melancholy tones when the last sentence fell from his lips. I had heard of the deep shadow that fell across the sunshine that once lighted up with gladness his eyes and face, and warmed his generous, loving heart.

# CHAPTER VIII.

The Underground Railway.—A Desperate Adventure.—Secession in Kentucky and Tennessee.—In a Bushwhackers' Den.—An Heroic Woman.—The Catastrophe.—A Graveyard Scene.—The Ghost.—A " Notiss."—A Woman's Eloquence and Matchless Patriotism.—A Monument to her Fame.

To discover agencies employed in effecting escapes by deserters, was eminently desirable. Within the hour that the exit of a fugitive from our army was discovered, his capture, we had learned, was impossible. He seemed spirited away. There was a mystery about it that excited keen inquiry and not a little anxiety among our commanders. I was instructed to put a period, if possible, to the process and resort to any means I might approve and employ any force required. I repaired at once to General Cleburne, who was my personal friend, and said to him that the easiest and surest, if most dangerous, mode of ascertaining the facts would be found by my own desertion. He approved the proposition, and, General Johnston assenting, I selected Doc Nooe, or Noah, a Kentuckian, as the sharer of my toils and of the hazards of the undertaking. He knew leading men in many portions of the Dark and Bloody Ground, as Spratling did not, and when questioned in reference to people or localities, would commit no blunders. He had been two years a citizen of Texas, and I knew him thoroughly. He was courageous, honest, and a devout believer in the justice of the Confederate cause. He loved the excitement of battle and was thoroughly tired of idleness in winter quarters. If arrested, he was to be the tale-bearer to account for our flight and assure our captors that our sole purpose was to return to our old homes and kindred in Kentucky. But for this, I would perhaps have preferred Spratling as my coadjutor in this scheme of desperate hazard.

With these general plans defined, Nooe and I left our lines about day-dawn. Even before sunrise, while moving rapidly along a little path leading toward Chattanooga and passing between Villanow and Ringgold Gap, we were hailed by a watcher in a thicket by the roadside. We stated at once the purpose of our flight. There was no danger incurred. If our captors were Confederates, we would be taken to Cleburne's or Johnston's headquarters and tried, convicted, and shot—with blank cartridges. If our captors were Federal scouts, we were certainly safe if our statements were accepted as truthful. We were hastily questioned and such was the overweening confidence of the common soldier of the North in the supreme, palpable justice of his cause that he never doubted when even hardened, fighting rebels pretended to approve it. In the loyalists' eyes it was almost impossible for a Kentuckian to be disloyal. There were genuine adherents, it was supposed, of Davis, Yancey, Ben Hill, and Bob Toombs, away down south, but very few, it was thought, in Kentucky and Tennessee.

At the rendezvous of Federal scouts and of bushwhackers not far away, to which we were hurried, we were rigidly questioned. A dozen men stood around and listened, intently scanning our faces. The sun was above the horizon, but its direct rays did not illumine our resting place till it was high in the heavens. In the gloom of the deep valley and beneath a great projecting stone that concealed perfectly the cavity in the mountain-side occupied by these daring men, we underwent this searching examination. The Kentuckian, Nooe, never hesitated. He never once faltered. His courage and intelligence alike were faultless. The most keen-sighted—and bushwhackers were more apt to suspect the honesty of others than Federal soldiers—were thoroughly satisfied of our perfect integrity. Every kindness was shown us. Cigars, liquors, and luxuries amazed and delighted us. We ate and drank prudently. Our lives were at hazard. Any blunder, even the slightest, would be instantly fatal.

The hiding place was wisely chosen. No visible road or path approached it. The beaten track we followed led near and beyond it. We bent low beneath dense undergrowth, and diverging abruptly from the path, we found, not far away, at the head of the deep ravine, the narrow entrance, between great stones, to the broad deep chasm beneath the northern side of the mountain. If enemies came from the south, occupants of the rendezvous could descend into the ravine and escape unseen ; if from the north, they could ascend the cliffs and pursuit was almost impossible. Sentinels, at each point of approach, were always on duty. Each week, late at night, guides, with deserters who had been gathered in, went forth to Chattanooga. The residence of Mrs. Shields, whose business it was to provide deserters with food and lodging, was the last resting place of deserters entering the Federal outposts.

We remained in the bushwhackers' den forty-eight hours, when we were consigned to the care of a guide and went directly toward the nearest pickets of Sherman's army. We had studied meanwhile, as carefully as possible, the topography of the country and watched every landmark closely, that we might make no mistake when we returned to requite with bullets every kindness shown us by our generous, confiding hosts.

How infinitely brutal and brutalizing is war! Lying, stealing, treason, and murder become foremost of fine arts.

We arrived at Mrs. Shields' covert, with our guide, before daylight. Her husband was absent, serving as a blacksmith, in Chattanooga. Both were living, I am told, not many weeks ago.

She was bright-eyed, shrewd, fearless, and active—eminently well fitted for the position she occupied. How keenly and earnestly she scanned our faces at breakfast! I had little to say, while Nooe talked volubly of Kentucky and of anticipated delights that would attend his arrival at home. He never seemed conscious of the presence or suspicious watchfulness of the adroit, wary, fiery, little woman. We ate ravenously and were greatly fatigued. Therefore, we stated to our guide, that we must sleep a few hours, before the resumption of our march, and that he might return, if he chose, to the bushwhackers' rendezvous. He assented.

We were left alone at Mrs. Shields'.

During the day we discovered that in the smoke-house, pantry, and in the loft, rich and abundant stores and supplies of all descriptions were deposited by Federal authority, for the use of bushwhackers and deserters. Federal picket lines were only two miles distant.

Just before sunset, a little boy, when we had bidden Mrs. Shields an affectionate adieu, was assigned the needless task of leading us to the nearest pickets. The boy was lazy and stupid. We gave him a few small coins, and telling him we could find our way without his assistance, induced his return.

Before leaving our headquarters we had so ordered events that a cavalry force of thirty men should come to meet us, by way of Ringgold Gap, at a little church within ten or twelve miles of Mrs. Shields'.

It was now very dark, and we soon lost our way and even feared that we might encounter Federal soldiers at every turn of the road. One's fancy, stimulated by reasonable apprehensions of danger and by darkness, becomes singularly productive of causes of alarm. Great stones and broken trees became silent, watchful horsemen, and shadows made by clouds and uncertain moonlight, falling through tree-tops, became ghostly wanderers, resting upon dense undergrowth along either side of our devious pathway. Our senses were keenly alive to the slightest impressions. Nooe detected, telling me of it in low tones, a faint, unsteady light not far from us. We feared we had lost our reckoning and discovered the resting place of a body of Federal pickets.

The forest was unbroken. No weary, somnolent winds, wooing sleep in silent solitudes, wandered by to disturb death-like repose that rested upon the great trees and stilled the pulse-beats of the voiceless woods.

Discovering at length that the pale, uncertain light came through crevices in a wretched log hut, we approached it very slowly and very cautiously. No sound came from within, and at length we were satisfied that the cabin was unoccupied. The fitful light we had seen was produced by an expiring blaze burning very low on the hearthstone. We went about the cabin and finally called out, "Who is here?" Again and again, when we called aloud, there was no response. We rebuilt the fire and found every evidence of the recent and hurried abandonment of the house. Roasted potatoes had been left on the hearth and two tin plates and knives and forks on the table. A blanket and mean bed-clothes were on a sort of bedstead attached to the walls of the hut. At length we discovered blood stains on the floor. A dead body had evidently been dragged out at the doorway.

It was now midnight. There was nothing to detain us. Hunger impelled us to take the potatoes, and we resumed our journey. The very stillness of the forest made me whisper to Nooe:

"Nature is shocked, stupefied, and silenced by witnessing the ghastly deed done here to-day in this wretched cabin. Bushwhackers have been here. It is their hideous work."

We passed near a little faded white church. The moon had risen and was now shining lustrously. We could see distinctly the few white gravestones in the church-yard, and fifty steps away, white palings, tipped with black, enclosed many graves, and now and then a rail pen encompassed some freshly raised hillock.

"See," I said, "even here there are newly made graves and wherever our footsteps lead, we soldiers are only digging graves. Mighty armies are engaged in this mournful task. Bushwhackers and freebooters and scouts—all of us—are now grave-diggers. I am sure, when looking upon these freshly reared, narrow mounds over which I have been walking every day since the spring of 1861, that blessed mother earth, stricken with grief, always heaves a little sigh when one of her children falls."

I had hardly spoken, when a white figure slowly rose up in the misty moonlight out of a grave in the remotest corner of this "God's acre." Very slowly it came forth, as it seemed to us, out of the earth. It stood still a moment, as if unused to the dim shadows of the silent night, and then glided slowly and silently, as if moved by the lazy winds, down the declivity.

It soon passed from sight.

Nooe and I stood still, staring with wide open eyes in stupefied silence in the direction the ghostly apparition had moved.

"What, in God's name, is that?" he asked.

"Let's follow it, and see," I answered. The suggestion restored manhood and excited a share of that ardor springing from the presence of danger over which courage is delighted to triumph.

We walked rapidly in the direction taken by the seeming shadow of death escaped from a newly made grave. As we passed the grave, we saw that no grass had grown over its little hillock and the clods had not been dissolved in nature's tears.

"Perhaps," I said, "somebody has been buried alive and we have witnessed this strange resurrection."

"God knows," answered Nooe; "I only know if I had not started to find out, I would gladly go back."

We slackened our speed when we again caught sight of the slowly moving figure.

"Who is that?" exclaimed Nooe, in nervous, quick tones.

The apparition turned and stood still. We advanced very slowly. I could hear distinctly the beating of my oppressed heart and think that my hair stood on end. Nooe hesitated.

" Shall we go on?" he asked, in unconsciously uttered words.

Desperate rather than heroic, I answered, "What, Nooe, do we fear?"

And yet in all my life, in a charge upon serried ranks of a solid phalanx, scaling a fort's walls as leader of a forlorn-hope, or meeting a cavalry charge, or when storming a battery, I had never been victimized by such unseemly terror.

"Surely," I thought, "graveyards do yawn and discontented spirits, in these troublous times, do revisit the land of the living."

We were now advancing very slowly and within ten paces of the apparition, standing still and facing us in a narrow path hedged in by dense thickets and overhanging tree-tops. Little, tremulous, narrow streaks of pale moonlight, penetrating dense shadows of forest foliage, fell upon the white-robed figure before us.

In husky tones, Nooe asked :

"Who—what are you?"

There was an age of silence, deeper than that of the breathless woods or of footfalls of the ghastly shadow before us. Like some great sorrow or weight of intolerable grief, this death-like stillness bore me down, and I felt that I was in the presence of a living death.

The answer came at last. In low, tremulous, painful accents of unutterable anguish, a woman's voice responded :

"I am most miserable, and helpless, and heart-broken of women."

There was an interval of silence.

"Why are you here, and why in that graveyard at this late hour?" I asked.

"We fled from bushwhackers in East Tennessee and only two days ago succeeded, by the merest accident and good fortune, as we thought, in passing through Sherman's lines. My husband was one of a squad of Confederate soldiers ordered to execute the decree of a court-martial at Greenville and hang an aged man who burned some railway bridge. His neighbors and friends swore they would avenge the 'patriot's' death. They resolved to kill every person who was a participant in the taking of that old man's life. Finding that we were nowhere safe in East Tennessee, and having been twice shot at, once in our own home at night, we came south. But ministers of vengeance were on our track. The worst of bushwhackers about Chattanooga are my old neighbors. I know them well. We were resting at the little cabin on the roadside, on that hill, there, when three of those terrible men from Green County—I recognized them— rode up to the door, and in my presence, shot my husband to death.

"Whether this happened to-day, or yesterday, or a week ago, I cannot tell. I know that people came, dug a shallow grave, and buried him in a blanket, and left me here. I only woke from a trance a little while ago, and when I looked up, I saw the gravestones about me, and the little church on the hill, and the path that led to the wretched cabin where we had rested a day.

"I am very, very cold, and going back to the little cabin, if I can find it. I don't know what is to become of me. I am friendless, helpless, and alone."

The wretched woman, as we learned afterward, had been seemingly unconscious when her husband was buried by the bushwhackers and two or three people of the vicinity, and these had hardly finished the irksome task of interment when a squad of Confederate cavalry was discovered taking possession of the church. Bushwhackers and pity-ing people fled, leaving the widowed woman where we first mistook her for a disembodied spirit.

The cavalrymen who frightened away the grave-diggers were the very body of men sought for by Nooe and myself. Uncertain as we were of the correctness of the course we had pursued through the night, guided by moon and stars, it happened that we had deviated very slightly from the direct route from Mrs. Shields' to the appointed place of rendezvous at the little church.

The helpless woman was to be cared for and we must move at once. She had been subjected to so many griefs and woes of war that this last great sorrow seemed only to invest her with a sort of dazed insensibility to suffering, giving a marble-like hardness to her features. She was very handsome and graceful. Her perfect self-possession and natural kindliness and intelligence won the regard and respect of the rudest soldiers. We "impressed" the wagon of a farmer for her use, and at sunrise moved rapidly toward our nearest outposts. The lady was sent to General Johnston's headquarters, while with fifty cavalry-men, having stationed a force at each point of exit, I made a descent upon the bushwhackers' stronghold. They had been warned of danger and fled. I found pinned securely to a tree at the entrance to their cavernous retreat a rudely written note of which I have a copy. It is couched in the following graceful terms :

"NOTISS.

" Ef we ever cum acrost you two dam rascals and spies again you dance on nuthin' and pul hemp like hell. We hang every Kaintuck we ketch. But want you sweet on old Kaintuck ! "

Kuklux warnings, of a later period, were modeled after this graceful proclamation of the outraged bushwhacker. Analyzing the proclamation I discovered that its writer was not wholly revengeful and malicious. While I am sure, if caught by him, I would have been hanged, yet, for all that, he appreciated the joke so deftly practised by Nooe, by means of his beautiful and heartfelt disquisitions in the bushwhackers' den, and at the bushwhackers' feasts, pronounced upon the delights of his "Old Kentucky Home."

The cavalry were sent to the outposts, while Nooe and I, with our orignal thirteen men, hurried back to Mrs. Shields'. We reached her hospitable dwelling before sunrise. An hour later my whole force, except Nooe and myself, never disguising the fact that they were rebels, were given an excellent breakfast. Mrs. Shields was a discreet woman and knew that twelve hungry soldiers are dangerous; but when they produced silver with which to pay for her kindness, she was coldly hospitable. The men having breakfasted, Nooe and I entered the gateway. Mrs. Shields stood in the door and stared at us, and then shading her eyes with her hand from the bright sunlight, and gazing intently in our faces, was assured of our identity. I never beheld such an exhibition of insane rage and malevolence. She had been restraining herself with the utmost difficulty while my men were at the table. She was forced to listen silently to their boastful stories, to recitals of their vaunted deeds, and to harsh criticisms upon the vices of bushwhackers. She was full of pent-up wrath, even before Nooe and I appeared. She was excited, too, because of denunciations heaped, on this occasion especially, on those who murdered the East Tennessee soldier in the hut at the little church. The young widow, the men said, though she moved about and talked and smiled, produced the impression that she was still asleep, having never become conscious of her latest and greatest grief. She was in that condition, her escort said, when they left her at army head-quarters.

The pent-up fury of Mrs. Shields broke down all restraints when I looked smilingly into her face, and asked her to give us breakfast. Her eyes and mouth, while she stared at me, were wide open. Then she exclaimed, in husky tones, her voice quivering with rage :

"I would see you both eternally d——d, first."

She turned to the table, and while she vilified us and the "one-horse Jeff Davis Confederacy," she hurled plates and viands out of the back door.

"I can feed honest, brave, rebel soldiers. That is bad enough for a woman who was born under the old flag and means to live and die under it, but would die a thousand deaths rather that let a pair of sneaking, lying, rebel spies sit at my table. Oh! how you two did love Kentucky! I thought from the first you were a pair of Texas cattle thieves. I watched you and when you bribed that stupid boy, Bill Callaway, to come back, I knew you were not going into Chattanooga. I sent the first honest man that came by down to the picket lines, to inquire whether you had gone in. I had you tracked towards Mount Pisgah Church. I sent word to the bushwhackers' cave that you were coming with one hundred men to capture and hang them. They were saved by me, and you pitiful fools were out-manœuvred by a woman. You might eat in my house if you hadn't been such a pair of stupendous asses. Outgeneraled by one little woman!'' And peals of mocking laughter rang through the house.

The men listened in amazed silence. She talked most volubly and her keen intelligence was wrought up to vigorous action. Nobody could long submit in silence to such a castigation as she administered. Her eyes blazed with unaccountable fury, while she gesticulated violently and reasoned with the precision and fierceness of a most skillful prosecutor. Every imprecation fitted its place and there was cunning logic in her frightfully fierce objurgations.

Seeing no end to the woman's vocabulary of epithets or themes of denunciation, I said to her that we had heard enough, and that we came, after paying for breakfast, to take charge of supplies deposited there by the northern army for the use of deserters and bushwhackers.

Mrs. Shields was silent. She stared at me as if bewildered. She turned suddenly to the fire-place and seizing a half-consumed fagot threw it violently at my head. Living coals were scattered every-where. She rushed out of the house, and when I went to the back door, she had already thrust a fire-brand into a little shed attached to the main building and filled with hay. Almost instantly the heroic little woman, with a bundle of valuables in a large satchel and her bonnet on her head, was standing in the road contemplating, with a degree of satisfaction too profound for utterance, the destruction of her com-fortable home.

We saved a few canvassed hams, several boxes of cheese, and a little canned food, but the brave, earnest, patriotic blacksmith's wife had again won a confessed victory by such a sacrifice as few men would have dreamed of making. She was then, and may be now, for aught I know, my mortal enemy, but she deserves a monument prouder and loftier than many that have been reared to perpetuate the memory of deeds infinitely less honorable and requiring infinitely less devotion and heroism than she illustrated when applying the torch to her own loved home.

While equestrian statues and bronze and marble everywhere, in Washington and other cities, tell of the grand achievements of men, why may not some artist's pencil or sculptor's chisel tell posterity of the deeds of this devoted woman, who sacrificed her wealth and all that she cherished, contemplating the conflagration with heartfelt joy, because she witnessed at the same moment the discomfiture of her country's enemies.

No single grand public attestation of woman's worth and patriotism, as illustrated in the war between the States, has been carved on mon-umental stone or set up in bronze or limned by artist's pencil. But war crowned its infernal vices and crimes by hanging an innocent woman, a deed so foul that it overshadowed the horrible crime it sought to avenge.    Through all ages, Mrs. Surratt's slender neck and clenched, motherly hands will hang out in the hot sunlight, swinging slowly round in their bundle of black rags.    Her upturned, pitiful face will never be banished from the conscience of the people. Partial amends to woman should be made by rearing a monument to fearless and devoted Mary Shields.

# CHAPTER IX.

Knowing that smoke and flames of the conflagration would attract the attention of Federal pickets and scouts within a few miles of us, we made a hasty departure, going directly towards La Fayette. When, next morning at ten o'clock, we approached the town, a countryman, coming out, informed us that the place was occupied by a small body of Federal cavalry.

A reconnaissance informed us that a courteous, kindly Federal soldier, Colonel Burke, of the Tenth Ohio Cavalry, was in charge of half a dozen Confederate ladies sent out of Nashville by Andrew Johnson, then, I believe, Military Governor of Tennessee. A like body of Confederates from our army head-quarters met Colonel Burke in La Fayette, they spent the night together, danced with the ladies from Nashville, and with all the pretty girls about La Fayette, stole the hearts of the choicest of them, and went away to return, not long afterward, to desolate the land with fire and sword. Soldierly hostility was purely political. It was never personal or social. The bushwhacker, on the contrary, was the personal, unrelenting foeman of every one who upheld the Confederacy. The reason was that a secessionist's fierceness and anxiety to consolidate southern opinions rendered him most intolerant. Before secession was accomplished, contumely, abuse, and social exclusiveness were employed, and, in the Gulf States, a Union man, in 1861—the people had been so instructed by fierce party leaders—was socially ostracized and despised. Unhappily for the conservatives of the South, their great leaders, Bell and Douglas, the former superannuated and incapable of exertion or usefulness when nominated for the Presidency, and the latter, a citizen of a northern state, exercised no potency in the South, while Yancey, Toombs, Tom and Howell Cobb, and every

Federal office holder in the South, as instructed by Davis and Quitman, Lamar and A. G. Brown, toiled side by side with Andrew Johnson and Isham G. Harris to consolidate the South. Andrew Johnson was hanged in effigy, in Memphis, by Whigs and Douglas men, in the fall of 1860. Afterward, when each southern Federal senator vacated his seat, and Johnson, hating Jefferson Davis, saw how infinitely conspicuous he himself became as the solitary southern senator, withdrew from association with his partisan friends, the adherents of Breckenridge, Davis, and Yancey, and pronounced for the Union. Therefore, the unmitigated abhorrence with which Johnson's personal and political character and conduct were contemplated by secessionists, and, therefore, the bitterness of this hostility between rebels and bushwhackers—the native southern fighting Union men.

Our most dangerous and fearless foemen, as scouts, were these bushwhackers, and yet among these we found loyal personal friends, and thoroughly honest, trustworthy gentlemen. It will be remembered that we encountered and captured and held as a prisoner, some days, a bushwhacker and ex-schoolmaster named Wade. After studying his character, I released him because of his accurately truthful statements, and in consideration of his promise to accompany Mamie Hughes, if she sought to come south, to her father's summer country seat, not far below Dalton and Tunnel Hill. While we were encamped in the woods near La Fayette, Wade came boldly to my sentry post, near the main road to Chattanooga, and asked to be conducted into my presence. I was pleased to meet him. I really liked the intelligent, honest, fearless Unionist, and then I was keenly anxious to hear from Mamie Hughes. We walked down to a little spring below the hill and there I asked impatiently:

"Have you seen Mamie?"

"Yes," answered Wade, "I went to her uncle's, near Charleston, on the Hiwassee. I pretended to be a sick East Tennessee Union soldier. She is the epitome of all rebeldom, and while her cousins came to hear me tell of my adventures, Mamie stood aloof. But I remarked at breakfast, while Mamie's face was half averted—she was my *vis-a-vis*—that I had been below Chattanooga and captured and held several days a prisoner by rebel scouts; and, my God, Captain," exclaimed Wade, "you should have seen the color come and go in Mamie's sweet face. She said not a word, and soon recovering herself, drank a little tea, and turning to see that I followed her with my eyes, she went out.

"I soon discovered an opportunity to confer with her alone. She was now as eager to hear as she had been persistent, for two days, in avoiding me. I was shunned, I now know, simply because I am your public enemy; she sought me because I am your personal friend."

"I think," I said, "you can always trust me as your friend."

"I repeated to Mamie what you said, telling her that whenever she wished to return to her home in Georgia, I would see her safely restored to her father's care.

5

" 'Oh!' she said, 'my poor father was already no more, and I did not know it, when I met the Captain beneath the stars and by moonlight, and danced with him so joyously on the hill-side beyond the Tennessee. My brother is in the Union army, a lieutenant in Colonel Cliff's regiment, and my poor mother is alone at the farm below Chattanooga. I must go to her and then I will be nearer'—

"She stopped; looked furtively in my face. I was watching and listening. She was instantly silent and her cheeks were redder than before. We were seated in a vine-clad summer house. Mamie turned away to hide her blushes among the rose leaves. When spring-time comes no bud will blossom there more bright or beautiful or sinless than the faultless girl you love. I am going, if you will trust me, because I now love Mamie as my own child, to see Mamie's mother, and with her assent, the poor child's wishes shall be executed. Her wretchedness, when she spoke of her mother's solitude, was measureless. Her cousins said she 'was always crying and always deploring the impossibility of reaching her own home.'

" But Mamie's mother doesn't know me. I must see her, with this letter from Mamie."

I could not help taking it, and would have kissed it, if Mr. Wade had not been looking at me.

"Certainly," I said, "I will see that you pass safely below our lines. General Cleburne, when I tell him what I want, will get a paper from head-quarters that will enable you to serve Mamie."

I sent a courier that night with dispatches to General Cleburne's head-quarters, telling him, among other things, that I wanted "a pass through the lines for Mr. Wade and for a rebel Georgia girl whom I loved."

Wade, the noted bushwhacker, slept that night beside my camp fire and beneath my blankets. He ate and drank with us and I am sure there was never a more reckless, thoughtless, joyous body of men, in either army than they who followed my fortunes and sought by every means to please the excellent bushwhacker. He was much older than any of us, had been a godly country pedagogue, but had acquired many soldierly tastes and habits. He could drink mountaineers' whiskey, told capital stories, and was an adept in Schenck's game of poker.

On the third day after his departure the courier returned with needful instructions and orders, and with the passport for Mr. Wade and Mamie Hughes.

I was perfectly blest.

# CHAPTER X.

When the passports were delivered by the courier, I called the bushwhacker and pedagogue and silently gave him the papers. I was dreaming of the day when I would meet Mamie Hughes, and was never conscious of keener delight than that given by my interview, as narrated in preceding pages, with the scholarly, modest, earnest bushwhacker. He read my heart and was silent, that I might dream uninterruptedly. Blissful visions were conjured up by the pedagogue's simple recitals. His pictures were exact copies of those my fancy had already etched a thousand times upon the clear blue sky when proximity of danger repelled sleep, and when I watched the stars, or discovered in white clouds, gorgeously gilded by moonbeams in this transparent atmosphere, the fancied outlines of Mamie's sweet face and matchless form.

I was still dreaming when the bushwhacker said :

"I saw General Sherman last Monday. He was visiting his outposts and inspecting his forces at Sweetwater and other points. I was at a fat and loyal widow's house on the roadside when he and his staff were passing. A soldier galloped by exclaiming :

" 'General Sherman is coming ! '

"I went to the door, but the widow almost ran over me. She rushed out into the midst of the highway, and there she stood bareheaded, her red, fat face shining, as if oiled, in the brilliant sunlight, her bosom filled by 'two churns,' as she mildly described them when fattening her twins, her body thrown back and arms akimbo. She stood with a protuberant avoirdupois of two hundred pounds squarely

and firmly in the midst of the highway. The foremost of the horsemen asked her :

" 'What can we do for you, madam? Why do you block up
the road?'

" 'I want to see Gineral Sherman,' was her firm answer.

"Another officer came up asking, 'What do you want madam?'

" 'I'm bound to see the Gineral,' was the sturdy response.

" 'I am his chief of staff, madam. Can't I serve you, and will you
not be good enough to leave the road that we may pass?'

" 'I'm bound to see Gineral Sherman,' persisted the good dame.
The front of her dress was apparently quite a foot shorter than the rear
that hardly touched the ground as she stood bending backwards with
naked arms akimbo, looking up and eagerly scanning the face of each
horseman. Her circumference, described by a cotton string around
her body—she had no waist—must have been five feet. Of course the
highway was effectively closed.

"The General rode up asking, when the obstruction to his progress
had been described by an aide-de-camp :

" 'What can I do for you, madam?'

" 'Is you the Gineral?'

" 'I am. How can I serve you?' he replied.

"She walked up, and standing beside the General's horse, held the
bridle reins and began :                                              •

" 'You see, Gineral, my old man and the three boys is in your army
afightin' agin Jeff Davis and for the old flag. I'm here a lone widder
with the two gals and the two twins, makin' a honest livin', I am ; and
lo ! and behold, Gineral, a lot of your soldiers keeps acomin' to see my
darters, Susan Ann and Maryer Jane, and acourtin' around here of
nights, and every time enny of 'em comes they tote away a turkey
or two tell I haint but one fat gobbler left. I've lost nigh onto
fifty turkeys, Gineral, and I'm ruinated and I don't know what's
to become of me and the gals and the two twins at these innercent
breasts.'

"Here the good dame lifted up the lower end of her striped,
homespun apron and wiped first one and then the other greasy, red eye.

"The General was evidently deeply affected. Natural nervous impa-
tience had been heightened by the endless multiplicity of just such
complaints as this preferred by the fat dame before him. He was disgusted, even furious.

"He straightened himself up, raised his plumed hat, stood in his
stirrups, and said:

" 'Look at me, madam ! Listen while I speak ! In your presence
and in that of these valiant men and of the bended heavens, madam,
I here swear and pledge myself to crush out the Great Rebellion if it
costs every damned turkey gobbler south of the Ohio !! '

"The General's manner was eminently and grandly theatrical,
solemn, and imposing.

"The woman, with earnest, inquiring gaze, stared wonderingly for

a moment at the General, and comprehending at last the trifling character of her sacrifices, said, as she slowly released the bridle rein :

"'Gineral, I have a fat gobbler left. It is your'n. Wait tell I go
and fetch him.'

"'With all my heart I thank you,' was the General's response, and
as he rode away, I heard the long, loud laughter of the rollicking staff.
One of them thoughtfully remained to get the turkey, for which the
courtesying dame, with eyes full of oily gratitude, accepted a five-
dollar greenback sent by the General.

"East Tennessee," continued the pedagogue, "is in a terrible
condition. The people are preyed upon by both armies and by
banded thieves and highwaymen that belong to neither. The morals
of the people are affected by these facts. The seat of war is the scene
of vice as well as suffering. I think many years must elapse, and a
new generation of men and women come upon the stage, before the
South can be restored to its original condition. The worst products
of the war will remain here ; the best return to their homes beyond the
Ohio. Poverty and vice and illiteracy will be dominant for many
years, and I dread peace as much as I abhor war. There is no future
in the South for men of my age, habits, tastes, and training. Dema-
gogues, of the revolutionary, violent sort, will win ignorant popular
favor ; and prejudices and hates of this lawless period will shape
results of popular elections. Discord, violence, and vendettas will
brood fatefully over this hapless land.

"I was infinitely amused, not long ago, by a little incident illustrative of what I have been saying. You know my school was broken
up, my home and books were burned, and I was thrust into prison at
Knoxville. For what, I never knew. I was furious, and swore
vengeance, and was wreaking it right and left when I fell under the
influence of your generosity and of the tender, filial confidence and
affection and marvelous beauty of Mamie Hughes.

"The story I would tell is simply this. It illustrates my lugubrious
philosophy, showing the tendency to evil of every incident of hateful,
vicious, red-handed war. One of the richest citizens of Carter County,
in Tennessee, is David Haines. His son, Landon C., is a brilliant,
facile talker, a lawyer of ability and pronounced success, and a violent,
original, "blood-drinking secessionist," so called in allusion to the
fact that political prophets used to tell the "submissionists," or Union
men, as you remember, that they, the prophets, would drink all the
blood to be shed in any war that would follow secession. Landon C.,
the son, is now a member of the Confederate Senate, at Richmond.
Then, too, the fortunate Mr. Haines, *pere*, has a son-in-law in the
person of Hon. Nat G. Taylor, the old Whig congressman and eloquent Unionist.

"Thus, you will observe, the elder Haines is braced up by a pair of
capable defenders in the son and son-in-law. Therefore, when Federal soldiers came plundering and seizing wagons, horses, and supplies
of every description, as is their wont in Carter County, Haines, senior,

announces the fact that his son-in-law, the congressman and preacher and orator, Taylor, has promised him ample protection and that his property shall not be molested. Taylor's name is potent among Union men.

"When Confederate guerrillas come dashing over the hills and hollows of Carter, robbing barn-yards and stables and smoke-houses, then the paternal Haines, with earnest, illiterate eloquence, his white locks streaming in the wind, tells that he is the father of the great Confederate senator, Landon C. Haines, and that Landon made Jeff Davis promise him immunity from these exactions levied by Confederate soldiers. The result has been that *pater-familias* Haines, until recently, has been effectually guarded by the son-in-law against Federal, and by the son against Confederate bandits. About two · weeks ago a squad of bushwhackers made a descent upon the old gentleman's pretty farm, and were about to desolate it. He came out and scanned their trappings closely. They gave no sign, but were badly appareled and armed, each man to suit his fancy. Mr. Haines concluded they were "rebels." He began his usual pretty little eulogium upon 'my eloquent, high-larnt son, Landon C., is a member of the Confederate States Senate, in Richmond, and he made Jeff Davis promise,' etc. The wicked bushwhackers would hear no more.

" 'Come, boys, help yourselves,' exclaimed their leader; 'this is the d——d old daddy of that howling fire-plug of hell, Landon C. Haines. Clean out the d——d old rascal.'

"Nothing visible was left. Mr. Haines loves money for its own sake. He was almost paralyzed by the blow. I did pity his sorrows.

"A few days later another squad of thieving soldiers came by. They bore no flag or other distinguishing marks of 'nationality.' They rode through the gate and up to the door. Mr. Haines sat there, eyeing them intently. He could not tell whether his unwelcome visitors were northern or southern.

" 'Tell me,' said the leader of the squad, after some trifling conversation, 'are you Union or rebel?'

"Mr. Haines, staring vacantly at his questioner, was silent for a moment, and then said very slowly:

" 'I'm jess nuthin, and sense I come to think about it, I'm d——d little of that.'

"The soldier was so amused—Mr. Haines is an illiterate old gentleman—that he laughingly ordered his men to 'feed their horses and let the old man alone.' "

# CHAPTER XI.

Next morning after the grand "international" ball in La Fayette the Federal cavalry set out to return to Chattanooga.

At the same time, my diminutive force, accompanied some distance by the East Tennessee shoolmaster who had agreed to do no further military service, moved toward Ringgold Gap.

Late in the afternoon we were moving leisurely through the woods two miles west from the town, Ringgold, when suddenly startled by the appearance, not far away, of a force of Federal mounted men. Ambulances followed them and we were amazed to discover, after a hasty reconnaissance, that this very calvacade left La Fayette when we did. In truth, it was the women's escort that pretended to leave for Chattanooga. It then occurred to us that the purpose of the. Colonel leading the force was to take advantage of the flag of truce to gather information. Secreting ourselves by the roadside till the ambulances went by, we moved rapidly to the high hills just west of the town of Ringgold. Satisfied that wrongful advantage was sought to be taken of the flag of truce, we proposed, soon after night-fall, to "stampede" the horses of the cavalry and ambulances and at least compel the cunning Ohio colonel to return to Chattanooga on foot. We watched the movements of the escort closely, and disposition of their horses.

The sun was going down and had just become invisible. Sitting on a fallen tree, smoking a cob-pipe, some little distance from my men, I was startled by the approach of two Union soldiers—infantry men—walking leisurely toward the spot where my men were lounging on their blankets. I advanced on the unexpected intruders and ordered them to halt. They failed to obey, but turned back. I called to Spratling or Lewis for a gun. The latter ran to me saying, in a whisper, "For God's sake, Captain, don't shoot. There is a brigade of Federal infantry just over the hill, there!"

There was no time to be lost. The two Union soldiers had not reached the top of the hill, going to their brigade, just below on the other side, when we were in full flight in the opposite direction. There were half a dozen Federal pickets, now discovered for the first time, between us and the bridge across the creek at the foot of the hill west of Ringgold.

It was now growing dark, and as my men wore Federal overcoats we slackened our speed thinking that we would be deemed stragglers and suffered to pass without molestation. If not, there were thirteen bullets for not more than five or six lazy-looking German sentinels. I passed within five paces of one of these. He simply grunted, when he looked at me, and I heard him mutter:

"Tam straeghlers!"

We were now within the Federal lines and almost in the midst of the enemy's encampment. I was never environed by such dangers, and never, when potent causes for gravest apprehensions were discovered, have I confessed, as on this clear, bright wintry night, a keener sense of genuine anxiety and even of alarm. Camp fires began to blaze everywhere. A division or corps of the Union army had evidently just reached the place and was bivouacking for the night.

Soldiers who were at Ringgold will remember the long-framed house, with its portico and rose vines, at the west end of the bridge across the deep creek. In the rear of this house was the kitchen and back of that was the smoke-house; behind this was the orchard, and then the open farm occupied the valley, extending nearly a mile to the base of the lofty wooded hills. The deep creek winds about through the farm in every conceivable direction. The owner of the place, a rebel, had left it in charge of an old colored servant and his wife. I had often stopped at the place and the good colored dame and her husband knew me well. She addressed me as "sonny," and I was accustomed to praise "Mammy's" ash-cakes—corn-cakes roasted in hot ashes—and buttermilk. I was hurrying to "Uncle Mose" and "Mammy" for information and that I might have their advice and assistance. Fortunate were we in first seeking the negroes' aid. "The 'big house' "—a designation commonly applied by negroes to the master's residence—"is chuck full of Yankees," said old Mose, after staring wildly at me for a moment.

"In the name of gorramity what you doin' yere, Marse Jim?" whispered "Mammy."

Her eyes protruded from her head till I could have knocked them
out with a board brought down edgewise perpendicularly.   By the
bright fire-light I could discover that her sooty face had assumed an
ashen hue.   She spoke in a hoarse whisper.

"Marse Jim," said the old man, "dar war some Yanks here yis-
tiddy, de fust dat cum.   Dey knode you and I said dey had you onct
and dat you fooled 'em and got clean away wid 'em.   Dey said dey
was gwine to hang you and Marse Nooe dar.   Dat's what skeers dis
niggah.   You must git cleer away."

"Show me the road to the mountains at once.   We can't talk
now," and old Mose led the way to the rear of the smoke-house, and
pointing across the creek and farm, told me to go.

Pressing the hard hand of the old negro and telling him to say to
"Mammy" that I would soon see her again, I leaped the fence, my
men following, and we ran at the top of our speed toward the creek.
Signal guns were firing and drums beating an alarm.   We could hear
the rattling of arms and movements of horses.   The moon was up, and
in the cloudless sky, diffused the light of day about us.   We had
emerged from the little orchard and gone two hundred yards in the
open field, each of us exerting himself to the utmost, when we heard
cavalrymen swearing, and tearing down the fence behind us.   Before
they entered the field, we reached the creek, five feet deep, and its
banks eight or ten feet high.   We never hesitated or looked to the right or
left.   Leaping in, we were immersed to the armpits.   The shock, heated
as we were by terrible exertion, almost paralyzed us.   The night was
bitterly cold, and words can never describe the unutterable anguish
we experienced when, slowly scrambling up the bank with limbs
hardly obeying volition, we began again the unequal race for life.

Thirty or more horsemen were in close pursuit.   When they came
to the stream, the shadows of moonlight may have exaggerated
its depth.   They halted and then rode up the stream to find a crossing
place.   Meanwhile we were recovering our capacity for flight and
moved rapidly.   The cavalrymen fired a harmless volley at us, and
then shouting triumphantly because a good ford was discovered, they
came rushing across the level field.   They were within one hundred
yards when we again plunged into the creek; and within fifty yards,
again did we cross it, and again our pursuers swore furiously, and
fired wildly at us, and rode madly up and down the creek to discover
a crossing place.

Our enemies were now scattered.   Five or six—probably more—
crossed the stream ahead of the rest, and as we were almost out of the
clearing and just as we entered the woods, these eager horsemen rode
rapidly to prevent our access to a place of security.   Spratling and I
had taken the lead in this furious flight.   He was strongest and I
most agile of the scouts.   As the horsemen began the ascent of the
declivity, we stopped that our whole force might encounter the
approaching pursuers.   Nooe and the rest soon stood by us in the
shadow of a few trees.   The reckless riders came within thirty paces

when we fired. I don't think one of those gallant, excited riders escaped unharmed. But we did not wait to see. We were not sure even then that the pursuit would be abandoned and therefore hurried through the forest up the ascent.

Utterly, helplessly exhausted, we rested at last on the mountain's summit. Weary beyond measure, our clothing frozen, and fearing, if we kindled fires, that pursuit would be renewed, we were reduced to the last extremity of suffering. We looked down upon endless lines of Federal camp fires and listened to musket firing about Murdock's Mills, south of Ringgold Gap, in the direction of Tunnel Hill. The configuration of endless lines of armed men could be defined by means of steady flashes of musketry and occasional explosions of field artillery. It was a splendid exhibition, but physical anguish rendered enjoyment of the dazzling, imposing spectacle, impossible.

In desperate straits men think rapidly. How absurd, I reflected. even then, had been my threat addressed to the two Federal stragglers an hour or two ago! how insane my vengeful little plan for the punishment of the flag-of-truce escort for its detour made, as I had supposed, to gather information! The Ohio Colonel knew more than I when he moved his cavalcade into the encampment of Palmer's Corps, sent to Ringgold Gap to compel the return of Cleburne's division suddenly ordered to Mississippi to arrest the march of a Union force across that state. Palmer's object was accomplished. As I learned later, Cleburne was even that night turning backward from Mobile and Meridian towards Atlanta and Dalton.

Cold, icy winds swept over the mountain top in freezing, fitful gusts. When we moved, our ice-incrusted clothes crackled, while our bodies had been superheated by this desperate flight and toilsome ascent. We were absolutely freezing to death. One of my men said, his lips trembling and teeth chattering:

"Boys, its a pity we hadn't surrendered. The devil will get us anyhow."

We were forced to have a fire; but there was not a match that could be ignited. We had been too often baptised. Fortu ately our cartridges were waterproof.

Just then Nooe discovered the glare of a fitful light down the mountain-side. Kendrick and I proposed to go in a body and capture those who enjoyed the warmth of the blazing fagots or die in the assault.

Nooe said "it were wiser if only one or two went forward. If these find everything right, they can whistle and the rest will join them. As you two proposed that all should venture to the spot, it is proper that you two should go forward."

I pressed Kendrick's foot with mine that he might be silent, and assented to Nooe's plans. If there were no danger, I was to whistle like a partridge and my comrades would come to me at once. If we fell into the clutches of bushwhackers, of course we would die and make no sign.

"Kendrick," I said, as soon as we left the scouts, "if we find everything comfortable, let us be silent and punish the boys for sending us helpless into hidden danger like this."

"Agreed," answered Kendrick, while we trudged along, ice-clad, our very bones shivering and freezing, down the steep declivity.

Reckless because of mortal suffering, we looked eagerly through crevices in the walls of a log hut and beheld a rudely clad country jade lighting an oven from a log-heap fire on the broad hearth. What spasms of hunger suddenly attacked me! I caught the fumes of the baking opossum. Kendrick hastily knocked at the closed door. I was still watching the woman. She dropped the pot-hooks upon the oven lid and turning toward the door, asked, in a sharp, shrill, husky voice:

"Who's dat?"

"Madam," I answered, "we are two starving men. We will give you a silver dollar for that 'possum and potatoes. Let us in. We will not harm you. We are freezing."

Slowly and doubtingly the ignorant creature removed the bar across the shutter and we entered, paid the woman the stipulated price, and in less than five minutes had devoured the opossum. No more delicious food ever delighted a hungry, weary, freezing soldier than this *summum bonum* of African luxuries—"baked 'possum and roasted sweet 'taters." But negroes are not singular in appreciation of this choicest southern luxury, that most abounds where persimmon trees flourish. When United States Senator Garland of Arkansas was asked by an eastern gormand how an opossum should be cooked, he answered:

"The bent of my mind is that if you would boil the 'possum in salt and pepper water until it is quite tender, and then brown it well in an old-fashioned oven, or skillet, wherein around its body a goodly number of potatoes are baked and browned, you would have a dish unrivaled, and more than Oriental, and a person who could not relish it, whether he took the 'possum hot or cold, would have no celestial fire or music in his soul." As to whether the 'possum is best eaten hot or cold, the Senator confessed his inability to decide. "Rather than miss it entirely," he added, "I would try to eat it in any way I could find it, and really I am of the opinion that it is best hot or cold, according to the state it is in when I last partake of it."

A daintier dish was never set before a king, and no sybarite ever enjoyed the costly viands of Lucullus' table as did we this baked opossum and potatoes.

We had hardly dispatched the grateful repast when we heard the footsteps of our comrades. They could endure mortal anguish no longer and came to share our unknown fate. We asked them to enter, telling the woman that she was safe and should be well rewarded for her kindness. The poor creature, staring stupidly and helplessly in my face, shrank, with a small yellow mop in her mouth, into the corner, and soon slept. Kendrick and I were well pleased to tell of the feast that had been spread for us.

"You sent us alone," I said, "to prison or death. We avenged the wrong by leaving you to freeze while we feasted."

We filled the fire-place with blazing logs, and Kendrick and I agreed to take the first watch. The boys drew lots to determine who should succeed us at midnight, and very soon profound rest dissipated every memory of the surprises, hopes, excitement, and keen anxiety of the memorable day and night at Ringgold Gap.

Our breakfast next morning was a reproduction of the supper of the preceding night. The good dame was surely objectionable as a cook. She was the ignorant widow of one of those ignorant, stupid fellows who are caressed and flattered by "great, good men," so called, and induced to become food for powder. The lackadaisical, yellow creature, with streaks of yellowish snuff trickling from a filthy mop in her mouth, said "she had heern he was kilt sumwhars in ole Ferginny."

She sniffled a little, and taking more snuff on the mop, filled her stained, yellow mouth and wiping supposed tears, with the corner of her greasy, homespun apron, proceeded with melancholy slothfulness to fry thick flitches of bacon and thinly sliced sweet potatoes, and bake corn-bread, and boil coffee.

Nine-tenths of the people of the Gulf States were preparing at this selfsame moment just such breakfasts of these selfsame simple materials. Our hostess was only peculiarly blest in having coffee furnished from the haversack of one of my comrades. Further south, rice constituted as in India, breakfasts, dinners, and suppers of an agricultural people cut off from commercial intercourse with all nations.

In the early summer of 1863, I descended the Tennessee River in a skiff with Major Hornor, of Helena, Arkansas, from Chattanooga to Decatur, Alabama, and thence crossed the country on foot from Decatur to Birmingham, known as Elyton, a wretched little village, and thence I went to Columbus, Mississippi. Even then there was neither sugar nor coffee, and only bacon and corn-bread, on the tables of the rural districts. The people of Northern and Central Alabama suffered most. They had the least possible communication with the exterior world. The women were appareled in the coarsest cotton fabrics, woven on rude domestic looms and spun on hand wheels, such as are only to be found to-day in collections of curious *bric-a-brac*. Salt, even at the period designated, could not be bought by the indigent population, and when a hog or beef was slaughtered, the people of each vicinage assembled and each took away a share that the whole might be used before decomposition began. These poverty-stricken districts were solidly democratic. They had been first for war, and only very old men, women, children and deserters occupied this broad district. Pitiful to the last degree was the condition of the country with its starving, rudely clad mothers and abandoned wives and yellow-legged, unwashed, unkempt, unattended children.

I spent the night with an old man, Elisha Short, in a district of Pickens County, Alabama, known as Bunkum. I gave him ten dollars in Confederate currency to kill a kid. I had a little salt and we fared sumptuously, having milk and corn-bread. Mr. Short seemed to think the condition of the country somewhat changed, but had no definite idea of the cause of calamities that befell him and his neighbors. He had been told, as he said to me, that "a feller named Abe Linkhorn had raised hell sumhows and was ruinatin' things, but he didn't know for certain." He had "heern of a feller what was a speakin' round for Kongris or sunthin' tellen the peepil to secesh and he heern they had seceshed and it looks like a hell of a bizness at this particular time. Thar's sunthin' about the nigger in it, but as we-uns haven't got any niggers, we don't know much about it. Everyboddy is Demmycrats in these yere parts, end of course we could get salt and things ef it wasn't for them Whigs and Abbylishermers."

These, substantially, were the words and sentences of the good old man who stammered fearfully. He had been falsely educated by party leaders and believed, till the day of his death, if he lives no longer, that Lincoln was the author of all the woes that befell the South.

The air was clear, sky cloudless, and sun shone brightly upon house-tops in the valley. Blue, spiral columns of smoke ascended, like incense, toward heaven, from chimneys of cottages, in the beautiful valley below, when we discovered, with a field-glass, that there were no Federal soldiers on the south side of the mountain. Ascending to the summit we beheld long blue lines of soldiers, like endless serpents, winding steadily and curving with the roads over the hills and along the valley toward Chattanooga. Palmer's spies and scouts had informed him that Cleburne was ordered back from Meridian, Mississippi, and Palmer, his object accomplished, was returning to his original position, We followed him a few miles to gather in stragglers and secure newspapers and possible valuable information.

Our purpose accomplished, we went to Tunnel Hill. Here we rested for a few days; in the meantime were ordered to report for active service to General B. J. Hill, Provost Marshal General of General Joseph E. Johnston's army.

We served General Cleburne no more.

From this time forth our toils and dangers, as we well knew, would be incessant. General Joseph E. Johnston, among his soldiers, was supposed to be omniscient. On the track of one there always followed another scout, to verify or correct statements made by the first. It was impossible to mislead the General, and nothing was surer to send a scout to service in the ranks than any exaggeration of the importance or number or value of facts he had ascertained. Most soldiers engaged in this business reported too much. They saw too much; they risked too much; they triumphed over insuperable obstacles and achieved results that the wily commander knew to be utterly impossible. I do not think that General Johnston was ever fatally misled. I was often amazed because of his possession of information which I thought nobody besides myself could give. Therefore, I never reported inferences for facts, and never anything that I did not know to be absolutely true. He was never unreasonable and never exacted impossibilities. I was ordered, when I made my first exit from our lines, to enter those of the enemy and report their strength at a given point. After earnest efforts to pass the Federal pickets during three successive nights, I returned at the time fixed, to General Johnston's head-quarters; and when I said I could not get through and gave the reasons, the General thanked me and at once sent me on a more dangerous mission.

It is not always possible for a scout to discover the disposition or strength of the enemy's troops. Patient watchfulness and slow, tedious movements along deep gullies and under the shadow of fences, crawling through briers and under-brush and crouching low when watchful sentinels grow restive, are least painful and tedious of tasks executed by scouts.

I am satisfied that the mere proximity of an unsuspected scout affects, unconsciously, the nerves of a sentinel. Of course the poor fellow does not know that, if discovered, I am ready to kill him. He can not be conscious of unseen dangers, but surely recognizes unconsciously the presence of fate impending. He begins to move as the scout draws nigh. The slightest sound made by a broken twig beneath my knees and hands, as I would creep silently by, would make the drowsy watcher start violently. Peering about him for a time into the darkness, he would again resume his ceaseless, steady march. Why, otherwise, do sentinels, when the stealthy, noiseless scout approaches, at once become silent? The melody that was chanted in low, soft tones while the sentinel was dreaming of the pretty girl that sang it at her own northern fireside, when at length I can almost see the color of his eyes, is heard no more, I have never drawn near enough to one of these watching, and therefore, nervously excited sentinels that I was not sure that he was told by some invisible scheme of telegraphy of my presence, of my purpose, and of imminent dangers that beset him. He whistled no more; his lowly uttered song that he was humming was silenced; and he was conscious surely of vague apprehensions of undiscoverable danger. In my inmost heart I have pitied an unhappy sentinel exposed to dangers he never measured and moved, by an instinct he did not comprehend, to tremble when he did not know that a bullet would pierce his brain at the very instant he discovered me. But the sentinel's death was no more painful to him than the mode and fact of taking his life were alike hateful to me. He would surely have killed me; therefore, I slew him. For all that, the necessity and the fact were alike horrible.

Henceforth we were to go on foot in pairs. We were to move by day and night. We were to live between the picket lines of the two armies. We were to deal with spies and scouts and bushwhackers and loyalists. Whatever the hour at which we reached our lines to make our reports, we were arrested and taken under guard to the provost marshal of the army and thence to General Johnston's head-quarters.

It happened on one occasion that one of my comrades was shot and killed, and his passports were secured by bushwhackers. I came immediately to head-quarters and reported the fact. Instantly General Johnston revoked all permits to pass the lines and every one seeking to enter was put under guard and sent to the provost marshal. We captured five men with forged copies of the dead scout's papers within our lines. They were all shot by decree of a drum-head court-martial. I was amazed to learn the next day, from a Yankee scout I captured, that he knew the fate of the five unhappy men who attempted to use copies of the passport that belonged to my dead comrade. He said:

"Your General Johnston is a wary old fox. We thought we had a safe and sure means of ingress and egress through your lines when we secured perfect *fac similes* of the paper signed by General Johnston himself. By his instant revocation of all passports, and thus, the capture and examination at head-quarters of all persons entering your lines, five ardent bushwhackers lost their lives."

Our picket lines were quite nine miles from Dalton, and many nights, walking this distance when the whole army slept, have I wished that I were reduced to the ranks. Weary and footsore I trudged, buoyed up by the hope that the intelligence I bore would serve or save the Confederate army. There was, however, a degree of fascination in risks constantly hazarded, and in this life of constant excitement, that made it inexpressibly fascinating.

Then, too, I was conscious that in the ranks, subjected to rigid discipline, and compelled to answer at roll-call, I could never achieve the leading purpose of my life, of which I dreamed day and night. The hour was drawing nigh when, if the good schoolmaster could execute his designs, I would meet Mamie Hughes and when, with her guide, she would be entrusted for a time to my guardianship.

General Johnston, when giving me orders and instructions late at night, said:

"You are the eyes and ears of my army."

I answered:

"My eyes will do perhaps, but I hope my ears are not big enough to provoke the suggestion."

The General smiled good naturedly, and I said,—and I could not help blushing frightfully,—"General, I want to get a young lady through the lines to her mother's, below Tunnel Hill."

"Is she of kin to you?"

"No, sir."

"What, then, is your reason for this evident anxiety on your part?"

Turning away, that he might not scan my face so intently with his keen, clear, kindly eyes, I said :

"If you have a moment's leisure, General, I'll tell the whole story."

His elbow rested upon the little, low, pine table before him, strewn with papers. His hand supported his massive head, and while a smile, half incredulous and half sympathetic, played about his face, he listened to the story of my love.

When I had recounted incidents of the dance by moonlight on the banks of the Tennessee and of our flight across Sequatchie Valley into the Cumberland Mountains, I told the story of the old scold and of her immersion by Spratling in the barrel-churn. The General could not contain himself, and forgetting, for the moment, the great burden of anxieties that weighed him down, he laughed till his sleeping staff aroused by the extraordinary incident, came to inquire what had happened.

I briefly told of the ex-bushwhacker Mr. Wade, and of the pass I wanted for him. My requests were granted with instructions to guide me for the ensuing week, when, saying, "I will always be grateful, General," I tipped my cap and bowed myself, at two o'clock in the morning, out of his presence.

# CHAPTER XII.

I had passed out of the lines, and with Spratling, awaited at the rendezvous, near La Fayette, the coming of Mr. Wade, the ex-bushwhacker and pedagogue. He reached our encampment at ten o'clock on the day fixed for our meeting. When I greeted him, extending my right, I held up the left hand, proffering the passport of General Joseph E. Johnston. I am sure the generous, good man never confessed in eyes and face a keener pleasure. His life had been devoted to the service of others. He was now a homeless wanderer. Incapable of any task save such as life-long schoolmasters assume and deprived of the privilege of waging war against the Confederacy, he was even grateful for that of serving Mamie and myself, and infinitely grateful for the confidence reposed in his truthfulness, integrity, and courage. When I gave him the passport, he said he had seen Mamie's mother, delivered Mamie's letter, and after spending a day and night beneath the roof of Mamie's hospitable home, conceived it his duty to fulfill, speedily and faithfully, promises given the mother and daughter.

"If not arrested and detained in the Federal lines at Charleston or its vicinity, I will meet you," he said, "three weeks hence at the old camping place near Tunnel Hill. I have no pass for Mamie granted by General Sherman's Provost Marshal, and if I find it difficult to secure or the task tedious, Mamie does not lack courage, and as a lad of fifteen years would gladly and naturally follow these gray hairs. I am so well known among the soldiers and officers at the Hiwassee bridge that I am sure I will encounter little hazard and that I can come south with Mamie having no other 'permit' than that which I have been accustomed to use. The worst that can happen will be the return to Mamie's present home on the north side of the river. Then she

6

must enact the role of a country boy and we will come down safely through that great, empty arm of the primeval sea now known as Sequatchie Valley. You crossed it, without a vessel and at night and dry shod, not very long ago, but the time was, at some remote period in the world's history, when mightiest ships could have floated serenely on the bosom of its fathomless waters. A little creek drains it to day. This stream I have followed from its source, gathering old, very old sea shells on its banks and counting deep, long, and parallel fissures worn by the ocean waves far up the mountain sides that hedge in this marvelous Sequatchie Valley. In studying this sublime history of a mighty sea, walled in on every hand, receiving great tributary streams through Cumberland and other Gaps, overspreading the district known as East Tennessee, and discharging its superabundant floods, in the olden eternity of the past, through Sequatchie Valley, she will confess the keenest and most intelligent interest. Then Sequatchie Valley was a Straits of Gibraltar at the entrance to another Mediterranean. In studying these marvelous pages of God's greatest Book—Nature—Mamie will forget dangers and fatigue and forget, now and then, that she ever danced with you by moonlight on the banks of the turbulent Tennessee. I have wandered again and again through this deep, broad valley, an ancient river's bed, and am sure I can escape from East Tennessee into Georgia by following it along the mountain's base or summit. I know the simple, honest mountaineers and no picket lines or armies can close countless paths along which they will guide me even to this very spot. Mamie's youthful vigor, her life in the open air, her eager anxiety to return to her widowed mother and to"—here the kindly pedagogue hesitated and looked furtively into my face, while I could see cunning smiles dancing hornpipes in his merry eyes—"to soothe her sorrows," he continued, "would enable her to withstand the fatigues and dangers of the toilsome; tedious journey.

"The climate of this mountainous region, where the sea itself was once bathed in sunlight, is faultless. It begets buoyancy of heart and spirit; and consciousness of existence, in this blessed valley, is an undefinable, delicious joy. The skies are roseate with eternal sunshine. The atmosphere, bereft of moisture by mountains on every hand, is so crystalline that distance fails, by half, as elsewhere, to lessen objects of vision. The sun rises in cloudless, gorgeous splendor and sets in a sea of golden glory. No shadow of cloud veils its glowing disc. The moon is wafted by night over an inverted, starry ocean, and glows with a brilliancy elsewhere unknown. The stars are blazing electric lights to illumine God's dwelling place and pathway.

"In a coming age, when peace and unity are restored, men and women will dwell here whose tastes and intelligence will be shaped by grand physical facts and aspects of nature about them, and the grandest race on God's footstool will dwell in Sequatchie Valley.

"Pardon my enthusiasm. I love East Tennessee, the land of my birth. I only wish to assure you that you need have no fears. Mamie has been climbing the hills, rowing a boat, learning how to use a repeater, and riding horses for months. Recently her industry, since she proposed to make the journey on foot to Tunnel Hill, has been redoubled, and I am persuaded that, when she reaches this place, she will be eager to join in one of your hazardous incursions into the Federal lines.

"And yet when I was leaving Mamie, she came and kissed my wrinkled brow and said that my face and conduct and the stories I told always inculcated the lesson which she had learned to lisp in childhood :

> " 'Naked on parents' knees, a new-born child,
> Weeping thou sat'st when all around thee smiled.
> So live that, sinking to thy last long sleep,
> Thou then canst smile while all around thee weep.'

"She has perfect health, and if a Mohammedan, instead of a Christian, would be pronounced horribly fanatical. Of fear she never knew an emotion, and is only timidly modest. Dismiss all anxiety. She will meet you in three weeks at Tunnel Hill. I was reading to Mamie the verse which tells that

> " 'Brutes find out where their talents lie ;
> A bear will not attempt to fly ;
> A foundered horse will oft debate,
> Before he tries a five-barred gate ;
> A dog by instinct turns aside,
> Who sees the ditch too deep and wide ;
> But man we find the only creature
> Who, led by folly, combats nature ;
> And when he loudly cries, forbear,
> With obstinacy fixes there ;
> And where his genius least inclines,
> Absurdly bends his whole designs.'

"She looked up when I closed the little volume in which the stanza was pasted, and asked if I sought to convey a lesson for her to study. " 'Do I propose,' she asked, ' "to combat nature" when I would ride the most unmanageable horse? My sex cannot vote, and yet I read with keenest interest discussions of political questions. I am taxed ; I toil to add to public wealth ; and yet I must fill only the meanest places in industrial life. We are paid less than men for the same and better service in public schools. We are used as nurses, but reviled as physicians. Barbarous codes of one thousand years ago, enacted by opinion and custom when men were mere fighting brutes and shaped the blessed Common Law, still fix the position and define the rights of my sex. Kept in ignorance, the calamity repeats itself forever ; and womanly ignorance and weakness refuse to demand woman's emancipation. I never felt the burden of fetters I wear as a woman till I wished to assert myself and, guarding myself and defying danger, return to my home in Georgia. "Brutes," as the poet tells, "find out where their talents lie ;" but women are not suffered to have talents. They can aspire to nothing higher or nobler or more useful than offices of washerwoman and housekeeper for despotic husbands who come home from ballot-boxes and public meetings for food we must cook and clothes we must cleanse. We are not even supposed to know why war rages or what you insane, selfish, wicked men are fighting about. My conviction is that the main cause of the measureless calamity is found in the fact that surfeited flies, feasting through forty years upon public pap, have been brushed away that another swarm, starved through nearly half a century, may prey upon the people. I have observed that every Federal office-holder ejected by Lincoln's election was instantly a howling, hooting secessionist. He set his neighbors, family, and friends in an uproar, and by sheer violence silenced opposition to the frenzied place-hunters. But isn't it singular that women, knowing nothing of questions involved and the least possible of results to follow, are most violent and earnest partisans either of the South or of the North. I can't help it,' said Mamie, 'but I do wish we women were differently educated and reared with higher and nobler purposes, and imbued with nobler convictions and loftier aims than those now hedging in our unworthy aspirations.

" 'When I was nearly fifteen years old, standing before the mirror at my sick mother's bedside, she was telling me of the terrors of this horrible inter-state war "precipitated by him who madly fired the gun at Sumter that set the continent aflame." "There are terrible days coming," said my mother. "Why do you weep?" I asked. Her answer was, "Because you are not my son rather than my daughter." I, too, wept. And every tear we shed was illustrative of the terrors of a code which has fixed the status and defined a sphere of inferior action for my sex from the Dark Ages even to this good hour. We have become at last separate property holders. We can testify in courts. We are at last, as wives, separable in matters of property from the man. We could not enter literary colleges or medical schools, but nearly all these are open to us at last. We have found access to the pulpit and bar, and our worth and equality and keenness of perception and skill in art and in the professions are confessed. We are advancing steadily and will be finally invested with every privilege of citizenship. The right will finally triumph, and mothers will weep no more that daughters are not sons.'

"Such was the substance, captain," said the schoolmaster, "of Mamie's earnest, vigorous speech made to me as her audience. I was delighted, because I believe as she does; and let me tell you, captain, that the exigencies of this war have stirred many an idle intellect to its profoundest depths. Even that little sweetheart of yours becomes a philosopher, dealing with questions of state-craft. She said to me one morning, and I don't understand it all yet, that the South pretended to fight because it couldn't take negroes to Kansas where nobody could or would have a slave, free labor being cheaper than that of slaves. Then she said:

" 'Within a life-time, after slavery is no more, the South will never believe that it ever approved the institution, and he will be execrated who asserts that the South fought that Mr. Toombs might "call the roll of his slaves," as he prophesied, "on Bunker Hill," or even in Georgia.    The negro, like my sex, has almost reached the proper period of preparation, and slow emancipation was coming, even if the bayonet had not intervened.'

"General Cleburne," said Mr. Wade, "and the ablest officers in your army illustrate the force and accuracy of this girl's reasoning. They propose, even now, to convert slaves into soldiers, making faithful soldierly service the price of negro freedom.    I am told that politicians who became generals, except Cleburne, oppose, but the greater number of officers and men approve the proposition.    A soldier is only a breathing machine.    One perfectly disciplined human creature is as valuable as another.    Confessing this fact, soldiers of the South do not object to the imposition of a share of their toils and dangers upon these slaves.    But Jefferson Davis, it is said, objects, and negroes may not be suffered, like other races, to fight for their own freedom.

# CHAPTER XIII.

Spratling, I well knew, was anxious to revisit the home of Bessie Starnes, the pretty, black-eyed mountaineer's daughter, who half promised and half refused to love him. It was part of my duty to learn whether the Federal army corps, encamped not far from Bessie's home, had changed its position. Spratling, advised of every order I was required to execute, gladly agreed to go alone and ascertain the facts, assuring me that Bessie would tell him everything that had occurred in that vicinity.

"Oh! she is bright-eyed and cunning and silent," said Spratling. "She told me, when I was coming away, that she often learned what I was most anxious to know. Bessie listens intently when Federal officers breakfast with the pretty, black-eyed, laughter-loving mountain lassie. She asks how long they will remain where they are, 'because she will be so idle and lonely when gallant men and officers leave the neighborhood.' She told me she would have a 'big lot of news to tell me' when I came back. Very many Union soldiers, of different Tennessee regiments, went from Bessie's neighborhood. These constantly revisit their homes and tell the seemingly careless, but curious girl all they know. She knows the strength of each Tennessee regiment and brigade, and who commands, and where they are encamped. She corresponds constantly with a young Georgian in Cliff's Tennessee 'loyal' regiment. The truth is, I think he is my rival; and if the fortunes of war so ordered, I would not not weep if his career were brief and brilliant. I have thought, when Bessie was gazing abstractedly in my face and when she was evidently measuring my virtues and worth, that she was weighing these against the admirable qualities of heart and person that distinguish, as she told me, the young Georgian in the Union army. But despite her possible love for him, she will be true to me as a rebel. Her sympathies are wholly with the South.''

The gigantic Spratling soon left us, moving down the long slope of the rocky hill-side with an elasticity in his movements and healthful vigor in his gigantic body and limbs that compelled us to watch and admire, as he went bounding rapidly down the declivity. His footsteps were hastened by anxiety to listen once more to the rich tones of Bessie's musical voice and gaze in the fathomless depths of her fascinating, brilliant eyes ; and perhaps he dreamed of dewy, pouting lips he had never kissed.

When Spratling had disappeared, Mr. Wade said to me that he had a newspaper containing an absurd and inaccurate and untruthful account of the shooting of the Confederate raider, General John H. Morgan.

''I was in Greenville when Gillem's command made its descent upon the place. Gillem himself did not know that Morgan was in the village. He was advised, which was true, that Morgan had gone to Abingdon, Virginia, to see his wife, who had just become a mother. But Morgan hastened back to Greenville, for reasons that became apparent when we secured his private and official papers, even the letters from his very passionately devoted wife.

''Morgan made no secret of his purpose to attack Gillem. In fact he was reduced to the necessity of executing at once some brilliant stroke of heroism or of retiring in disgrace from the Confederate service. His exactions, levied alike upon friend and foe, and outrages, practised even upon rebels or upon the wives and children of Confederate soldiers, forced General Echols to order him to transfer his authority to his next in command. Morgan resolved to fight, and if possible, destroy Gillem, and thus win such *eclat* that Echols would be compelled to revoke this order. Unhappily for Morgan, he was induced to spend a night at the elegant home of his aide-de-camp, Major Williams, whose widowed mother resides in Greenville. Cards, wine, and most accomplished women—one of these, Miss N. N. Scott, a granddaughter of H. L. White, Andrew Jackson's great rival—made sleep, till a late hour, impossible.

''About sunrise, Mrs. Williams, finding her home surrounded by East Tennessee Union soldiers led by Colonel John B. Brownlow and others, hurried to Morgan's room. She knocked. He awoke and came in his night clothes to learn that he must fly or be put to death.

'''These men will not spare you,' she said. 'I hear them, even now, threatening to burn my home. They have learned that you are here.'

''Mrs Williams told me all this,'' said Mr. Wade.

''Morgan hastily drew on his pantaloons, and leaving his coat and vest, the former having on the collar the insignia of his rank, ran down stairs and out through the back door and down the high, broad steps that led into a garden and vineyard in the rear of the building.

"'Meanwhile, Major Williams, instead of following Morgan to the small, frame church under which Morgan proposed to conceal himself and thence escape into the woods not far away,—the church was quite fifty or sixty yards from the residence,—took refuge under the steps which Morgan descended into the vineyard. A good-natured dog's family here had their bed of sticks and straw. Williams, almost suffocated by the process, covered himself with the dog's bed, remaining there till ten or eleven o'clock, when the Union soldiers left the yard. Then he crawled into an empty cistern, and shuddered when a Union soldier walked over it, saying, as he lifted the cover and looked down into the darkness, that he would 'get a squad to fire into that d——d hole ; it may be half full of thieving Morgan's men.'

" Williams deeming the place unhealthy," continued the pedagogue, "crept out and, entering the kitchen, was concealed by his 'black mammy,' the fat queen of the kitchen, beneath the floor. Meanwhile, Brownlow's soldiers captured Captain Clay,* grandson of the matchless popular leader, Henry Clay, of Kentucky. From him I learned many facts which I now recite.

"'General Morgan was seen, when approaching the rear of the church, by one of Colonel Brownlow's men and forced to return towards Mrs. Williams' residence. He had retraced half the distance to the house and was in the little vineyard, the vines waist high, when Andrew Campbell, a private, on the outside of the enclosure, fired upon Morgan, who was moving rapidly. Morgan fell, dying instantly. Members of Mrs. Williams' household at once made the fact known to our soldiers that the great guerrilla was slain. Meanwhile, many of Colonel Brownlow's men,—the brigade was an East Tennessee organization,—having unrestrained access to the whiskey shops of the town, were half drunken. Morgan's dead body, still bleeding,—the blood issuing from the orifice made by the musket ball in his back,—was taken from the garden by Captain Northington, placed across the bow of his saddle, and thus borne on horse-back through the streets of Greenville. This was done that the people and soldiers might know that the terrible raider and plunderer was dead.

" Morgan may have been a better man than they deemed him, but he was abhorred, as a lawless robber, ruffian, and heartless freebooter, by the common people of East Tennessee. Horrible stories were told of his brutalities and crimes, and whether well founded or not, it is certainly true that his alleged lawless deeds caused the promulgation of the order depriving him of his command, which we found among his papers in Mrs. Williams' house.

"It is proper to say that General Gillem was of obscure origin. His mother was keeper of an apple-stand in Grainesborough, Jackson County, East Tennessee. He was the protege of General Alvin

---

*Captain Clay is still living in East Tennessee.

Cullum, formerly circuit judge at Gainesborough and, later, member of Congress. While sitting in Congress, Cullum sent Gillem to West Point and Andrew Johnson, because Gillem was an East Tennesseean, caused him to be transferred from a quarter-master's to a brigadier general's position. Gillem's nomination was still unconfirmed by the Senate when his command moved upon Greenville.

"Gillem, when Colonels Brownlow, Miller, and Ingerton urged him to attack Morgan's command in Greenville, when they supposed Morgan to be in Abingdon, refused to do so. He finally agreed. that the attack might be made. When his subordinate officers mentioned moved upon the place through a pitiless and ceaseless rain-storm, marching at night over the worst possible roads, to attack a force twice as strong as their own, Gillem said to Brownlow that it was 'a d———d wild goose chase and he would have nothing to do with it.'

"Brownlow answered, 'If we don't attack Morgan, we know he means to attack us. Then we will be surely beaten. As assailants, we will be victorious.'

"But Gillem refused at last to participate in the assault upon Greenville, remaining several miles away at a country farmhouse. When he came into Greenville he encountered Colonel Brownlow who had pursued Morgan's flying men more than five miles toward Jonesboro' and returned to Greenville.

"Brownlow said to Gillem, 'We have killed General Morgan.'

"Gillem supposed Morgan to be in Abingdon where he was seen by Gillem's spies. Therefore, he believed that Brownlow was jesting.

" 'There,' said Brownlow, 'is Captain Clay, of General Morgan's staff. Let me introduce you. He will confirm my statements.'

"Gillem was amazed and the more delighted. The United States Senate had recently refused to confirm his nomination as brigadier general. He knew that this sublime luck, in the achievement of which he had not the slightest agency, assured his confirmation."

Gillem was not mistaken. The taking off of the rebel raider made Gillem a major general and, after peace, a colonel in the regular army. He will be remembered for the defeat he suffered in the lava beds at the hands of the red warrior Captain Jack.

It should be stated perhaps, in connection with this recital of facts by the ex-bushwhacker, that it may be colored somewhat by his prejudices, but he could have no selfish motive impelling him to do injustice to Gillem who was loaded, it seems, with honors for a deed of which he was wholly innocent. Even so of a woman who left Mrs. Williams' house the evening that Morgan arrived. She, or others for her, caused the story to go abroad that she went to Gillem's head-quarters that night and telling him that Morgan, unguarded, slept at Mrs. Williams' house, induced Gillem to assail the town. Nothing is further from the truth.

Colonels Brownlow, Miller, and Ingerton did induce Gillem to assent to the assault upon Morgan's greater force than their own, but the argument they made, as already given, was that, in Morgan's absence, his command would be much more easily discomfited, and they knew that Morgan or they themselves must be beaten. Their only security rested in an offensive, aggressive campaign. But Gillem shrank from it and at the last moment stood aloof, and neither conceived nor proposed nor executed and only assented to the plans of his subordinates, Colonels Brownlow, Miller, and Ingerton.

"It may be proper to say," added the schoolmaster, "that special credit is due Captains Wilcox and Northington who commanded the squad of 50 men that surrounded Mrs. Williams' residence and prevented the escape of Morgan and his staff. Major Newell, commanding about 100 of the Tenth Michigan Cavalry, actively co-operated in the assault upon Morgan's 2200 men, our whole force numbering 1100.

"I wish to add that, for the first time in this unhappy war, a surgeon, A. E. Gibson, here distinguished himself by acts of personal valor. He brought down his man with a musket instead of a dissecting knife; and then, when the fighting was done, was as generous and kindly to prisoners he captured as to the soldiers of his own (Colonel John B. Brownlow's) regiment. By the way, I have a theory that doctors, as well as poets, are born not made. Dr. Frank A. Ramsay, of Knoxville, would have been the first pathologist of the age if he had never read a book or managed countless hospitals or sat through all the years of his busy life at bedsides of the sick and dying. He reads one's disease when he reads his face, and ministers to that of mind or body with matchless art."

The schoolmaster and I were resting on blankets near a fire that burned against the body of a great fallen oak. We heard the clatter of horses' hoofs at the base of the hill. Knowing that these horsemen would surely see the smoke and flame and inspect our resting place, we gathered up guns and baggage and went into denser woods in the valley below, following the course of the road that we might discover the character and purposes of the horsemen. They proved to be general officers of the Confederate army on a tour of inspection. They were accompanied by aides-de-camp and a small body of cavalry. Generals Bate, Walthall, Cleburne, Walker, Mercer, and perhaps others were of the number. I was delighted to meet General Cleburne, and as soon as I heard his voice and before I recognized his face, ran into the road to greet him. Cleburne dismounting, grasped my hand, and commended me, in a kindly little speech, to his comrades, telling them how long and well I had served him as a scout. I was pleased to see with General Bate the newspaper man who had assisted at baptismal services on the Cumberland Mountains. He was evidently delighted to encounter me. He said his brother John was a private in Pinson's Mississippi Cavalry, and that he was spending a week or two with John and with General Bate. I suggested to the journalist the possibility of exciting adventures between the lines, and proposed his participation in dangers of an incursion into Tennessee. I adverted to the delightful companionship of the pedagogue, who spun interminable yarns, in a modest, unobtrusive way, through days and nights by glowing camp fires. The editor was captured, I think, by the pedagogue. He gave his horse to his brother and even after swimming the icy Tennessee at Bridgeport, was pleased to renew modes of life peculiar to those who never dared to sleep beneath a roof and rarely twice within a month at the same place. The journalist and I, after arranging for a future meeting with his brother, and after I had given General Cleburne a hurried description of the country and told him that he was then six miles from the enemy's nearest outposts and twelve from his own, bade adieu to officers and men and soon joined the pedagogue at the camp fire.

We moved that afternoon five miles toward Starnes' place. Starnes' pretty daughter, it will be remembered, had fascinated Spratling when we captured the supposed deserter Ellison. To this new encampment Spratling was to return the next day. Here clearest, most delicious chalybeate water gushed from between great flat stones in a deep narrow valley, and from the summit of the high hill above the spring we could see the road a mile along its tortuous course that led to Chattanooga. The schoolmaster was rapidly recovering from the effects of his toilsome journey, and the newspaper man ready for any adventure.

Making a fire of materials that would blaze little and glow in living coals, we sat, half-reclining upon blankets, a fallen tree serving as a pillow. Broiled bacon, hard tack, and coffee taken from Mrs. Shields' depository of supplies constituted materials for an excellent evening repast. This disposed of, we lighted our pipes, and the editor and the schoolmaster began to discuss the course of public and military events. I had given the journalist a brief sketch of Mr. Wade's career, and in order to account for the presence of such a man in such a place, had shown how valuable he had become.

"In 1860-61," said the journalist, "I was as devout a Unionist as yourself, Mr. Wade. I then abhorred, even as I was taught in childhood to hate Benedict Arnold, those who advocated the secession of the South. It was in June, 1861, that I inserted a paragraph in the newspaper of which I was then a youthful editor, in which I said there was no practical difference between Jefferson Davis, a secessionist, and Wendell Phillips, an abolitionist. In other words, I declared secessionism and abolitionism identical in purpose and results. I was arrested under a decree emanating from the despotic vigilance committee, and when taken before that body, was informed by the president, Frazer Titus, an honest, good citizen, who had gone mad with many like him, that if the conduct of the *Daily Bulletin* were not conformed to the necessities of the Confederacy, the newspaper should not exist. I was told that if I had not been born, reared, and educated in the South, and if my social position were different, I would be imprisoned and exiled. This occurred just before Tennessee finally agreed to co-operate with the Gulf States.

"What are we going to do about it?" continued the newspaper

man. "Suppose we win this fight, which does not seem very probable. We will have two Unions instead of one. Each, jealous of the other, will maintain a great standing army. White people are tired of fighting and abhor already, every fact and incident of the war. It is stated that two-thirds of those enlisted as Confederate soldiers since 1861 have deserted. Admitting, however, that the South win, will it retain its winnings? Will not two Unions, if we fly from one, be doubly intolerable? Will the people endure quadrupled burdens of taxation? The truth is I don't see very clearly what we are fighting for.

"We are not waging war for negro property. Those owning twenty negroes are exempt from military service. Then no father or mother would give a son's life for all the blacks on the continent. Then, too, negro slavery has become negro 'servitude' and if there had never been an abolitionist or secessionist to keep the country in an uproar, thus enabling them to secure offices and honors by the consolidation of parties and sections, if the right of petition had never been denied, the slave codes of the several southern states would have been mollified and the process of emancipation, as Henry Clay advised, been begun. Even with these fierce slave codes nominally operative and now and then enforced, prohibiting the education of negroes and subjecting them to restraints and penalties too horrible to approve, negroes on every plantation are taught to read and write, and in wide districts the best preachers are hired to minister to their spiritual wants.

"The negroes know what will be the result of Federal triumph in this conflict and yet they are content to toil industriously and create supplies in the absence of masters and overseers everywhere, for the armies of Jefferson Davis. Luckily our wives, mothers, sisters, and sweethearts are left at home under the guardianship of 'servants' and not of 'slaves.' The next step in African redemption should be a modification of the Mexican system of peonage, and then should come perfect liberty. President Lincoln entertains proper opinions on this subject, and General Cleburne and others of our leaders propose to give absolute freedom to those negroes who serve in our army. Many of our general officers oppose the scheme of negro conscription, but such multitudes of capable white men now escape by nameless and numberless subterfuges and deserters become so innumerable, that the negro will soon be required to do more than feed and clothe and care for the families of these soldiers. General Cleburne is not singular in advocating negro conscription and then negro emancipation.

"White men are weary of the toils and dangers and hardships of these terrible campaigns and begin to think that as soldiers are veriest slaves, so slaves should be faultless soldiers. I am persuaded that, however the war result, the negro will be the gainer. If we win, it will be through negro intervention as a soldier and because negroes fed and clothed us and have taken care of our families while we fought. In the county in which my father, mother, and sisters live in Eastern Mississippi there are at this hour thirty thousand negroes and less than four thousand whites, and two-thirds of these whites are helpless old men and women and children. I have never dreamed of danger to befall those I love. In fact, the more perfect the liberty given this peculiar race the stronger the development of those singular virtues of patience and kindliness that everywhere distinguish the African. I saw a letter in *Harpers' Weekly* written in 1860 from New Orleans, by James Harper, in which he said the planters of the South were most anxious because of the conduct of their slaves; pruning-hooks, scythes, axes, and all implements that might be used for murderous purposes were carefully removed at night from the negroes' reach and that servile insurrections were greatly dreaded. Some knave imposed upon Mr. Harper. I have never heard man or woman in the south refer to the negro except in kindness, and never heard a suspicion of negro fidelity to his master suggested, and now quite one half of our generals would gladly convert the blacks into soldiers, giving freedom to each family whose head serves a year or falls in the ranks.''

I asked the journalist if he believed negro servitude would end if we won victory at last. .

"Certainly;'' he answered. "Each of the two rival Unions, Lincoln's and Jeff Davis', must maintain great armies and fleets. Each 'nation' will fear the other. White men are already weary of military life, and its duties will be assumed, north and south, by negroes. Lincoln and Davis will finally become two starveling, lean, lank, lantern-jawed grand Turks, upheld by two grand armies of black janizaries. Lincoln, like Andrew Johnson, is a native-born 'plebeian,' and Jefferson Davis an aristocrat. But whatever their impulses or purposes, they will be helpless. The two Unions, because of retro-active pressure, must become consolidated, costly despotisms. Burdens of taxation will be enormous and the people, remembering the time, prior to 1860, when we did not know, except that the politicians howled mightily, that we had a government, will force their masters to reconstruct the Federal Union. Therefore I could never see any use in secession or in all this terrible fighting. The end defined is inevitable, If the North triumph, the Union will be restored, less slavery; if the South, the Union will be as surely reproduced with gradual emancipation.

"But there is a fight progressing. I can't stop it and I couldn't prevent it. I am only for the under dog in the fight. It is my d——d dog," said the journalist laughingly, while he contemplated the smiling face of the drowsy pedagogue, who said:

"I don't see that we differ widely enough to render further discussion a necessity, and I am only led to reflect by what you have stated, that when the disgusted, weary people of the South no longer sing that horrible, dolorous ditty which has utterly unmanned your soldiers and broken the spirit of your women, whose pitiful refrain is

'Maryland, my Maryland!'—when you have substituted aggressive, vigorous popular melodies, like that which I have heard chanted by ten thousand voices of earnest men whose heavy tread shook the earth, while earth, air, and ocean caught the refrain, 'Old John Brown's soul is marching on'—when you have reproduced the spirit of the army and courage of the people by showing them that there is some grand end to be attained by fighting,—then, and not till then, will Lee and Johnston win victories.

NOTE.—In confirmation of the pedagogue's statement that General Gillem had nought to do with the killing of General Morgan, it is stated on page 540 of General Basil Duke's " History of Morgan's Cavalry," that Morgan's "body was taken from hands which defiled it by General Gillem, as soon as that officer arrived at Greenville and sent to us under a flag of truce. It was buried at Abingdon and afterward in Hollywood at Richmond." Thus it seems that Adjutant General Duke knows that General Gillem was not at Greenville when Morgan was slain.

General Duke recites the story that a daughter-in-law of Mrs. Williams conveyed to Gillem the news that Morgan was in Greenville. In this General D. is wholly wrong. Greenville was assailed because Morgan was supposed to be absent, and that therefore his command would be easily routed.

General Duke feelingly insists, and he knew Morgan thoroughly well, that he was incapable of wrongs and robberies ascribed to his supposed vices by the people of East Tennessee. But General Duke tells, as the school-master stated, that Morgan was about to be " court-martialed " for alleged lawless exactions imposed upon people and banks.

# CHAPTER XIV.

Bessie Starnes.—Spratling's Story.—His Enormous Strength saves his Life.—Two Prisoners.—Two Dead Scouts.—Spratling's Confession.

Spratling reached the modest log house, in which Bessie Starnes budded into young womanhood, late in the afternoon. His habits as a scout made him cautious and watchful. He refused to sleep in the house, not because he feared betrayal by its inmates, but capture and death at the hands of implacable, cunning bushwhackers. These "loyalists" ascribed to Spratling's extraordinary physical strength the peculiar mode of execution to which the captors of the bushwhacker, whose neck was broken by an elastic hickory tree, had resorted. The story went abroad that Spratling, when enraged, was capable of any terrible act of demonism. He was hated as he was feared, and never did one suffer more unjustly at the bar of opinion. There was never a soldier more fearless, and never one more kindly and generous or less capable of cruelty or injustice. He condemned the conduct of the drunken men who broke the neck of the dastardly assassin by tying it to the bent tree, even more harshly than I who reported the outrage at head-quarters, that the drunken malefactors might be, as they were, severely punished.

But to Spratling's miraculous muscular strength was ascribed the horrible deed, and he knew that assassins plotted his destruction. At night-fall he left Starnes' house, going down into the valley. Entering the woods, he ascended the hill and slept on its summit. When he awoke at day dawn, seeing two men get out of a light wagon drawn by a single horse and enter the house, he went down to the road in front of the house. They wore pistols in their belts, having no other visible weapons. They remained in the house perhaps half an hour, and came out with Bessie Starnes walking very slowly and doubtingly between them towards the wagon. Spratling could not comprehend the propriety or necessity for Bessie's departure, seated between two blue-coated Federal soldiers. Presenting his repeater he stood at the horse's head, telling the two men they were "Spratling's prisoners. Obey me, and if you are friends of Bessie Starnes, you shall go free; if you mean any harm to her, I'll cut your throats"

The aspect of Spratling when excited and when he drew himself up to his full height and spoke with curt fierceness was even awe-inspiring.

"Come, Bessie, tell me what all this means. Drop your weapons instantly," he continued, addressing the two soldiers in a voice of thunder. "Bring me those pistols, Bessie. Your friends are in no danger; but I am while they are armed. I don't understand this proceeding, and because I love you and I see your mother wringing her hands and crying in the house, I don't intend to let you go away till I know why you go."

The two men had dropped their pistols and Bessie stood motionless, staring vacantly in Spratling's face. There was no time for any discussion of the facts. With a cocked repeater in each hand Spratling advanced toward her. Ordering the men to stand aside, he secured the weapons, made the men mount into the wagon while he held the horse, and conferred with Bessie. Spratling reciting the facts afterward, said:

"I had heard Bessie speak of several Federal officers from Chattanooga who had visited her. She had often adverted to a quarter-master whose marked and persistent demonstrations of love and admiration annoyed and even offended her. He made Bessie costly presents, and she loved finery only too well and could not repel the generous 'major' as decisively as she should have done. The 'major' had learned at last that Charley Hughes, a lieutenant in Colonel Cliff's Union regiment, was desperately enamored of Bessie and that she lavished upon Charley all the wealth of her boundless love. Once when this quarter-master was at Starnes' house, while Bessie was in the kitchen, the quarter-master discovered in Bessie's table drawer a package of well-worn letters. He hastily read one of these ardently affectionate epistles and thinking that its possession might in some way invest him with power over the beautiful girl, he appropriated it. Soon afterward he conceived the plot now sought to be executed. He forged a skillfully drawn letter from Charley Hughes. This was the paper which Bessie held tightly in her grasp when I made the two soldiers drop their pistols and get into the wagon.

" 'Bessie,' I said, 'you must tell me what this means. Why do you propose to leave with those two villainous-looking fellows? You know I am your friend and even more than friend. This is not right or safe, and unless you make me understand that it is, I will take that wagon and those two soldiers to our rendezvous at once and have these men sent in as prisoners of war.'

" 'Bessie still hesitating and frightened, at length came to my side and placed the crushed letter in my hand. I opened it and read as follows:

"'HOSPITAL No. 6, CHATTANOOGA, *February 2, 1864.*

"'MY DEAREST BESSIE:—I was severely wounded in a skirmish on the picket line last Monday. I thought I would be well enough to reach your home and be perfectly blest as the object of your tender care. But the inflammation of the wound makes it threaten my life, and the surgeon says I cannot go to you. Will you not come to me before I die? You can return to your home in the evening. The kind doctor lends me his horse and ambulance, and you can trust the two men I send to guard you. Ever your own,

"'CHARLEY.'

"'Bessie,' I said, after slowly reading Charley's note, 'Charley didn't write that letter. It wasn't written by a dying man. It don't sound right or honest. It is too long and stiff and particular, and those fellows in that wagon there must tell me who wrote that letter or I will string them to the limb of that oak. There is some d——d scoundrel at the bottom of this rascally business. Bessie,' I said, 'read it over again. Are you sure Charley wrote it?'

"She looked at me vacantly and then at the letter most intently. Hesitating, and evidently doubting the genuineness of the paper, she said:

"'Oh! yes; Charley wrote it. Nobody could be wicked enough to write me such a story if it were false.'

"'It is false, and those men in that wagon are hired to place you in the power of some villain in Chattanooga.'

"The pair of knaves grew pale when I gazed in their faces. The devil was in me and I wonder I had not killed them at the instant.

"Just then three bushwhackers who left Chattanooga as scouts, and had followed closely after the wagon containing the two soldiers, came riding rapidly toward me. My repeaters were in my belt and I held a Henry rifle in my hand. The scouts were within fifty yards or less when I turned and ordered them to halt. They obeyed, and then seeing at length that I stood alone with Bessie, and that two Federal soldiers, armed, as they supposed, were in the wagon, they began to advance. The horse attached to the ambulance had been turned and was ready to move toward Chattanooga.

"Then it was, gentlemen," continued Spratling, "that my great strength saved my life and prevented the seizure and ruin of Bessie Starnes by those dreadful villains.

"When the three bushwhackers suddenly raised their carbines to their faces I shoved Bessie violently out of harm's way. She fell almost senseless in the corner of the fence. I leaped to the rear of the wagon and the two knaves in it struck the horse, a gaunt, bony animal he was, thinking to expose me to the aim of the scouts. But my blood was up. Bessie was in danger and I was savage. I seized the rear axle of the wagon with my left hand and held the wagon as still as if it had been anchored there from all eternity. The two soldiers in it struck and cursed the struggling horse, and when he

7

jerked and reared, standing on his hindmost legs, and fell back helpless, they turned and saw my arm holding them fast. They looked pitifully and helplessly into my face. They were paralyzed by overwhelming amazement that begets nameless terror. The Federal scouts, expecting the struggling horse to move the wagon out of the way that they might shoot me down, stared in mute amazement at the helpless animal. As soon as he was still for an instant, I fired, and one of the scouts fell from his saddle. The other two turned to fly. I shot a second, and the third alone escaped. Neither of them fired a shot.

"Bessie still lay frightened and stunned by the roadside. I was not absolutely sure that the men in the wagon had no weapons and feared, if I turned away to raise her up, they might fire on me and drive back to Chattanooga. Dropping my rifle and seizing the rear axle of the wagon with both hands, I raised it suddenly—the horse's head was turned down the hill toward Chattanooga—and overturned it, with the men in it, upon the horse's back. The men, stunned and bruised, rolled down the declivity; the frightened horse, with the wagon body on his back, fled in terror. His speed down that hill was never eclipsed. The wagon body soon fell off and the wheels took their places in the road and the frightened horse was found dead nearly a mile from the spot.

"The two knaves were almost killed by their sudden elevation and fall. I made them come to me and, while Mrs. Starnes attended to Bessie, I tied their hands together behind their backs. They were perfectly helpless because perfectly unmanned by amazement and terror. I never saw faces full of such helpless agony as the two knaves wore when they found I was stronger than the horse that struggled in vain to move the wagon. It was this that struck the approaching bushwhackers dumb with astonishment and made them stop a moment to stare at the struggling animal. They could not believe their eyes when they saw the venerable brute straining every sinew of body and legs and plunging forward madly and yet fixed to the spot where I held him. The horse trembled either from terror, or it may have been from tremendous exertion of strength. But he shuddered visibly. I felt the wagon tremble after each vain effort made by the horse to move it."

"What wonderful stories the fellow that escaped told of your deeds in Chattanooga," said the schoolmaster to Spratling, "and if ever those two knaves and pimps for the villainous quarter-master escape or return to their command won't they noise abroad the fame and deeds of Spratling !

"I am almost tempted, Captain, to ask you to turn them loose. I would, were it not that they are such infamous knaves. They were hired by that remorseless villain, the quarter-master, to bring that forged letter to Bessie, and take her to some den of iniquity in Chattanooga. When tied and questioned separately they finally confessed the whole truth."

"There's something else I want to tell," said Spratling. "I am not sure that Bessie would have me tell it, but there is no harm in it, and as I will never see Bessie again she should not care. Then the newspaper man and the schoolmaster will never meet her or tell anybody who will repeat it in Bessie's neighborhood, and I might as well finish my story.

"You know, Captain, I loved Bessie. I do think she is too good and too beautiful for this world. When she came to her senses, after that bloody work this morning and looked up so gratefully in my face and when I was watching the color come and go in her pale, sweet face, and the lights and shadows that fled from one another across the great depths of her beautiful eyes—when she said to me in low, soft, musical tones :

"'Do you know now that I owe you more than my life, and that I am ready to give even that to you.' She put her little brown hand in mine, and looked up in my face with such a dreamy look of grateful love, that I—I couldn't help it, Captain—I kissed the pretty girl and pressed her passionately to my heart.

"But I began to think, and knew I was doing wrong. I began to recall the incidents of the morning. I remembered that Bessie was impelled by irresistible affection to risk her life and fame that she might watch at the bedside of the man she really loved. 'Spratling,' I said to myself, 'you have no right to take advantage of this pretty girl's gratitude. She loves another and if you really love Bessie you must not make her wretched by inducing her to become your own because she thinks she owes you a debt that cannot otherwise be paid.'

"I stood up, Captain, and told Bessie I was an honest man, and that I loved her with all my heart, but that I had forced her that morning to tell me why she proposed to go to Chattanooga. 'I can not, Bessie, save your life in order to make it wretched. I love you madly enough, God knows, but you love Charley, and you shall wed Charley.'

"I bade her good bye, Captain, and she wept with a pitiful sort of smile, significant, I thought, of her gratitude, playing about her pale, sweet face—gratitude because I had now given her to perfect blessedness and to Charley Hughes.

"Holding both her hands and gazing long and rapturously into those wonderful eyes, I kissed her again and ran away."

I, who rewrite the story of the adventures of these scouts, am impelled to say that Spratling and Bessie and Mamie and Bessie's Federal lieutenant and the captain all met, and not very many weeks after the occurrences. just recited. How these men and women were brought together, and what strange consequences sprang from personal interviews, subsequent pages will tell.

# CHAPTER XV.

> With flowers we deck our soldiers' graves,
> With drooping folds our standard waves
> Where flowers and lawn the dew-drop laves
> And breath of spring is softly blown
> O'er mounds where, on a simple stone,
> The record says they were—" Unknown."
>
> *Emily Hawthorne.*

Spratling's almost incredible account of his sojourn at Starnes' farmhouse begat profound silence about the camp fire. We sat gazing moodily into the burning, glowing heap of wood and ashes, watching intently the weird shapes assumed, and brilliant, quivering forms that danced, and castles, towers, domes, and minarets that rose and gleamed and fell among the living coals. The captain rose at length and went away saying :

"If everything is quiet we should sleep. We must march to-morrow."

The newspaper man said he had been writing, before Spratling returned, an account of the woes of a poor soldier whom he had encountered twice since the war began.

"There is such an admixture of mirth and sadness," said the editor, "begotten of the simple facts that I cannot tell, when recalling the incidents, whether I should laugh or weep. I was pursuing my life-long vocation," he continued, "when I stood upon the heights at Columbus, Kentucky, and witnessed the descent of U. S. Grant's brigade—Iowa and Illinois troops, I think they were—upon Colonel

Tappan's Arkansas regiment and a squadron of cavalry encamped on the low, flat shore of the Mississippi. Confederate official reports of that battle did not confess the fact; but my impression was that Grant played his cards for all they were worth, and by this first little game of "poker" with bayonets, Bishop General Polk, being his *vis-a-vis*, demonstrated his capacity to "hold his hand" and play it skillfully even when R. E. Lee sits facing him, as he does to-night in front of Richmond. After the fight, I went to the adjutant or colonel of each Confederate regiment engaged, to ascertain the names of the killed and wounded. It was late at night when I reached Colonel Jem Cole's quarters. He led, in this action, raw Tennessee troops, and several were killed or wounded. I was sitting beside him at the entrance to the tent, and had made full memoranda for the night's telegrams, when an old man, hat in hand, and holding a lantern close to my face, said:

"I wish, Capting, you would put me down among the dead."

"Why?" I asked.

"Oh, it doesn't signify," answered Gibbons, Cole's orderly, "but you see, I'm gwine onto fifty yeahs or mo' and I was fool enough to marry a nice young gal. She ain't more'n twenty-eight; she's down to Vicksburg whar I live. Well, she kinder got tired ov me somehow and scolded a heap, and made it hot for the old feller, sometimes, and I didn't like her carryings-on with the boys like, and when the drums beat and fifes shrieked in the streets, day and night, you see, Capting, I thought mebbe Mary Ann would be sorry and kinder come round a little if an old feller like me dressed up like a soger in fine toggery and went to the wars and she knowed what made me go. She knowed home wasn't comfortable. She was sorter sorry, I reckon, when I marched away to the steamboat to come here; but she didn't say much and she don't write to me, and I think ef you'll help me, Capting, I can bring her. Ef you'll print in the papers that I'm dead, she'll know she killed me. She knows I'm here because she wasn't good to me. Will you kill me in the papers, Capting?"

"I haven't the slightest objection," I said. "You are in earnest," I asked, "and you want me to say that you were shot between the eyes fighting gallantly beside Colonel Cole, and that you fell dead in the front rank of your brave regiment?"

"That's the very way to put it," answered Gibbons.

I met Bassett, soon afterward, the clever and kindly correspondent of the *Appeal*. We interchanged memoranda, and Bassett, as well as I, telegraphed the story of Gibbons' heroic death. This happened on the night of the 7th of November, 1861, when telegraphic wires north and south were made tremulous by the exciting story of the first battle fought in the war between the States, in the valley of the Mississippi.

More than two years had elapsed, when, not many days ago, I sought the quarters of General Preston Smith, that I might encounter friends left at Columbus, Kentucky, late in November, 1861. I was riding along placidly enough, and within our lines, occasionally accosted by a sentinel, to whom I exhibited a passport from the Provost Marshal, General ———. At length an aged man, stepping out from behind a tree and looking intently in my face, exclaimed, nervously and quickly:

"Halt there!"

I drew the rein and at the same instant extended my right hand with the passport. The gray-haired sentinel only stared at me and at length said, as if soliloquizing:

"D——d ef it ain't him!"

"Ain't who?" I asked.

"You are the feller what killed me at the battle of Belmont, ain't you?"

Seeing that the old fellow was still living and yet talked of himself as dead, I knew he was a lunatic, and saw that he was well armed. I had no weapon of any description, and confess I felt anxious. He still held his musket at a "present arms." Constantly, through two years, in the midst of ever-recurring excitements, of course I had utterly forgotten that I had ever advertised any one as dead at Belmont, and there was nothing in this rude, bent, gray old soldier to recall the neatly clad, erect Mr. Gibbons, who was acting as Colonel Cole's orderly in November, 1861, at Columbus, Kentucky.

He still stared at me. I said to him, soothingly:

"Are you not mistaken? I don't think I killed anybody in the battle of Belmont. I only crossed the river in the afternoon and saw the fighting at the boats, when Grant's troops were going away."

"Oh, I'm not talking about that," said Gibbons. "You killed me by telegraph. Don't you remember it?"

I now knew that I was arrested by a maniac. The bare suggestion of death by telegraph instead of by railway implied hopeless, irremediable insanity.

I was at my wit's end and could only suggest that I had "almost forgotten it."

"D——n it," exclaimed the old fellow, bringing his musket down till its muzzle almost touched my face, "I'm Gibbons, Colonel Cole's orderly, and you sent my death to the *Avalanche*, and the *Whig*, at Vicksburg, copied it, and every other newspaper in the wurruld, I think. I thought my wife would sorter cum round and be sorry like, and that she'd be glad when I resurrected, and sorter went home outer the graveyard like. But you played h——l, you did."

The fun involved in the queer facts now began to dawn upon me. I remembered Gibbons and his supposititious heroic death, and how poor Bassett and I slew him with our little pencils.

"Mr. Gibbons," I remarked, solemnly, "you told me to publish the story."

"Yes, that may be, but you shan't laff about it. You played h——l, I tell you! The news went, and kept agoin' and everybody knowed I was dead, very dead. I was, sir, d——d dead," exclaimed the old man, and he stamped the ground as if his hated corpse was beneath it.

I could not repress signs of laughter.

"Look here," exclaimed the old fellow, "I won't have any of that. You'll be shot deader than I am, except in the newspapers, ef you don't cork up."

He was profoundly in earnest. His eyes blazed, and I "corked up." I was, in fact, profoundly solemn. The musket was coming up to my face.

"I'll do anything I can for you, Mr. Gibbons."

"Well, then, git down and resurrect me."

I was again puzzled. It occurred to me that surely the man was a maniac. How was I to "resurrect" him?

"Git down," he repeated, "and write it all out and sign your name to it, and tell 'em it was all a d——d lie, and that I ain't dead. The old 'oman and the infernal lawyers has done administered to my e-state. She sold my fo' niggahs, and she was about marryin' another feller when I last hearn from her. Be quick and straighten it all out. When I writes, or rayther when I gits some other feller to write and I makes my mark to the letter they sends back word, they can't be humbugged. They knows I'm dead and that no swindling rascal can git money outen her. I'm ben miserable, mighty miserable, ever sense you killed me in the newspapers. I lost home, wife, property, everything, and I am gettin' very old, and now I'm buried alive, and out'n the wurruld, and still knows I was in it."

Tears came into the old man's eyes, his voice faltered, he bowed his head, and I pitied him with all my heart. In broken accents, he went on:

"Last summer I got a furlow to go home for thirty days, and took sick and lay thar in a horspital at Jackson till I only had one day left. I staggered down, a skelly-ton, to the railroad, and rode on the kyars to my farm, whar my wife lives sense she sold my house and lot in town, twelve miles outen Vicksburg. I got thar about dusk, and staggered along till I got to the house. I looked jest like a dead man, for all the wurruld. I staggered in. The front door was open and thar sot my wife. She knowed I was dead. She was aholdin' a young feller's hand, and her sister was in the room. It looked free and easy like, as if they was used to it. I stood and looked and listened a minnit and hearn the gal say, 'Oh, he's ben dead more'n a year and a half,' when I got mad. I knowed they was atalkin' about me, and I stepped into the room, and stood thar silent, holdin' up my bony hands.

"Never, in all my born days, did I hear setch screams as them two wimmin give. Both keeled over, dead; deader'n ever I was. That ar nice young man knowed it was me. He used to know me in Vicksburg before I died. His eyes stood an inch or two outen his nice little head, and har riz up and stood like hog bristles, and he wur whiter than his liver. He stared at me half a minnit, and then went fur the winder. I think it's more'n probable he is arunnin' yet. He never looked back, nary a time.

"Them horspital folks at Jackson had telegraphed the conscript officer at my railroad dippo to catch me as a deserter. When I started to get some whiskey for the wimmin and to be out of sight when they opened their eyes that they mightent be skeered agin, I was ordered to halt. At that very minnit here come the train. The conscript officer tuk me with him and fetched me to Jackson, and the next week I was sent with six more deserters under guard to my rigiment. Noboddy seen me at home but them thar people. That feller what was gwine to marry my wife—well, I know he's clean gone. He was, perhaps, the wust scart man that has lit out anywhare sense this skeery war begun, and cowardly legs have ben mightily imposed upon and stretched all over these hyar states. He knows I'm a ghost, and my wife and her sister jest swares all the time that it was my ghost which they seed, and the nabers believed it, and that I got up outen my grave at Columbus, Kentucky, and traveled to Vicksburg jest to keep the old 'oman from marryin' that skeery chap. You see how very dead I am. You must help me, won't you? I don't want to be dead, when I know I am living, and now everyboddy swars I am buried and forgotten at Columbus, Kentucky, and that my ghost has been seen agin and agin. My wife has the ager whenever she hyars my name."

I dismounted, and asked the heart-broken old man to sit beside me at the root of the great oak, through whose branches winds sighed sadly, while tears fell rapidly from the old man's eyes.

I wrote of his griefs as I read of them now. I will publish this story and the old soldier may yet make the world confess that, like Daniel Webster, "he still lives."

# CHAPTER XVI.

The Newspaper Man spins another Yarn.—A Porcine Steed.—Sim Sneed in the Role of John Gilpin.—He disperses a Battery.—A Dead Dog.—"The Divel Sure."—Denouement.

At noon, next day, we rested on the banks of a little mountain stream fifty yards from the country roadway we had followed, leading towards Tunnel Hill. Two men on foot and one on horseback, as tracks in the highway indicated, were not far ahead. Whether enemies or friends we could not tell. Spratling went forward to ascertain their character. What befell him and how extraordinary was his action may be imagined when one reflects that he was now imbued with indestructible and boundless confidence in his own powers and in his iron muscles. And then he was reckless because he deemed his separation from Bessie final.

We were eating hard bread and broiled bacon and sipping strong coffee when the newspaper man said he was "in Chattanooga about a year ago, when the daring Federal Captain, Andrews, almost succeeded in giving General Mitchell possession of the place. Generals Kirby Smith and Leadbetter were in command, Leadbetter, a supposed engineer, engaged in fortifying the stronghold."

"I don't think," said the journalist, "there were more than five hundred soldiers in the ragged, ricketty, weather-boarded town. These were raw, half-armed, undisciplined Georgians encamped at the end of the railroad track on the river bank half a mile from the Crutchfield tavern, occupied by Generals Smith and Leadbetter.

Here, in this Crutchfield tavern, occurred the conflict between 'Bill' Crutchfield and General Vaughn of which I was telling some time ago, and in its immediate vicinity happened the most ludicrous incident that will be illustrated in all the annals of this absurd and ghastly war. While the word Chattanooga, signifying crow's nest,— the rounded hills in the valley representing, in red men's eyes, the eggs of the bird,—is held down in its place on the map of the earth's surface by that mighty paper weight, Lookout Mountain, this story will be ever memorable. The news came to the Confederate generals, by telegraph from Big Shanty, that a Federal Captain, Andrews, and a dozen gallant men, disguised as country clodhoppers, had seized the locomotive at that place and were coming north. Three hundred passengers, and cars with reinforcements for Chattanooga, were thus left at Big Shanty, while Captain Andrews, coming north, was destroying each bridge and culvert behind him. The Federal General, Mitchell, was at Bridgeport, west of Chattanooga, intending, as soon as he was advised of the success of Captain Andrews, to attack and capture the feebly garrisoned stronghold. He proposed to carry it by storm before bridges and culverts could be repaired, and before men and munitions could be sent up from Atlanta.

"Andrews failing to cut the telegraph wire when he first left Big Shanty, full dispatches, telling what he had done, came to us in Chattanooga. A train of platform, open cars was at once freighted with two hundred raw militiamen and sent down the road to capture Andrews.

"I had slept through the night on a blanket, with Rolfe S. Saunders, beside the railway at the southern end of the Crutchfield house, afterwards burned. In an alley running at right angles to the railway and behind the tavern, slept a sick soldier named Sim Sneed. He was very small, short of stature, round of person, and bald-headed. Just before the train started out to intercept Captain Andrews, coming up from Big Shanty toward Chattanooga, Sim was suffering greatly. I gave him a large share of the exhilarating contents of Saunders' canteen and discovered that Sim, besides being very sick, was exceedingly drunk. The train was now coming down toward the hotel. Two hundred men on it rattling guns and shouting, and the roaring of cars and locomotive, begat a mighty noise. A huge sow, weighing quite four hundred pounds, was roused from her matutinal slumbers in a mud-hole by this dreadful uproar. She was greatly frightened, and came snorting and leaping along the railroad track, ahead of the locomotive, to our resting place. Fearing that the immense brute would run over and cover us with greasy slime, in which she had been bathing, Saunders and I stood erect. Sim Sneed, at the instant, with clothes wholly unloosened about him, because of the pain he suffered, hearing the noise made by the huge hog, rose up on his knees and elbows. He was facing the flying hog. The animal, frightened by Saunders and myself, turned suddenly and rapidly into the alley-way. Her nose passed under Sim's body, and between it and his pantaloons that dropped under the hog's throat. He clasped his arms about her, and thus, lying on his face, pinioned to the huge brute's back, he went careering backwards down the alley.

"The thoroughly affrighted beast, with her involuntary rider, snorted like a hippopotamus. Sim's shirt floated as a flag of truce above his back, as he hurried, wrong end foremost, down the hill.

At the foot of this declivity, Captain Claib Kane's gallant battery was encamped.

"The railway train now stood still, and three hundred men, amazed and silent at first, contemplated the stupendous flight of that dumbfounded hog. At last the supreme ridiculousness of Sim Sneed's attitude struck the soldiers. Many had seen him caught up on the animal's snout and fastened on her back, and shouts and laughter rent the air.

"Chattanooga was as full of dogs and fleas as Constantinople. These dogs all barked and howled, a fact I would not have observed at the moment, but many of these curious curs came rushing toward the tavern to see what had happened. Saunders, from a platform car which we had mounted, directed my attention to a big, black cur, with a very short tail, rushing madly along a garden fence at right angles to the course pursued by Sneed and the Flying Childers he bestrode. Just as the dog turned the corner, the hog reached it. That dog had never seen any living thing whose physiognomy bore the remotest resemblance to features made up of a sow's grim head thrust between a man's pantaloons and body, and this body constituting a full, white, round forehead for the unaccountable beast. When the dog rushed round the corner, to face the hog, his hair was all turned the wrong way; his short, stiff tail worn off by having good Sunday-school boys of Chattanooga tie tin buckets to it, was turned up stiff and straight, at right angles to his rigid backbone. The dog was terribly excited when he suddenly faced the sow and Sneed inverted. He stopped dead still; his hair and tail instantly fell; he shook; his spine gave way; his head sank; he dropped upon the sod, and turning gently upon his side, his legs quivered, and there was a dead dog.

"Captain Kane's battery of eight guns, one hundred and fifty horses, and as many men, was at the foot of the hill. The great, grim grunter, now ridden by Sneed, was well known there. She foraged among Captain Kane's horses; but as she came down the hill, bearing Sim upon her back, she was wholly unrecognized by Irishmen and horses.

"'An', what is it, Pathrick?'

"'An', faith, an' will ye be afther tellin' me, Jemmy?'

"'An', bejazes, I niver seen the loikes of it before.'

"'Oh, it's the divel sure, with his face white-washed.'

"Meanwhile, the echo of voices of shouting crowds reached these artillerymen. They stood upon guns and caissons when the old sow rushed down the declivity. Horses broke away from their fastenings and fled in all directions, and the sow was crossing the encampment before the artillerymen saw how Sim Sneed became a sort of inverted centaur.

"They had hardly recovered from their alarm and ceased making signs of the cross and invoking the Holy Virgin, when the sow passed out of sight under the negro shanty where her dozen pigs reposed in dusty blissfulness. As she went under, Sim's fat person struck the sleeper of the house. The sow never halted. Sim's breeches were rent in twain, one-half remaining on either leg. He lay some time senseless in the dust. A comrade ran to him with a blanket, and Sim soon afterward was furloughed by Leadbetter as an insane John Gilpin."

# CHAPTER XVII.

Spratling makes a Descent upon the Bushwhackers.—An Extraordinay Meeting.— Spratling suddenly loses his Appetite.—At Headquarters.—Camp Life.—Woman in War and Politics.—Why this Book was written.—Camp Fire Morals.—An Illustration.—A Ludicrous and Pitiful Story.—An Old Woman Eloquent.—"The Foremostest Sin that God Almighty will go about Forgiving."

While the journalist was talking, as recited in preceding pages, Spratling followed rapidly in the footsteps of the three persons just ahead of us. He came upon them within a mile of our resting place. They had kindled a fire some distance from the highway and prepared their noon-day meal. Spratling concealed himself on the summit of the hill, watched their actions, and soon ascertained that one was a young soldier and officer and the others bushwhackers. He said afterwards that he was satisfied, while watching the movements of these three men, that one was the very bushwhacker who escaped when his two comrades fell at Starnes' home. This conviction excited a keen desire, Spratling said, to "capture the rascal." He had sought to slay Spratling, and if the latter had not held the wagon, thus guarding his own person despite the horse's exertions to move the vehicle, he would have been shot to death by his three assailants.

·"Therefore," said Spratling, "I could not help watching and waiting to-day for an opportunity to resent the thwarted purposes of this bushwhacker who had escaped from me at Starnes'."

When the soldier and bushwhackers had appeased hunger, they sought each a spot on which to rest. The soldier came to a great tree hardly fifty paces from Spratling's place of concealment. The two bushwhackers stretched themselves on blankets side by side. Within ten minutes, all were so still that Spratling believed they slept. He crept, stealthily and noiselessly, to the tree. One of its roots was the soldier's pillow. Spratling, of whose strength, as we learned afterwards, the sleeping soldier had heard marvelous accounts, leaped, when within a yard or two of his victim, upon the unconscious youth and seizing his throat said in a whisper:

"Be silent.   You are my prisoner and are safe."

The soldier said afterward there was no need for these injunctions of silence, that Spratling's grasp about his throat almost crushed every bone in it.

In an instant Spratling raised the young soldier and held him, disarmed and helpless as he was, as a shield with one hand, while, presenting his repeater in the other, he ordered the two bushwhackers to rise and hold up their hands.

The man who had sought to kill Spratling at Starnes' looked up, grew pale, and shuddering, said, in husky tones:

"It's him!   It's Spratling!"

The name was magical in its potency.   The two men rose with hands uplifted, their guns and pistols lying on their blankets.   If they had been fearless as Spratling and resisted, one or both would have fallen instantly and in no event could Spratling have been killed except by a bullet that was first fatal to the young officer.   The bushwhackers comprehended the exigencies of the moment and, in obedience to Spratling's orders, moved toward the road, fifty yards distant.   The young officer having been disarmed, was ordered to join his two associates, and Spratling, with a cocked repeater in each hand and his Henry rifle strapped on his back, followed his prisoners to the creek where he had left us.

We were not a little amazed when he laughingly ordered us to "open ranks" and receive his prisoners.   The trio came to us pitifully crestfallen.   They confessed in their faces a sense of shame that they had succumbed to the tact, courage, and notorious strength of one man.   Meanwhile we could hardly conceal from Spratling and his prisoners our amazement.   We supposed he would bring accurate information, and that we might assail these supposed scouts, but never dreamed that he would undertake the task he had effected.   Spratling's good nature, when he discovered the chagrin of the young Federal lieutenant, made him say that "he knew that his own success depended upon the deprivation of the young officer of every means of resistance and of escape.   I, therefore, first disposed of him.   When he was helpless, of course the others surrendered."

The bushwhackers captured recognized the pedagogue as a former comrade, the latter stating that he was a paroled prisoner.   The youthful officer, seeing that the pedagogue was on the best possible terms with the captain, Spratling, and the newspaper man, said to him that he had "supposed prisoners of war would be kept under guard."

"We have no guardsmen," interposed the captain.   "Now and then we hold as prisoners men whom we can trust implicitly, and Mr. Wade is of the number.   I am not perfectly sure, but think it needless to use handcuffs or cords in dealing with you.   Tell me as a man of honor and as a soldier that you will not attempt to escape and you can go where you please.   The others, I am sorry to say, since there are only three of us and the editor there is a volunteer aide-de-camp, and we now have six prisoners, must be tied together."

The lieutenant, looking into the captain's face, said that his "widowed mother's home was not far from Tunnel Hill. These loyal scouts had agreed to guide me safely thither. If you will suffer me to visit my home, I will promise anything. Here is my furlough. It lasts"——

A sudden light shone in the captain's eyes. He gazed into the lieutenant's face with suddenly awakened interest and earnestness that startled the young soldier.

"Keep your furlough," said the captain. "I know who you are and your mother's name."

The captain rose, and walking away, said, "See the schoolmaster, there. I accept your pledge. You can hear from Mr. Wade much that you would gladly know. Possibly it is most fortunate that we have met. I am engaged in serving those you love. The fact that we are public enemies need not affect our personal relations. Our duties and obligations as soldiers need not clash with those that rest upon us as men. You are paroled," continued the captain, "and I would only advise you to remain with us and especially that you confer with Mr. Wade.

Spratling had overheard none of this colloquy. He was providing for the security of his prisoners. When his task was done, he came and sat near the editor, and was devouring bacon and bread with that energy which distinguished him when marching and fighting.

"Do you know, Sprat," asked the journalist, "the name of that handsome young officer whom you almost choked to death a little while ago?"

"No," he answered, glancing at him and Wade, who were engrossed in matters they discussed, "but I don't see why the captain releases him on parole and at the same time handcuffs his comrades. He is much more dangerous than these two clodhoppers who only know the woods and roads and are too timid, if watched, to be murderous."

"But do you know the name of that gentleman?"

"No," answered Spratling, "and I don't care to know; but I don't think, since it cost me so much risk to catch him, that he should be turned loose."

"Let me tell you, Sprat. Come near that no one else may hear. That is Lieutenant Hughes, the young man Bessie Starnes talked about, and let me tell you further—Oh, sit still and don't get excited, Sprat—he is Mamie Hughes' brother."

Spratling's nerves and muscles were unstrung. Bread and bacon fell from his unconscious fingers. He slowly returned his ugly knife to its sheath in his belt, drew the back of his hand across his face, and straightening himself, as he sat, turned to stare at his prisoner.

"Suppose," said Spratling, as if talking to himself, while he stared at the lieutenant, "suppose I had cut his throat, as I once thought of doing, while he slept, or suppose I had actually killed him, as I might have done, when I held his throat! My God! what would Bessie have thought of me!"

Forgetful of my existence, Spratling rose, and approaching the lieutenant, said to him:

"You don't know how glad I am that I didn't kill you and how sorry because I had to make you a prisoner. I didn't know your name or that you knew Bessie."

A new leaf in the volume of human nature was suddenly turned by the lieutenant. Bessie, only the day before, had told him of Spratling's honest devotion to herself, but the lieutenant deemed the gigantic rebel a mere animal, full of courage as of physical strength. He never dreamed of ascribing to the rude ranchero and herdsman of Texas a generosity of purpose and true nobility of character, now partially unfolded, such as few men have illustrated in acts or words.

The lieutenant rose up and, slowly extending his hand, looked searchingly into Spratling's large, transparent blue eyes that never faltered while the two men studied one another's virtues as written in their faces.

Spratling drew the lieutenant aside and said to him, "You don't know how sorry I am for what has happened; but I couldn't help it. I did not know that you are Bessie's lover. She has told you about me, I reckon, and what a fool I was; but she told you I was an honest man and that I would serve her or even a dog that she loved. Don't forget that while Spratling is above ground and you are true to Bessie, you have a friend who would storm hell if you asked it."

Two days after the events just narrated, the captain left Spratling, the pedagogue, and lieutenant not far from our pickets, and with the journalist and the two soldiers captured by Spratling at Starnes' and the two bushwhackers found with the lieutenant, proceeded to General Cleburne's head-quarters. Every leading incident of the preceding month was here narrated, and the general, as requested, applied for passports required for the use of the paroled lieutenant. When these came, two days later, from the provost marshal general, the captain returned to Spratling's bivouac. The journalist sought the encampment of Pinson's Mississippi cavalry, having agreed to rejoin the captain when the schoolmaster returned from East Tennessee with Mamie Hughes. The editor was also to recover possession of his horse and spend a week, in the interim, with the Federal lieutenant at the home of the latter, below Tunnel Hill. Communication between all these was to be maintained through General Cleburne's head-quarters.

Nothing is more intolerably irksome to those accustomed to daily newspaper work than the incomparably stupid and monotonous life of a soldier. Tattoo, reveille, dress-parade, drill, service on the out-posts or as sentinels, ditch-digging, greasy cards, musty, hard bread and tough beef, with no books and rarely a newspaper, are hourly facts that invest with horror, when nearly twenty years have elapsed, memories of life in camp. There is nothing to elevate or refine and everything to degrade, the intellects and tastes and brutalize one's habits and modes of thinking. There were many educated, excellent gentlemen, sons of rich cotton planters, acting as private soldiers in Pinson's regiment. Even among these the journalist said he heard stories hourly by the camp fire that shocked his sensibilities. The great evils of war are those that result from the separation of the sexes; husbands from wives, brothers from sisters, lovers from sweethearts. Vices consequent upon these facts are discovered in the homes of the people as well as in conversations on tented fields.

To the very extent that woman gains potency in the church, in society, in social life, or in government, to that extent man as an individual and as a citizen is made worthier of God's approval. There is a divinity in woman that may be demonized by man, but while she remains herself she elevates, refines, and deifies our race. Her influence would be as beneficent in law and government as war showed it to be in social life; and woman's morals, tastes, and purity should be injected into the ballot-box.

These memoranda, made concurrently with the events of which they tell, are now exploited that a new generation may have some inadequate apprehension of codes of morals and tastes and habits of every-day life that obtained everywhere in states that became seats of war. Many generals, and countless writers of every grade of intelligence and truthfulness have written of campaigns and battles. This unpretending volume only assumes to tell how soldiers and people talked and ate and slept and loved and hated when grim-visaged war stalked abroad leaving its blackest curse upon the morals of homes and churches and of woman. In digging graves for myriads of men whose depravity was as steadily progressive as the strokes of Death were violent, spasmodic, and numberless, War achieved least of its measureless calamities.

Of the character of stories commonly told by camp fires I can not give a perfect illustration. The journalist, when he, Spratling, the captain, and the pedagogue had again met and were seated about blazing logs during a cold evening in February, 1864, with half a dozen cavalrymen—the journalist's brother among the number—assigned to temporary service as scouts—the journalist told a story that smacked of the morals of the age when Mars was the god of the people as of armies.

"I was telling, some time ago, of my flight from Knoxville to Kingston and how I was forced," said the editor, "to win the favor and confidence of the people by becoming a preacher. I had spent three years at a theological college. My father proposed to make me an educated preacher. I did not assent; but thought that I would please him if possible. But the more I saw of preachers in embryo the less I was inclined to adopt their profession. I left theology and took to literature at the university, and thence, after I was graduated, was inducted into a law school. But I never forgot the forms or lessons of the theological institution, or the two or three sermons I had written with infinite care. How I pronounced one of these discourses, and its effects, I may tell to-morrow night.

"I won the confidence of a good Union methodist to such an extent at Kingston, that, though I was a baptist, he conveyed me in his wagon twenty miles toward Chattanooga. Burnside's cavalry held the railway below Knoxville and I was forced to make a *detour*, as formerly explained, by way of Kingston. My methodist friend commended me, as a devout young baptist brother, to one Deacon Applegate, of my church, whose guest I now became. With much shamefacedness and most unwillingly did I repeat a prayer, night and morning, in the presence of the household and the more was I chagrined when I went to church and was made to occupy a seat in the pulpit while a venerable and godly man expounded the scriptures to his homely flock. I had begun to practice the odious deception and wear this false character when no other course would have saved me from incarceration of indefinite duration. Having entered upon the wrongful and false line of conduct I dared not turn backward. I aided modestly in the services and then was asked to remain and witness the trial by the church of Julia Adams, a 'good girl,' so the brethren and sisters said, but 'unfortunate.' I inquired of one of the brethren whether Julia was to be tried for some 'misfortune.' He answered, with a puzzled look:

" 'Not adzactly; but its somehow that way.'

"The baptist polity is that of a pure republic. Every church member, white or black, male or female, old or young, is invested with the 'privilege' of suffrage which thus becomes a 'right'—because of its universality. It happened, however, that the good and aged pastor, Mr. Robinson, when the conference was opened, advised the unmarried and youthful members of the church of both sexes to go out. I observed that Mr. Applegate's son, about seven or eight years of age, a handsome, intelligent child, was much excited and very loth to obey his mother and make his exit with the rest. He had attended a country school with Julia Adams and though the girl was eighteen years of age, Jimmy Applegate was her sworn lover. Jimmy had heard that Julia had loved, as the newspapers commonly have it, 'not wisely, but too well;' but Jimmy, in the innocence of his nature, did not see in what Julia was not as good and beautiful as before. Julia, unhappy child as she was, sat beside her faithful old mother in a corner of the little log church, crying as if her heart would break. Jimmy looked wistfully toward her, his eyes swimming in tears, as he went out of the door. Not many minutes later I observed that Jimmy had crawled between two logs into the goods box of a pulpit and was quietly ensconced where he could see Julia's sweet, tearful face and watch the progress of the impending trial. The gray-haired preacher sat, when holding the business meeting, at a little table in front of the pulpit. He announced to the 'bretheren and sisterin' that the 'object of this session of the conference meeting is to say what shall be done in the case of sister Julia Adams. You've all hearn about it and there's no use talking. Thar she sits aweeping by her aged, heart-broken mother, who loves her child and holds her hand, and cries even more bitterly than her unhappy daughter. What have you to say about it, my bretheren and sisterin?'

"One after another the half dozen male members and saints of the church rose and insisted that there was nothing to be said in defence of the girl. She was a church member and forgetful of obligations to society, to the church, and her own family and fame, had suffered herself to be betrayed by that scapegrace, Jim Carter.

"The truth is, the brethren and sisters confessed no pity for the poor girl, and all denounced her in harshest terms.

"Meanwhile Julia's grief was painful to contemplate. She threw her arms about her aged mother's neck and sobbed aloud. She had never before comprehended the frightful enormity of her misdeeds. Nearly every old member of the church had spoken concurrently, urging Julia's expulsion and the gray-haired pastor would groan out, as each speaker sat down, a deep, sonorous, solemn 'Amen.'

"Evidently Julia was undone, and she, the mother, and the faithful little lad in the pulpit, who loved her most ardently, were overwhelmed by this great grief and impending and incurable disgrace.

"There was profound silence and everybody watched earnestly the slow deliberation with which Mrs. Nancy Ransom, an aged widow, rose in her place. She removed her homespun sun-bonnet and her long, white, unconfined hair fell down her back and over her shoulders curved by the weight of eighty years.

"'Brethren and sisters,' she began, 'I want to say something, but aint used to saying what I think before the church, and yet I can't be silent when I listen to these unchristianlike speeches you have been making. Poor Julia! with all my heart do I pity her! I always loved the warm-hearted, confiding, generous child, and I love her just the same to-day as a year ago. She is just as good and true and honest to-day, as she was before this black cloud cast its hateful shadow on her path, and before this tempest burst upon her sunshiny home. See her bitter tears and pale, sweet face and the black sorrow that sits on her stainless forehead.

"'Admit she sinned. Has she not repented? Look and see!' exclaimed the old dame, pointing at Julia clasped in her mother's arms.

"'Brethren,' she continued, 'I don't think you read your bibles. I don't think you know anything about the Savior. You are governed by your resentments and not by that charity which God taught us to practice. Don't you remember when that unhappy widow, another poor Julia, was brought before God? When it was sought to have Him condemn her—expel her from God's church and from God's presence and from God's mercy, what was His answer? I repeat it here to-day in reply to all that these brethren have said.

" 'Let him who is without sin cast the first stone.' Who among you men or women dare cast the first stone at Julia?'

"Here the old woman straightened herself up to her full height. Her great blue eyes dimmed by years, blazed with the fires of renovated youth. She shook her bony forefinger at the old preacher, and in deep tones and measured accents, said:

" 'Brethren and sisters, it is my honest opinion, in the presence of Christ's example and of our own natures and of the fact that God made us and not we ourselves, that Sister Julia's is the foremostest sin that God Almighty will go about forgiving.'

" 'The last were her precise, exact, earnest words.

"Silence. profound and lasting, that followed, told of the effects of her simple eloquence. The old preacher groaned audibly.

"I observed that little Jimmy Applegate, as he sat in the pulpit, was in ecstasies. He rubbed his sunburnt hands together. His long hair was brushed away from his smiling nut-brown face. His tearful eyes shone lustrously and lovingly while he listened and watched intently each movement and caught every simple, earnest word that fell from the tremulous lips of wrinkled, time-worn Mrs. Ransom. Meanwhile, poor, unhappy Julia's eyes almost smiled through tears that stood still at last.

"Her wretched mother stared wonderingly, amazed beyond measure that one woman had at last pitied and forgiven another.

"There was protracted and death-like silence when Mrs. Ransom sat down.

"At length Dr. Joe Prewitt, a gray-haired, most influential deacon, rose in his place, and said:

" 'Bretheren, there is no use talking. Sister Ransom is right. We forgot Christ. We forgot that none of us can "cast the first stone." I move that Sister Adams' name, she having repented of her sin, remain on the church book.'

" 'Amen! Amen! Bless the Lord!' sang out the aged preacher.

"The motion was carried, *mem. con.* The doxology was sung; the old preacher pronounced his benediction upon the assembly, and all were going out when Jimmy Applegate ran, and grasping the bony hand of Mrs. Ransom, kissed it. He then followed closely after Julia. I watched the little fellow whose tenderness and fidelity were even touching. He said to Julia, when she turned and kissed him:

" 'The oldest and youngest of us, Mrs. Ransom and Jimmy, knew you were good and true and we loved you, and now everybody loves you, and you won't cry any more, will you, Julia?'

"Julia again kissed her big-hearted, honest little lover, as tenderly and gratefully as she did the aged Mrs. Ransom who came to bid her good bye, and tell her to be a 'good girl' and she would never want friends.

"I am much inclined to believe, boys," said the editor, "after studying her sweet, pretty face and watching the tears that fell from her great blue eyes, that Julia Adams is still one of the best and truest and most stainless of her sex. Her soul, if not her body, is uncontaminated, and I must say that until I heard Mrs. Ransom's simple, earnest defence of Julia, I had never translated liberally the words that fell from Jesus' lips:

"'*Qui sine peccato est prius in illam lapidem mittet.*'

"It is hardly necessary to say that the venerable dame, Mrs. Ransom, gave to the proper translation of these words a specific application to the offence she discussed, perhaps wholly unwarranted. 'He who is without sin' can condemn the guilty. It is not asserted that he who is guiltless of this special offence is alone fit to pronounce sentence upon the weak, unfortunate, and fallen."

# CHAPTER XVIII.

The lieutenant, while we were resting at noon, was telling that he was sent at one time on special duty and as a bearer of dispatches to New Madrid in Southeastern Missouri. He said that, returning to Nashville, he was accompanied by an old citizen of Spring Hill, a village thirty miles, perhaps, southwest of Columbia, in Tennessee. My newly made friend was a sensible, sturdy farmer, who, it seems, had been a surgeon in the United States Army. His account of the killing of the Confederate Major General Van Dorn greatly interested me. I had been reading of this terrible affair in northern newspapers, one of which stated truthfully that Van Dorn in all physical and social respects was a perfect knight, belonging to the middle ages rather than to modern times. He was quite young when killed,—perhaps thirty-six,—but had been distinguished in the old army, before the war, as a peerless Indian fighter. Marvelous statements are told of his horsemanship and how he would ride down upon Commanches, Navajahoes, and other bands, sabering right and left.

"On the field of battle he was the coolest man I ever saw," said the doctor. "Often when I have felt sick at the stomach and wanted to compress my shoulders and ribs into a little space, I have seen Van Dorn sit there under a rain of bullets, absolutely enjoying himself. He was a knightly fellow to look at. His hair was a clear golden color, and in natural ringlets, it fell around his shoulders and neck and looked like a King Charles wig. He had a rich golden mustache which sprung across the whole upper part of his face, and then he wore a chin whisker. He had the softest blue eyes, clean-cut features, and good teeth. He was rather below middle size and a splendid horseman and man-at-arms. Besides, he could blush like a girl.

This, with his winning address, made him absolutely irresistible among women. Wherever he went, they gave way.

"He was one of the few men in either army that could sing and play musical instruments with a sweet, rich voice and accomplished hand. He wrote poetry. In his dress he was neat as a pin. As soon as he entered a household his bearing attracted, his address delighted, his accomplishments made the women worship him, and I am sorry to say that he was a lawless *roue*.

"His father was an old Mississippi judge, and I suppose of Dutch descent. The old man was just about the son's size, and often used to come over to our camp, and he was almost invariably full of whiskey. One day he said to me, 'Doctor, do you hear what some of these chaps have been saying about me—that I drink a good deal of whiskey? They don't know, doctor, what an unquenchable thirst I have!' Van Dorn had married in Alabama, I think, and his conduct aggrieved his wife, although I believe she sent for his body after his death and took it back to Alabama and buried it on her farm, in a field, where I suppose he lies without a stone.

"Doctor Peters was a practicing physician at Spring Hill. He had married his second wife, considerably younger than himself—a giddy, pretty woman. It was absolutely certain that when such a creature should be seen by Van Dorn, and listened to him, there would be a flirtation and perhaps an intrigue. It happened of course. Peters was one of those silent, deadly men you meet with in Tennessee and derivative states; he had a pair of cold gray eyes, which in ordinary times were nearly expressionless, but would start up demoniacally. Inflict a personal wrong on such a person and he would be worse than an Indian. He had a lean, listless look, but turned into iron when excited. Van Dorn came into this vicinity laboring under a bad reputation. He had been accused of seducing two fair daughters of Vicksburg, and it was said of him at Memphis that with the family of a leading citizen there, mother and daughter, he had been treacherous. Van Dorn didn't care about it. He lived in his own personality and believed, to some extent, that all within his command was his. I mention these facts to answer your question as to whether he was much regarded. By those of his officers who had received his favors and knew him intimately he was lamented, but by the general public and by public opinion, I think not.

"He rose very rapidly in the Mexican war from second lieutenant to be a captain at Cerro Gordo and a major at Cherubusco. From the very beginning he was one of the most dauntless officers in our army. I think I am in error about his age. I believe he was born in 1823. In 1858, in an attack on the Commanches, he killed fifty-six Indians, and was dangerously wounded in four places. No man in the old army was more intense in his devotion to slave property on account of his family, marriage, birth, and temperament. As Early as January, 1861, he resigned his commission, became a colonel in the Confederate service, and took a leading part in Texas in capturing other regulars. He took the *Star of the West* steamer, received the sword of Major Sibley, and almost immediately became a major general, when he was put in charge of the Trans-Mississippi District. He fought his leading battle, which was a reverse, at Pea Ridge.

"Van Dorn was a favorite of Mr. Jefferson Davis, and had command in the battle at Corinth, which was also unfortunate in results. He was court-martialed at that time.

"Afterward he had his head-quarters at Spring Hill several weeks. I am of the belief that nothing criminal happened between himself and this woman, Mrs. Peters, though I do not acquit him of bad intentions. The woman, however, but recently wedded to Peters, had sufficiently inspired his mind with the idea that a criminal intrigue had commenced. Peters then deliberately arranged the assassination of Van Dorn and his own escape. He established relays of horses to carry him into the Federal lines by rapid flight. He went from his house to Van Dorn's quarters, and, saying that he had some business just inside the Federal lines, would like to have a pass to get through. Probably glad to get him out of reach, with that interesting wife behind him, Van Dorn cheerfully consented, and leaned forward on his desk to write the pass, and signed his name to it. At this moment Dr. Peters, leaning on the desk on his left hand, drew his pistol while Van Dorn was leaning forward over his signature, and shot the general through the spinal marrow at the back of the head. The ball did not pierce the brain but produced paralysis, and he died in two hours. Peters seized the pass, got on his horse, and was far on the road to the Federal lines before it was discovered that Van Dorn had been shot. One of his staff coming in, found him leaning over the table muttering incoherently, and bleeding. They placed him on a lounge and heard him say, 'Peters has murdered me.'

"Peters passed into the Federal lines. There it was no harm to have killed Van Dorn. He was not molested. After the war it was not thought proper to indict him for a murder committed during hostilities under the circumstances. He condoned his wife's offence at the end of the war, and took her back, and they moved to Arkansas. In a little while the woman began to coquette again, and again aroused Peters' ire. He took her next supposed paramour by the chin, with a bowie-knife in the other hand, and literally guillotined him. That is the last known of Dr. Peters."

Such is the story that has been popularized in northern newspapers. It is untrue in every respect. The assertion that Peters, after killing Van Dorn, cut the throat of a lover of his wife in Arkansas is a sheer fabrication. He is a quiet, sober, unobtrusive, educated gentleman, and he and his wife have never been talked about save because of the killing of Van Dorn. He was an ardent secessionist and had been a leading member of the Tennessee legislature. After killing Van Dorn, he fled to Nashville, pursued by Van Dorn's staff officers.

"When he came to Nashville, I happened to be there," continued Lieutenant Hughes. "He was brought before General Rosecrans, to whom he applied for a passport to St. Louis. The general at first refused because Peters had been a conspicuous secessionist in the legislature of Tennessee. But Governor Brownlow and ex-Governor William B. Campbell interposed in Peters' behalf, and the passport was conceded.

"Peters recited the story, in my presence, of the taking off of Van Dorn. He suspected the progress of an intrigue. He knew Van Dorn's character and Peters' wife was famed for her personal charms, exquisite taste in dress, taste and coquetry. At Ben Weller's boarding house, on Cherry Street in Nashville, where Brownlow and Campbell lived, I heard Peters tell that he had suspected Van Dorn's infamous purposes, and in order to satisfy himself as to the facts, he announced his intention to be absent from home several days. He made every preparation for a journey, but returned the night of the day of his departure, and concealed himself in the ice-house, where he remained till about midnight. He then heard Van Dorn's horse's feet and soon afterward, the clanking of Van Dorn's heavy spurs as he came upon the back porch. Van Dorn himself had given Peters a passport through the Confederate lines, that he might enter Kentucky.

"Peters ascended the ladder from the ice-pit, and looking out, beheld Van Dorn's plumed hat. At this instant, as the Confederate chieftain entered the house, admitted by the wife, Peters having a pistol in his hand, was almost impelled to kill both the wife and her lover. But instead, Peters only followed quietly, and telling Van Dorn, 'Now, you d——d scouudrel, I have caught you, but I will spare your life and prevent gossip and the degradation of this woman and the stain upon my fame if you will write and sign the statement that you have corrupted my wife.'

"Van Dorn hesitated, but the cold steel gleamed in Peters' eyes and the cocked pistol was ready to do its deadly office, and Van Dorn said, 'I will sign the paper.'

"Next morning Peters called ·at Van Dorn's marquee. Van Dorn asked Peters what he proposed to do with the paper to be signed by himself. Peters replied that its contents should never be known to the public, but that he would take it to Richmond and learn whether the Confederate government were base enough and so depraved that it invested men with high offices and honors who professionally debauched the wives and daughters of those serving the government, however humbly, with tireless fidelity.

" 'Van Dorn asked me,' said Peters, 'to wait till two o'clock, when he would certainly execute the paper as I required. I am satisfied now that he thought that my passion would be dispelled by the lapse of a few hours and that he would easily escape the necessity I sought to impose. At two, p. m., I was again at Van Dorn's tent. His adjutant general was with him. This gentleman withdrew at once and Van Dorn and I were alone together. I had not attempted to kill Van Dorn in my own home and had postponed the final concession of my exactions, and Van Dorn thought there was no risk at last in refusing to do as he had promised. I had the fleetest, finest horse in Tennessee at hand. I did not know what was coming and did not intend, in any event, to be caught by Van Dorn's stipendiaries and clerks.

" 'When I approached Van Dorn, he said, quietly, that he had concluded not to give me any such "G—d d——d paper" as I required. Then I answered,' said Peters, "You are a d——d scoundrel," and shot him before he rose up. The bullet, I think, broke his neck. I rode several hundred yards before the alarm was given. Van Dorn's staff-officers and several soldiers pursued me. I don't think they were very anxious to catch me. I could not have been taken alive and was so armed that I was dangerous, and they knew it.'

" But Rosecrans was finally induced, as I have stated," said the lieutenant, "by Governor Brownlow and ex-Governor W. B. Campbell to grant the passport asked for by Peters, and the reason given was that though Peters was a devout secessionist and for this might properly be hanged, yet he had done God and the country such a service, by ridding the earth of Van Dorn, that Peters deserved well of his country and race. Peters did not believe that his wife was debauched but Van Dorn's criminality was none the less. He did not even deny his purpose. Peters' forbearance grew out of this fact and that other that he sought to evade scandal-mongers and newspaper notoriety."

It is needless to say that, like the lieutenant, his listeners approved Dr. Peters' conduct; and, therefore, the people concurring with us in opinion, Dr. Peters was never prosecuted.

This story is told not made because of its reference to prominent men of the war period; but, like many other narratives in this volume, to illustrate the force and direction and training of public opinion in the South.

# CHAPTER XIX.

The pedagogue was a delightful *raconteur.* Though his stories were
tinctured always, and naturally enough, with his political prejudices,
we were never offended. In fact, the old Whigs and Union men
in the Confederate service often gave expression to views never
tolerated among officers and placeholders. With the common soldiers
the people sympathized, and when, in 1863–4, the whole country was
singing a lackadaisical, sorrowful ditty, with the refrain,

> "When this cruel war is over,
> Maryland, my Maryland!"

the people were thoroughly beaten. There was nothing to commend
the horrible, dolorous ditty except its invocation of peace, and yet
every child, negro, and woman was singing it. Men went humming it
to the fields and workshops, and soldiers, catching the sickly, pitiful
melody, that over-ran more pitiful words, deserted their colors till Mr.
Jefferson Davis, at Macon, Georgia, announced, in the spring or early
summer of 1864, that two-thirds of his soldiers had deserted their
colors. It made one's heart sick to hear everywhere of the woes of
military despotism and this heart-rending cry for peace that came
welling up in this wretched song from the great fountain of popular
griefs. The vigorous, heroic verses of Father Ryan, of Lide Merri-
wether, and of Harry Timrod, and John Mitchell's eloquent portrayal
of the woes of "conquered" Ireland, availed nothing. The common
people persistently sang the dolorous ditty, and the Confederacy was
undone. Spratling began to recite, "Maryland, my Maryland," his

deep, strong, musical voice investing the monotonous music with a share of attractiveness, when the schoolmaster quoted the philosopher who said that "he is master of the country who writes its songs and not he who makes its laws." Spratling was silenced and the pedagogue began to tell of the marvelous campaign of moral effects to which he had alluded in former conversations. He said that Leadbetter, in Eastern Tennessee, a Confedederate Department Commander, in 1862-3, was weak, violent, and tyrannical. The post commander at Knoxville, Morrisette, was an artillery officer. He had been reared a banker's clerk, was a speculator, broker, and auctioneer. He had never fired a gun or pistol, and when appointed captain of artillery and given in charge six, and then twelve, field-pieces, had never seen a battery. Of course he knew absolutely nothing of gunnery or of artillery drill and practice. He selected as his first lieutenant one Baker, an *eleve* of a German military school and an adept in the art of war. I used to attend the dress parades of this "Morrisette Battery" to watch the captain's efforts to catch the whispered words of command given by Baker. Then Morrisette would repeat the words in the swelling, sonorous accents of a brigadier. When the "manual of the piece" was gone through with and duties of dress parade were discharged, then Morrisette, arrayed in all the feathers and toggery of glorious war and mounted on a magnificent charger, would lead his battery, guns, caissons, and men and horses through the streets of staring, wondering Knoxville.

Morrisette told me that the "moral effect upon the disloyal population of the place was very fine." I used to think the moral effect of Leadbetter's profuse administration of the oath of loyalty most unfortunate. In this, Morrisette concurred. But Leadbetter was singularly well pleased when Morrisette's polished guns went gleaming through the streets in the gorgeous sunlight of East Tennessee. Bootblacks, newsboys, and idlers about the bar-rooms swore roundly, when Morrisette strutted by, that his was the finest, bravest battery in the world.

Morrisette would look neither to the right nor left. He was intent on duty. His bosom was swelling with emotions of purest patriotism. He was the impersonation of lofty aspirations, and every inch a soldier. He was small of stature, had a huge nose and little legs, and dressed gorgeously. While Morrisette was thus appealing to the fears of Union men, Leadbetter was briskly imprisoning their consciences by "swearing them in," and East Tennessee was slowly lapsing, it seemed, into secessionism.

The jail, meanwhile, was full to overflowing. A magistrate of the place named Tillson, a vulgar, ignorant, noisy, whiskey-drinking fellow, became the partner of a vigorous lawyer of the town. A cavalry commander was also interested in the cruel, nefarious business.

The magistrate asserting jurisdiction in political cases, mountains and valleys were searched and every suspected individual was arrested, without warrant, by the cavalryman Blackburne and brought before the red-haired "squire." This grave and solemn sot always advised "culprits" to see the "great and good lawyer," who managed to scare simple people till they gave him all their money. Now and then he acquired a pretty farm in compensation for arduous "professional services."

I was at the Lamar House late in the afternoon, when Blackburne, the lawless myrmidon of the squire, brought in twenty or more "disloyal people." Colonel Casey Young, now an ex-M. C. and then Adjutant General on the staff of Brigadier General William H. Carroll, happened to be on the street when Blackburne came with his prisoners. He was accustomed to deliver them to Fox, the jailor, another "good and true man" of the period, so called in official papers at department headquarters. Dismayed and helpless, these Union men were moving toward Fox's dungeons. Colonel Young addressed one of them, an intelligent preacher—a presbyterian, I think. I heard him say that he had been teaching school and preaching and had nothing to do with war ; that he never spoke of it, but devoted himself to the service of God, his church, and his pupils. Colonel Young at once instructed the guards to leave this gentleman at the hotel. It was understood that the facts affecting his arrest would be investigated next morning. The preacher's two daughters, charming girls, had followed him to Knoxville. Late at night they came weeping to Colonel Young's apartment. The lawyer and the jailor, Fox, were in their father's room. They had given the lawyer a thousand dollars in gold which they had brought from home to save their father from Fox's clutches. The lawyer demanded more.

Young, half dressed, went to the preacher's room. The lawyer had disappeared, but the pug-nosed, squarely built jailor was with the prisoner, and in the act of leading him to jail, as instructed by the justice of the peace at the instigation of the learned lawyer. Young ordered Fox to leave the hotel, telling him that if he imprisoned political offenders under a *mittimus* from a state court, he (Young) would have him shot. Fox slunk away ; but the lawyer still enjoys riches that sprang from the hard-earned $1,000 filched from these pretty presbyterian girls.

Next morning I visited the jail. Young had frightened Fox, who was a cringing supplicant when I entered the prison yard. He was made to understand how he was violating the law in obeying the magistrate's decrees. Fox said that a prominent lawyer of the town (naming him) was the magistrate's adviser, and that he, the poor jailor, knew nothing about it. On the contrary, Fox robbed each prisoner mercilessly, and starved those who were without money, so they stated, remorselessly. Those suspected of having money or known to have rich friends were consigned to the iron cage till Fox's exactions were complied with. Mr. William Hunt, many years clerk and master of the chancery court at Cleveland, was robbed of four thousand dollars by Fox and his associates in the nefarious business. Mr. Hunt said that a secessionist furnished him part of the money with which he finally bought his liberty. There was never a jailor so abhorred by prisoners as this man Fox. I may do him injustice, since I tell what I heard from his victims. I would not wrong his memory, but there was joy in many modest homes in bright, peaceful valleys of East Tennessee when Burnside captured Fox at Bristol and consigned him to his own iron box in the jail at Knoxville. A few days later, when the turnkey made his usual rounds, he found Fox dead in his cage. Nobody seemed to care about it, and I never learned whether he committed suicide, as was rumored, or died of terror. He feared, when he fled from Knoxville, that the people of East Tennessee would wreak vengeance upon him for the outrages and robberies practiced by himself, the lawyer, the magistrate, and the cavalry leader. Hence the story that he took poison. The magistrate of whom I tell died a frightful death in Texas. Raving mad, tortured by visions of helpless women begging for mercy for those they loved, pursued by hideous phantoms to which whiskey gives birth and clothes with nameless terrors, the wretched man cursed God and himself and was no more. The lawyer, who profited most by the crimes of Fox and the justice of the peace, still lives, but not in Knoxville.

Among prisoners at this time in Fox's charge was William G. Brownlow, afterward governor and United States Senator. He was emaciated to the last degree. I remember that he showed me a "running seaton" on his breast and said that his condition was such that, if he were not taken from the cold, comfortless prison and supplied with better food, he would soon die. In the same apartment with Mr. Brownlow were many farmers, Confederate deserters, and all classes of people, victims of Fox's cupidity. Colonel Young, in conversing with these people, became satisfied that their imprisonment was needless as well as lawless and wrongful. The next day there was a general jail delivery. Brownlow himself was sent to his residence on Cumberland Street, and not many weeks later, when his health was somewhat improved, in charge of an escort commanded by Colonel Young and Captain O'Brien, he was sent through Chattanooga and Shelbyville to Nashville, then occupied by Union armies. Curious, staring, wondering, and untraveled southern soldiers hearing that the famous editor, preacher, and Unionist, Brownlow, was on the train at Chattanooga, sought to discover his identity. One of them, bolder than the rest, gained access to Brownlow's car and asked Brownlow himself, pale, wan, and mild-mannered as he was, to designate the terrible parson. Brownlow pointed to Colonel Young. "Johnny Reb" stared at Young a moment most intently and then, drawing a long sigh, exclaimed :

"Well it beats Judas Iscariot, by G—d."

Brownlow laughed till his life was almost despaired of, but I never heard that Colonel Young, confessedly good-looking as he is, enjoyed the joke.

I began this story to illustrate evils incident to military government conducted with a view to moral rather than physical results.

Morrisette and Leadbetter proposed to achieve the conquest of East Tennessee by every species of moral force, in which the one would make a parade of power, the other employing moral suasion. In both instances there was only a grand parade. Neither ever snuffed the breath of battle. When that fatal day at Fishing Creek dawned upon the hapless South, when Zollicoffer fell, a part of Morrisette's battery escaped from the wreck, but Morrisette himself was still commanding the fort and holding it bravely one hundred and fifty miles away, at Knoxville. When those daring, adventurous men who were hanged in Atlanta seized the railway train at Big Shanty, below Chattanooga, and leaving the passengers at breakfast, came north, tearing away bridges and culverts behind them that General Mitchell might capture Chattanooga, it being impossible to draw reinforcements from the south, Leadbetter was in Chattanooga almost frightened to death. He was never nearer the enemy or in greater danger than on that occasion. Of his conduct and of a memorable incident that befell the ragged town of that day the reader has been informed.

But Morrisette and Leadbetter in Knoxville finally grew weary of inaction. The latter found the task of ceaseless administration of oaths of loyalty tiresome. The people had already pronounced it exceedingly monotonous. Morrisette's battery—that portion of it which did not accompany Crittenden and Zollicoffer to Fishing Creek—when it went rattling and roaring along the stony streets of Knoxville, no longer attracted the slightest attention. In this desperate condition of affairs, Morrisette planned a grand expedition into Chucky Valley. Along the little river of this name, were pretty farms and delightful homes. Here, in Washington County, David Crockett was born, and the people were devoted to the "old flag."

They had never seen the new, and loved the Federal Union as our fathers made it. They were sons and grandsons of men who fought at King's Mountain and Eutaw Court-House. Their prayer was to be let alone. They were unwilling to fight their neighbors and kindred and had pledged themselves, in private conversations at methodist and baptist meeting-houses, never to strike down the stars and stripes. In every house there was Weems' "Life of Washington," Jefferson's "Notes on Virginia," the *National Intelligencer*, and Brownlow's *Whig*. Morrisette and Leadbetter had often been told of the charms of Chucky Valley and of the devout Unionism of the people. The two Confederate chieftains, wielding absolute power in East Tennessee, conferred secretly about it. With profound solemnity and injunctions of secrecy, they held several councils of war. They consulted Lieutenant Colonel Hugh Green, the rollicking, fun-loving leader of a half-drilled, half-armed regiment encamped at Knoxville. All, for one or another reason, approved the grand scheme of Morrisette and Leadbetter, and it was agreed to show the innocent dwellers along the banks of the bright and brawling Chucky how great and powerful was the mighty Richmond government.

Chucky Valley would thenceforth be ashamed that it had dreamed of resistance to the authority of Jefferson Davis.

Bill Carter was from Nashville. He was brave. He had fought many battles, in each of which he fell, but rose again, only to fall whenever he met his mortal enemy. Whiskey slew him at last in a frightful conflict that occurred in Knoxville. Bill was found dead one morning in the gutter, his eyes bloodshot, hair matted, clothes in tatters, and shoes, like those who gave him whiskey, soleless. He was reared a lawyer and thoroughly educated. He was the only child of his parents, inherited a good estate, and won a beautiful wife. Five years afterward, Bill was a beggar and his wife soon happily divorced by Bill's death.

Meanwhile, Bill was General Crittenden's orderly. Crittenden loved Bill for his weaknesses as well as wit. There were broad realms of sympathy in which they met. Both worshipped Bacchus. Bill was uglier than this god, who had distorted Bill's features. A horse had kicked and broken the lower maxillary bone on one side of his face, and a drunken Patlander had fractured the same bone on the other, and the two sides of this jaw-bone had been separated from one another until the lower part of Bill's face was a foot wide. His long nose was pressed upward by toothless gums. He ate with difficulty and, therefore, drank enormously. But he talked well and wittily. The slightest provocation to mirth emanating from a hairy turtle set up on end would surely provoke infinite laughter, and Bill's face had been compressed and widened till one always had visions of turtle soup while Bill poured forth the contents of an exhaustless vocabulary. Bill, in Crittenden's absence, had attached himself, as a sort of volunteer aide-de-camp, to Morrisette. In fact I heard him telling Morrisette, with great solemnity that he would be his Sancho Panza in the coming Chucky campaign.

Lieutenant Colonel Hugh Green had about six hundred good men. Of these Leadbetter took command. Leadbetter insisted that he must have artillery. Morrisette, giving him two brass six-pounders, had four left, in charge of about one hundred men. They moved slowly across the country from Morristown, firing morning and evening guns. The roar of artillery, both commanders insisted, exercised a fine "moral effect" upon a rebellious people.

It may be proper to state that I did not participate in this most eventful and disastrous campaign. I am indebted for the facts to memoranda made by Morrisette and to recitals of those who returned safely to Knoxville.

Having reached the seat of war, Morrisette followed the course of the River, while Leadbetter marched on a parallel and converging line three miles from the stream. Morrisette moved along the base of mountainous precipices next to the river, the shining guns reflected in its crystal waters. Leadbetter and Lieutenant Colonel Green, on steeds splendidly caparisoned, and in all the pomp and circumstance of glorious war, went careering across the country. They were stared at by women, and unkempt, wondering children.   Fearing conscription, the men of the country, it was observed by the leaders of the expedition, were never visible.   It was concluded at first that they had fled into the mountains; and, secondly, that an attack by night upon the forces of the Confederacy was contemplated by the innocent country bumpkins of Chucky Valley.

Soon after the sun went down, the moon, full-orbed, came up in gorgeous glory.   The air is clearer in East Tennessee—bereft of moisture, as it is, by mountains on every hand—than elsewhere in the United States.   It may be as transparent for like reasons in Western Texas and Southern Colorado, but the stars are brighter and the moon shines more lustrously down into the valleys and gilds the hills, and sheds a softer, sweeter radiance upon the rivers of East Tennessee, investing mountains and valleys with a diviner splendor, than elsewhere in America.   When moon and stars were borne away on bounding, sparkling waves of the boisterous river, Morrisette, unconsciously charmed by the scene and wedded to the spot, turned majestically in his saddle and ordered a halt.   The air of November was cold, clear, and crisp, and the soldiers soon lighted fires along the perpendicular banks of the rapid river.   Twenty feet away the mountains rose up precipitously, almost overhanging the stream.   In the next valley, two and a half miles distant, Leadbetter and Green had encamped. It soon occurred to Morrisette, who sat like Agamemnon, gloomily in his tent, that he had selected unwisely a spot for his resting place. "Lincolnites," as adherents of the Union were termed in the vulgar partisan jargon of the time, might readily overwhelm him and even crush his beautiful brass field-pieces by rolling stones down the mountain sides.   A bird, disturbed by the flames in the valley, rose out of its nest, and countless stones, their number growing as they descended, almost overwhelmed Morrisette's pretty tent.   He could not sleep. That Leadbetter might know where he was, he ordered a field-piece to be discharged.

The concussion shook the hills, and countless stones came leaping into the valley.   Leadbetter, inferring that Morrisette was assailed, fired his guns that the enemy might be aware of his presence and power.   Morrisette's guns responded; and thus, in the solemn, still, bright November night of 1861, was the "Campaign of Moral Effects" signalized by furious cannonading in the silent, happy valley of Chucky.   The listening people, thinking the rebels amused themselves wasting gunpowder, slept well.   But Morrisette and Leadbetter were thoroughly alarmed.   Each believed the other involved in a desperate conflict, and both fired away furiously.   At length each was silent that he might hear from the other and profound stillness rested upon river, mountains, and valley.

It was after midnight when Morrisette's soldiers slept nervously beside camp fires and guns.   He himself was haunted by the demon of unrest.   He was not satisfied that bushwhackers were not hidden among the stunted cedars and great stones on mountain sides above

9

his head. His nerves were unstrung, and he wandered forth to assure himself that sentinels were at their posts.

He had seen the one most distant from his encampment and was coming away when he heard the voice of Bill Carter. He stopped and saw Carter proffer a canteen to the sentinel. The musket dropped, the canteen was eloquent, and Carter and the sentinel silent. Carter's canteen thus gave the countersign. He entered, having a dozen like it filled with whiskey and brandy distilled in the mountains. Carter was heavily freighted, too, with fowls. Morrisette watched him as he staggered into the encampment. He reeled along and soon slept soundly beside a glowing camp fire. An orderly named Villere was dispatched to Carter's resting place with instructions to empty the canteens, otherwise half of the command would become intoxicated before breakfast. Villere, finding Carter asleep, baptised him and the chickens in whiskey and brandy. Carter's clothes, hair, and whiskers were thoroughly saturated.

Villere and his master at last rested, and Carter slept profoundly.

Carter's baptised birds were not comfortable. They fluttered about the fire, and at length, blue flames danced over one and then another of the frightened, roasting poultry, fastened to Carter by cords that confined their legs. Lambent blue lights danced at last over his garments and played over his thick, heavy hair and whiskers. He screamed, rose up, blinded, frightened, and dumfounded. Each chicken was a fluttering great blue torch-light, and a column of blue flame rose far above Carter's head. He shrieked and ran blindly along the river's edge. Sentinels fired their guns. Every man was on his feet.

The devil, robed in flames, fresh from abodes of the damned, was before their eyes. Carter's senses partially restored, he leaped into the river. But the encampment was "stampeded." Everybody sought to be first to escape from the infernal presence. Morrisette and Villere alone knew that Carter, wrapped in flickering blue flames of alcohol, innocently personated the Evil One. There was no time for explanations. "The devil take the hindmost," was the literal impulse that moved Morrisette's unlettered command. It was hopelessly dispersed. All efforts to rally the discomfited soldiery were unavailing.

When straggling soldiers of the dispersed battery, engaged in the grand "Campaign of Moral Effects," came in pairs and trios, ragged, hungry, and foot-sore, into Knoxville, I enquired eagerly for news from their noble commander. His soldiers were unwilling to talk.

"Where is your captain? Where is your battery? What has been the fate of the military expedition?" the first ever organized without the remotest design of hurting anybody.

I finally induced a moody, silent Irishman who had utterly refused to talk, to accompany me to my private apartment. I gave him a gill of whiskey, and promising another, asked him what had happened.

The Irishman's face wore an aspect of profound melancholy. I had never before seen, outside of the confessional, a truly solemn Irishman. But, wiping his lips with his sleeve, and with wide open eyes, Mike said:

"Captain, we won't talk because nobody will belave us; but may the divel sazè me if I didn't see him, wid eyes like braziers, breathing blue flames as he rose up out of the earth. He sazed the captain and ran away wid him, and laped into the river wid him, and the water biled. He shook the mountain, and stones and trees fell down upon us. Nobody but these you see here got away. Our guns and horses are all gone. The divel flew away wid 'em. The men fired at him, and bullets made holes through him, but he walked away all the same down the river and laped in at last, as I was tellin' ye."

· I asked Mike if it were possible that a campaign planned to produce "grand moral effects" had ended in a disgraceful drunken debauch.

Mike answered that there was not a drunken soldier in Chucky Valley.

I sent Mike for his associates in flight. They came and concurred in all that he had said. Each had seen a gigantic figure, clothed in blue flames, countless little angelic devils fluttering about it, rise out of the earth, shake the everlasting hills, and disappear in the blue waves of Chucky River. I was puzzled. Twelve sane, sober men, each examined separately, testified, with profound earnestness and unwillingly, to the same extraordinary facts. These men never dreaming of desertion came as frightened fugitives from a terrible battle field. The Irishman was not free from superstition. His religion was mystical and vague, as well as formal and ceremonial. He was heard to say that if the devil was with the South, he would go north. He soon crossed the mountains, and afterward, in fighting the South, never doubted, I imagine, that he was "whackin'" the devil that appeared in Chucky Valley.

Some weeks elapsed, after the return of Leadbetter and Morrisette with the wreck of their demoralized forces, before any demonstration of military ardor was made. Leadbetter was less vehement and less active and earnest in administering oaths of loyalty than when planning the Chucky campaign. Morrisette's vanity had been sorely wounded. The people would talk and laugh. Bill Carter would pretend to be very drunk, and hairless and whiskerless as he was, his face terribly scarred by flames of alcohol that almost consumed his life, sauntered about head-quarters, reciting criticisms he heard in bar-rooms. Bill was the great sufferer. He was, too, the innocent cause of the utter discomfiture and dissolution of Morrisette's command. He hated Morrisette because he had ordered Villere to empty the whiskey-filled canteens. He had witnessed the flight of Morrisette's terrified men. Though he had been painfully, and even dangerously burned and thoroughly frightened, he comprehended and enjoyed the supreme absurdity of the expedition. He sat many nights, surrounded by half-drunken listeners, telling with infinite delight, of the marvelous "Campaign of Moral Effects." Everybody in Knoxville had laughed again and again when Bill Carter, as chief of staff and Morrisette's Sancho Panza, recounted the story of absurd adventures. Morrisette knew all this, and for a time shrank from public gaze. Leadbetter was moody, violent, and silent. But the pair of heroes finally talked the matter over. They had heard of Bill Carter's eloquent descriptions of the overthrow of the battery and discussed the propriety of having Carter consigned to the tender mercies of Fox, the jailor.

But this would not silence Carter. He must be shot or conciliated. Pacific measures were preferred, and Carter was supplied with whiskey, *ad libitum*. He advised Morrisette to put on a bold face and show that he was unaffected by the absurd disaster. The result was that a grand dress parade was ordered for the next Sunday.

It came, a cold December morning, when church bells were ringing and people, arrayed in the finery of peace, already fading in the presence of war, were going in pairs along the sunny streets. Morrisette's battery, guns, caissons, horses, and men rattled and roared over the stony roadway from the hills in the suburbs down into the valley, ascending Gay Street into Knoxville.

Idlers in throngs sauntered leisurely along the side-walks while Morrisette, glittering with gold lace and bestriding his gaily caparisoned war horse, led the gorgeous column.

It was a sad day for Morrisette. It was long to be remembered by many dwellers in Knoxville. He led the battery toward University Place, and turning to re-enter Gay Street, a caisson, filled with gunpowder and shells exploded. What caused the disaster no one ever knew. All the shells were not exploded at once, but forced in all directions, at intervals hurled fragments of iron into the air and into houses. Morrisette's men fled, as, not long before, in Chucky Valley. The battery was again dissolved. Artillerymen leaped from horses and from ammunition chests and hurried away. Morrisette, overcome, as he afterward explained, by "grief" and "rage," dismounted and in a private residence found relief in whiskey. Two men and four horses were killed and many persons injured, while Morrisette was so unnerved that he was unable to bestride his steed.

He had enlisted only for a year, and his term of service expiring in 1862, he retired to private life.

Poor Bill! His hair and whiskers had been burned off by flames of alcohol in Chucky Valley. His eyelids hideously red, he was of horrible aspect. Men gave him money to induce him to leave their presence. It was painful to look upon him, and therefore was he supplied with means of endless inebriety. The end came, as I have stated, and Bill, not long afterward, died in the gutter.

# CHAPTER XX.

"A taste for archæological inquiries was rapidly developed, even in this country, until Dickens ridiculed its devotees mercilessly and successfully in his Pickwick Papers; but gentlemen of taste, learning, and leisure, like Alexander B. Meek, Benj. F. Porter, Joseph B. Cobb, and especially the late Governor and United States Senator from this State, George R. Gilmer, were devoted to the prosecution of inquiries affecting primeval dwellers in America. I was reading a paragraph to-day," said the journalist, "in the *Tallahassee* (Fla.) *Sentinel,* that tells of the discovery, two miles from that city, of a Spanish horseman's heavy spur. On either side of the rowel, an inch and a half in diameter, little bells dangled. Such spurs are still used in Mexico, and, I presume, in Spain. More recently a farmer plowing in the field, and near the spot at which the spur was found, unearthed a solid, shapeless mass, which proved to be a bronze stirrup, of heavy, ancient pattern. It is as massive, relatively, as the spur. This stirrup was firmly imbedded in the ground, and thick coatings of rust enveloped it. Raised figures on the stirrup still stood out in strong relief. Its sides are Ethiopian statuettes, facing each other, and leaning forward till they almost meet. Their uplifted clasped hands hold the leathern strap that attached the stirrup to the saddle. The Florida editor says: 'So unlike are both these relics to anything known to this generation, and, both being found near the same place, it is not unreasonable to ascribe them to the same era and artisan. Nor is the supposition at all improbable that one of the knightly followers of, De Soto was allured on through this then unknown region and wilderness,

like that dauntless son of Spain, by a thirst for yellow heaps of
gleaming gold that loomed up ahead of them in vain visions and
heated fancies,  Here he fell a victim to the tomahawk and scalping-
knife of the wronged and revengeful red man ; and, no doubt, some
one of the "Tallahassee Tribe," of which "Tiger Tail" claimed to
be a descendant, boasted, as he displayed at his belt a yet bloody
scalp, that he had here killed a pale-face.'

"Beyond the fact that trifling discoveries of this character define
with a share of probable accuracy the route of De Soto, they have
little value, and yet to such an extent is the taste for the old and
curious indulged, that I am told I cannot secure this old stirrup and
spur save at great cost.  My purpose was to send models of them to
Castelar, the Spanish scholar and statesman, that he might discover
when and where such spurs and stirrups were manufactured.  We
should not forget, while noting the spot at which such remains of De
Soto are found, that Indians may have stolen and lost this property of
Spaniards, and it is not impossible that some Floridian, who served in
the Mexican war of 1846-47, may have brought the spur and stirrup
from Mexico.  Are there such evidences of decay that this supposition cannot be well founded?

"After Governor Gilmer had served many years in each branch of the
United States Congress, he devoted his old age to the perfection of
an archæological and mineralogical cabinet.  When a boy, I was often
at his attractive home in the ancient village of Lexington, Georgia.
The Spanish consul at Charleston visited the venerable statesman,
who was not well enough to designate for the stranger the wonders of
the cabinet.  Of this I was telling the curious Spaniard all I knew,
when he stopped me suddenly, and holding up a blood-red, beautiful
carnelian between his fingers, asked whence it came.  I had heard
Governor Gilmer tell that it was plowed up by a negro in a field near
Macon, Georgia.  I remembered, too, that the governor had paid ten
dollars for the stone and an old musket stock found about the same
time, near the same spot.  The stone was perforated longitudinally.
Its length was about five and a half or six inches, and its transverse
diameter about one and a half inches.  The stone was very beautiful,
but Governor Gilmer had no conception of its design as shaped, or of
its value.  He often wondered why it was so deftly carved and what old
race of artisans did this cunning work.  He said it was strange that
such an old-fashioned musket stock had been unearthed near the same
spot.

" 'This,' said the Spaniard, as I conducted him to Governor Gilmer's
private apartment, 'is a Castilian dagger handle.  Very few were
ever made.  Noblemen of Spain wore them there four hundred years
ago.'  Brilliant light, in Governor Gilmer's eyes, fell from the Spaniard's lips upon the pretty carnelian.  It shone with lustrous glory as the
stranger held it in the bright sunbeams falling through the open window, and flooding the apartment.  The gleaming stone became as
eloquent as beautiful, and Governor Gilmer deemed it invaluable.  It

may not be improper to say that a few years ago I caused the cabinet of Governor Gilmer, now the property of the University of Georgia, at Athens, to be examined by Mrs. General King, of Chalky Level, that I might photograph the stone and publish its history in *Harper's Monthly*. The carnelian dagger handle had disappeared. It could not be used or exposed in this country. There is not another like it. Is it not barely probable that it finally found its way, through Charleston, back to Spain? Though I was a little boy at the time, I remember how eagerly that courtly gentleman, the Spanish consul, with his great lustrous black eyes devoured that brilliant stone. But any rude soldier of this dreary age would have deported such a carnelian for its beauty and uniqueness.

" From old books gathered in the admirably well-selected and costly library of the University of Alabama, of about 150,000 volumes, I had gathered a share of information affecting religious creeds and 'superstitions,' as we are pleased to term them, of Oriental peoples.* I had read of the crude faith that clings everywhere to the horseshoe as an emblem of good fortune. Our ancestors, as do we, through many centuries, persisted in hanging old horseshoes over gateways. Lord Nelson sailed into the battle of the Nile with a horseshoe nailed to the masthead of his ship. Recently, the vague, undefined superstition has gathered fresh vigor, Young gentlemen, strangely enough, have scarf pins fashioned after horseshoes, Fairest dames, more wonderfully, knowing not what they do, deck miniature horseshoes with brightest jewels, worn as amulets. Old horseshoes, found in the highway, are gilded with gold and suspended over mantels in fashionable *salons* of wealth and taste. Hindu maidens originally set the example. They have muttered prayers, through many centuries, looking to the horseshoe as the vehicle of supreme delights. Who can tell in what facts the vague, but universally accepted superstition had origin? What does it signify, and what is this significance? The Eastern and Asian origin of the Irish race has been asserted, because Irishmen are especially addicted to that faith in the capacity of old horseshoes to ward off evil which obtained among Phœnecians everywhere in the Orient. It was not a horseshoe, as such, that won, originally, this superstitious regard. But the horseshoe either represented the crescent moon or probably symbolized that depraved nature-worship practiced by devotees of Siva in Hindustan. I saw Spratling pluck a worn-out horseshoe from its deep burial place in the roadway only yesterday, and carefully suspend it from the body of the oak beneath which he slept. He said his father did such things, and he only followed in his footsteps.

"But all this is simply a prelude to an account of two discoveries,

---

*Soon after the date of conversations here recited, the University of Alabama, with all its costly structures, observatory, dormitories, professor's residences, and the old Roman pantheon, containing the library, was destroyed by fire. The torch was applied by the specific orders of a commanding general.

supposed to define De Soto's route from Florida to Arkansas and Texas.

"William Richardson is an old and intelligent citizen of Pickens County, in Eastern Alabama. Plowing in his field along an old road-way, not many miles from the little village of Yorkville, and, perhaps, twenty miles east of Columbus, Mississippi, he unearthed a package of twelve rust-eaten horseshoes. They were superimposed upon one another in the edge of this old roadway which was used at some period and by some race before Mr. Richardson was born, and before his farm was cleared and cultivated. I have what is left, by the corroding tooth of time, of one of these horseshoes. It is quite one-half broader than a modern horseshoe. It had no 'heel' and no groove or depression for the heads of the nails. We are not told by any chronicler of De Soto's wanderings and battles how his horses were shod or that he brought horseshoes from Europe and I am curious to know whether horseshoes of this description were made three hundred and fifty years ago in Spain. Since Indians never shod ponies, and no army ever invaded Pickens County, and these iron platings were designed for the hoofs of the largest horses and not for Indian ponies, and Mr. Richardson and his neighbors were always puzzled about the origin of the queer old rust-eaten horseshoes. Dr. Alexander Agnew, a gentleman of singular learning and literary taste, living in Richardson's neighborhood, carefully preserved the 'relic' which I have. It gained value in his eyes when he learned that in the same old roadway several miles west of Richardson's and near the village of Yorkville, another discovery had been made which shed light upon the mystery attached to the horseshoes and to the origin of the 'old road.' Indians made no roads, only 'paths,' and yet here was a road evidently carved out as a wagon-way, its outlines perpetuated by rain-falls along the hill-sides, in primeval forests and beside this old road, at the foot of a hill, and at a bright, sparkling spring, perhaps seven or eight miles from Richardson's farm, a pair of apothecary's scales were found. A great chestnut tree was blown down, shown by consecutive rings of annual production to have been more than two hundred and fifty years old. It had drawn its life from the fountain of which I tell, and fell that a thirsty farmer might find the scales, guarded through centuries beneath its roots. The scales themselves and the weights, having on them Spanish inscriptions and numerals naming the King of Spain and the Pope of the period, and dated, if I remember accurately, 1534, had rested two and three feet below the earth's surface, and below the great tree, from the day the thirsty Spanish pharmaceutist, who accompanied De Soto, drank, and ate chestnuts at this spot. The tree sprang up. Its roots covered and guarded the scales till the tempest overthrew this monarch of the forest. The farmer, Mr. Alexander, who discovered the scales, took one of the weights to Carrollton, the capital of Pickens County, that the inscription might be translated. A Mexican war veteran said that the words were Spanish and that it was very strange that implements of druggists' art, as old as these, should be found in such a spot. It never occurred to him that De Soto's followers lost the scales and thus designated a point in his route to the Mississippi. It can hardly be supposed that the Indians stole or seized in battle and lost both the horseshoes and the apothocary's scales found so near the same spot, and I have ever believed, since I became conversant with the facts here recited, that De Soto passed through Pickens County and crossed the Tombecbee, of which his chroniclers tell, at Barton, a little village a few miles above Columbus. Many persons of the neighborhood of Yorkville saw the scales and horseshoes of which I tell. They gossiped about the inscriptions, and this inter-state war came, and when I sought, not very long ago, to secure the relics, the finder had moved away. His grandson, a citizen of Columbus, Mississippi, wrote very recently that he had not abandoned hope of their recovery. But do not forget," added the journalist, "that I have the oldest horseshoe in the world, and that it belonged to De Soto. I have heard most intelligent officers and many soldiers, since the inception of inter-state hostilities, and since we began to march over the country in all directions, ascribe the erection of the old stone fort in Kentucky, and of that, more wonderful, at Winchester, Tennessee, to De Soto. General Bragg examined the ancient fortress at Winchester, and stated when I asked him what he thought of it, that it was constructed in accordance with the most approved rules of the highest military art, and that with guns, even of a century ago, it was absolutely impregnable. Who reared this massive structure, and who carved out this stone and lifted up those enduring walls and when was the mighty task accomplished? Great earthworks, fortifications, and mounds in Eastern Tennessee have been ignorantly ascribed to De Soto as their builder. He was never in East Tennessee, or at Winchester, or in Kentucky and nobody pretends that red men of our time ever executed these tasks comparable with works of highest civilization; and I am persuaded that as Indians have been valueless and incapable, since 1492, when Columbus came, even so were they always averse to toil; and, digging few graves, were addicted to no species of industry. They were always nomadic and homeless as the Apaches, Creeks, and Sioux, and I have never believed that any Indian tribe, except the bearded Natchez, ever reared mounds like that at Florence, Alabama. The Natchez alone had beards like white men; and, claiming descent from white men, were always, like the moundbuilders, fire-worshippers. They were most civilized of all the red race. They gave La Salle a grand festival, sitting at tables covered with buckskin as white as linen. They used chopsticks, as do Chinese, and were greatly frightened when the Frenchmen of two hundred years ago drew broad, glittering knives from sheaths and thrust them with food into their mouths. They said their original king and queen came down from the skies, and that they were white; that they lighted the sacred fires on the summit of the great mound just below Natchez which would burn while the Natchez were free, and no longer. The

French made the priests drunken, extinguished the fires, the dispirited Natchez were easily beaten in battle, and migrated west, and became extinct. These Natchez Indians said that their fathers, who may have been the moundbuilders, once reigned over the whole continent, and that the land, covered with great cities, extended, unbroken by the sea, an infinite distance toward the east. There came a great convulsion of nature, and the Gulf of Mexico supplanted their sunken domains which had extended far out into the Southern Atlantic towards Africa.

"When Commodore Maury surveyed the ocean's bottom from Cuba towards the western coast of Africa, he found abrupt chasms and shallow depressions, and there were those who believed that sunken cities rested in the ocean's depths, and that the Natchez were not mistaken, and that Solon and Diodorus Siculus were not misled by Egyptian priests who told them of the sunken continent, Atlantis, lying west of Africa. Isn't it strange that traditional lore of our red men was conformed to that communicated by Egyptian priests, five hundred years before Christ, to the Greek philosopher? Plutarch tells the story in his life of Solon.

"If you would listen and know what I think about it," continued the newspaper man, "I would designate upon the map the route of De Soto, as I have defined it. We are constantly marching blindly over the country, and it invests one's movements with peculiar, intelligent interest, if we may read the history of men and battles of a former age in geographical facts. That we may not err and ascribe to the Spanish hero the works of primeval races found almost everywhere in America, I will give you a succinct definition of the route pursued by the heroic Spaniard. I was reading, even in Smithsonian papers, the grave statement that De Soto reared those skillfully constructed ancient fortifications, described by Edwin M. Grant, in Eastern Tennessee. The story was once told that De Soto built the great mounds at Birmingham, Alabama, and opened the tunnel as a means of underground communication, said by the people of the vicinity, when Lord Lyell was there in 1846, to connect the mounds with the spring, three hundred yards distant. The greater Birmingham mound is a parallelogram having an area of more than an acre on its summit. It is lifted up fifty or sixty feet above the valley in which Birmingham rests idly in the sunshine between mountain ranges five miles apart, of coal on the one hand and of iron on the other, each stratum thirty feet in thickness. I visited the place, when a boy, with 'Mr.' Lyell, the English geologist, but gave little attention to peculiar facts now discussed. I only know that there is nothing in books or in the peculiarities of the ancient earth-works at Birmingham to induce the belief that De Soto visited the spot. It is hardly necessary to suggest the reflection that, as these greatest mounds commonly designate centers of moundbuilders' wealth and population, so, in our time, they mark sites of most prosperous town and cities, and we may yet discover evidences of the use of coal and iron which must have attracted primeval inhabitants of the continent, if they used these minerals, to the beautiful valley in which Birmingham reposes. Whether they did or not, it is nevertheless true that the site of each great city in the valley of the Mississippi was designated for our race by great mounds, showing that the same commercial laws and facts begat aggregations of wealth and population in the moundbuilders' age as in ours. Did they have steamers and railways? Surely they were not modern red men who had no commercial ideas and located towns and villages without reference to facilities for navigation or proximity of productive districts. I have said this that one may not confound works of primeval races with those of the heroic Spanish knight.

"Using Theodore Irving's translations of old records preserved in Spain, and applying data somewhat vague to geographical and topical facts familiar to those who have traversed the Gulf States as often as most Confederate soldiers, and then cognizant of each antiquarian's discovery that designates a spot visited by the Spanish adventurers, I would state that De Soto left Tampa Bay, Florida, going northwest, June 31, 1539. De Soto's route was parallel to or near the road from Tampa to Fort King. He crossed the Withlacoochee and Suwanee Rivers. He moved into Georgia and passed the winter of 1539-40 on the Bay of St. Marks. March 3, 1540, he left Appalachee and following up the east bank of the Flint River, crossed into Baker County, Georgia. The Alabama poet and literateur, Alexander B. Meek, in his book entitled, 'Romantic Passages in Southwestern History,' published in 1837, says that De Soto passed very near the site of the present beautiful city of Macon. But Judge Meek never heard of Governor Gilmer's carnelian dagger handle or of the discovery more recently made at Macon, in this State.

"When the place was partially fortified not many months ago, Dr. I. E. Nagle, now of New Orleans, was sent thither to organize army hospitals and provide for the sick and wounded. He was watching Confederate soldiers employed in perfecting old military earthworks planned and upheaved by prehistoric races in the suburbs of Macon. These earthworks were made after the models used in our time and it was only necessary to repair them. They may have been planned and built by De Soto, but it is much more probable that he, as did these Confederate soldiers, used here, as the latter did the mounds to resist Grant's gunboats along Yazoo Pass, these old strongholds of primeval occupants of the country. In any event, while the Confederates were digging away the base of a broad, earthen wall, they came upon a grave, its occupants' skeletons encased in rust-eaten coats of mail. Dr. Nagle sought to secure the relics, but these were claimed and retained by the owner of the spot, and the doctor was only suffered to have a broken rosary twined about a skeleton's neck. This rosary adorns to-day, so Dr. N. tells me, the walls of the priest's rooms attached to the cathedral in Memphis, Tennessee. A part of the sword of an armored knight remained undestroyed by time; but the armor itself was only a series of layers of iron rust. But full details of this discovery may be obtained by the curious in such matters by addressing Dr. I. E. Nagle, No. 13 St. Charles Street, New Orleans, Louisiana, as W. B. Bryan, of Columbus, Mississippi, will tell of the discovery of the Spanish apothecary's scales by his grandfather at Yorkville, Alabama.

"Leaving Macon, where he probably fought the Indians, using moundbuilders' earthworks, he passed near Milledgeville, and crossed the Ocmulgee and Oconee Rivers, entering the province of Cofachiqui lying within the fork of the Broad and Savannah Rivers. May 3, 1540, the Spaniards moved northwest and were five days crossing the mountains of Habersham County, in the midst of which the late Texas soldier and senator, Rusk,—Houston's peer,—was born. In De Soto's time, this Cherokee County was known as Chalaque. He came to Canasauga, after several days' march, on the banks of the Etowah. June 25, 1540, the Spaniard encamped at Chiaha situated on the upper end of an island, as described by De Soto's chroniclers, fifteen miles in length. There is no such island in the Coosa River, but the Spaniard probably mistook the peninsula formed by the Coosa and Chattooga for an island, or these rivers were originally united, creating an island above the point of confluence. Farmers of the district say that such was the case. In any event there is no doubt that the indian town and stronghold, Chiaha, was but a short distance above the junction of the Coosa and Chattooga.

"Leaving Chiaha July 2, 1540, De Soto on the same day reached Acoste on the southern extremity of the island. The next day he crossed the Coosa River, marching several days through a province of that name—it is sometimes spelled Cosa—embracing Benton, Talladega, Coosa, and Tallapoosa Counties, in Alabama. He rested at an indian town called Cosa, till August 20, 1540, when he began to move through Tallamuchassie Ullobali and Toasi. He reached Tallise, in the curve of the Tallapoosa River at the site of the present village of Tallase, September 18, 1540. From Tallise he went to Tuscaluza, on the banks of the Alabama, in Clarke County, where he fought his most terrible battle. November 18, 1540, he moved northwardly and, in five days, arrived at Cabusto, in the province of Pafalaya on the Black Warrior River in Green County near the village of Erie. After a few days' anabasis, he crossed the Tombigbee in a province called Chicasa, in a few days encamping at a town of the same name. Northern Mississippi and Western Tennessee were dwelling places of the heroic Chicsas or Chicasaws. We only known that after a terrific battle with these red men, De Soto was six days in reaching the Mississippi. Whether this battle was fought, as many suppose, near Tupelo or at Carrollton, in Mississippi, I am not prepared to say. From either point the great river might have been reached at Memphis after a six days' march. He crossed it forty miles above Memphis. With much accuracy the district known as Surrounded Hill, in Arkansas, sixty miles west of Memphis, is described by those who recited the story of De Soto's adventures. Beyond this, it is needless to follow him.

Except Surrounded Hill, no place of encampment or of battle west of the river has been identified, except, as I have shown, that he was buried below Helena, at the base of Crowley's Ridge, in the channel occupied by the river at that date, now known as Old Town Lake.

"When Arkansas and Texas and the Indian Territory are more densely populated, and broader areas are cultivated, the plow and spade may make discoveries to define paths as made west of the Mississipi by the daring, resolute Spaniard."

"Will you not tell me," asked the schoolmaster, "how you know that De Soto was entombed in Old Town Lake. I never heard the assertion before. I have seen many pictures of the sad burial scene, but never one representing the locality as now identified."

The newspaper man replied :

"We have heard enough of De Soto for to-night. Remind me to-morrow evening or at noon that the story should have its proper conclusion, and I will tell all I know of De Soto that has not been published in countless books and magazine articles devoted to this attractive theme."

# CHAPTER XXI.

Occasional days, even now, in February, presaged the coming of spring. Delights of sunny latitudes were discovered in Favonian breezes occasionally coming up from the sea, and in the ethereal mildness of southern summer skies. Verse and book makers tell of "smiling sunlight" and "fertilizing showers" when spring-time comes in hyperborean regions. The imagination of weary, restless wealth and fashion is excited, and never learns the truth that the fiery fierceness of the summer's sun and hot-air baths of cloudy afternoons are infinitely more intolerable at Cape May and Saratoga, than cooling winds that climb the mountains and descend into the valleys and come toying with roses and dancing about cottages of dwellers in East Tennessee. Each inhabitant sooner or later falls under the spell of enchantment and is ready to exclaim, "The fairest land beneath the sun." Spring expands into summer, and summer is the rest of the year. East Tennessee is poetically eloquent of the charms of delightful valleys, the sweep of verdure-clad plains, the witchery of beautiful rivers, and impressive majesty of environing mountains. The face of the country is fascinating, strong, rugged, full of character, and never to be forgotten.

Glad and gracious days, through an entire twelve-month, have here been illumined with sweetest sunlight, and shed upon us continuous luster. Not elsewhere do flowers blossom more brightly or fruits ripen more generously or waters murmur more sweetly or birds sing more charmingly through all the months of the delightful year.

To rise when those mountains environing East Tennessee are flushed with splendors of earliest dawn; to traverse smiling valleys and deep green fields while scarlet flowers clasp the gliding feet; to watch purple wraiths of rain haunting the fairness of the parti-colored mountains; to see the shadows chase the sun's rays on the dusky sides of the Blue Ridge or Smoky or Cumberland range; to feel the living light of the cloudless day beat as with a million pulses; to go out in the luster of the night aflame with astral splendors, until the dark still plains and deep and darker valleys blaze like a phosphorescent sea; to breathe this wondrous air, soft as the first impassioned kisses of young love, and rich as wine with the delicious odors of a world of flowers—these, as was written of Italy, have been our joys at once of the senses and of the soul.

Eastern Tennessee is the dream-land of the continent. Cold, fierce, wintry blasts that came, not long ago, from icy caverns beneath hyperborean snows and made us shiver on the mountain's brow, only serve to excite stronger affection for the homes we have in deep valleys, beneath cloudless skies, fanned by delicious breezes coming, warm with the life-blood of the equator, and tripping away, with laps full of roses, from rich, green fields almost tropical in their exuberance.

Such was the land of which Mr. Wade, the good pedagogue, was delighted to tell. He had revisited Eastern Tennessee. Encountering no difficulty at the Hiwassee bridge and having passports for himself and Mamie Hughes from General Johnston, he had complied with Mamie's wishes and proceeded directly to Tunnel Hill and thence to Mamie's home. Her anxiety to return to Georgia, the pedagogue said, was infinitely heightened when she was informed by him that her brother had preceded her to her mother's home with a safe conduct given by the captain.

"The captain, it seems," said Mamie, "and that gigantic Spratling who participated in delights of the dance by moonlight on the banks of the Tennessee, are my brother's benefactors. It makes me shudder when I think of my brother's neck in the grasp of that giant; but I can't forget his simple, earnest, big-hearted generosity, and how he loves my brother because this brother is beloved by his own pretty sweetheart. How infinite must be the ardor of his devotion to that charming Bessie Starnes of whom my brother has often written. And what an extraordinary creature is this gigantic Spratling. Devoid of jealousy, and in utter self-abnegation he becomes the more than friend of my brother because he thinks Bessie Starnes would have him serve her preferred suitor. If Bessie were cognizant of the facts and capable of measuring and properly valuing such devotion I greatly fear she would prefer the giant and even forget my handsome brother. I am sure I don't know how I could withstand such assertions of devotion made by such a soldier as you describe when telling of the daring deeds and generous acts and words of this wonderful Spratling."

"Instead of coming out on foot through Sequatchie Valley as I proposed," continued the schoolmaster, "of which I spoke in order that the captain might be prepared for the worst, we traveled very comfortably and very safely in a condemned ambulance given me by a quarter-master. Mamie, instead of the *role* of a rollicking country boy, enacted the part of a staid country dame. I had no difficulty in distinguishing rebel from Union scouts, and was provided, as you know, with papers eminently satisfactory to either. I am here, now, on a mission of peace and instructed to invite the captain, Spratling, the newspaper man and his brother to spend a day or weeks with the lieutenant at his mother's home."

Very certainly no message ever gave greater satisfaction. Spratling alone failed to assert his glad acceptance. He became moody, and was silent. He said, at last, that before going to Tunnel Hill, we must go in the opposite direction toward Chattanooga. We must know what the enemy are doing, and that no great movement is on foot, before we devote a day to idleness.

There was no evading the necessity and yet we suspected that the suggestion sprang from Spratling's anxiety to meet Bessie Starnes. But armies could not remain idle. The sun was shining brightly, and now and then, we caught faint breathings of dawning spring-time.

Next morning, at day-dawn, the captain and Spratling set out on foot to traverse the distance between the two armies. Their purpose was to go as far as Chattanooga Creek between Rossville and Chattanooga, and, returning, spend the night at Starnes'. They would not be absent more than three days and on their return we proposed to accept the hospitality of Lieutenant Hughes. We knew well enough that the expedition, now entered upon by the captain, would be as speedily ended as possible.

It lasted just three days and none fuller of grave incidents ever befell the two scouts. They said, when they returned, Spratling severely but not dangerously wounded by a bullet that pierced his left shoulder, that they were induced by anxiety to learn what movement was contemplated by the Union army, to cross Chattanooga Creek not far from Rossville. They were greatly fatigued and had mounted, each, an ill-used, emaciated horse, purchased for a trifling sum from an innocent countryman, who had certainly stolen the animals. When they had turned back, and were within five miles of the creek, flooded by recent rainstorms, they discovered that a squad of Union cavalry followed.

Flight and pursuit were instantly begun. The worn-down horses soon began to flag. Fleet enough at first, and out-stripping pursuit, it was found at the end of two and a half miles that the horses must be abandoned.

The two flying scouts had entered a long, narrow lane. Some distance ahead was a carriage occupied by a gentleman and his wife. This was overtaken. There was no other recourse. The captain said to Spratling:

"Tell the gentleman we must exchange horses, and that a fair exchange, under such circumstances, is no robbery."

Spratling having the better horse was slightly ahead. He rode beside the carriage, a negro driving it, and apologizing for the necessity, ordered a halt. The frightened negro leaped from his seat, and Spratling, when the captain came up, had cut the 'hame strings' and thrown the harness from one horse. This the captain mounted. Looking back, he beheld the flying cavalry enter the lane. In an instant the other horse was stripped. There was no need for saddles, and the captain and Spratling on fresh horses outsped pursuit. Protected for a time against shots of the enemy by the carriage and its occupants, they fled, at last under fire, down the long lane. The aim of men pursuing, at men pursued, all on horseback, is not accurate; and firearms, thus used, are not dangerous; but when twenty or thirty bullets come, in successive showers, designed to fall upon a fugitive's unprotected spine, he is much inclined to be uncomfortable. He imagines there are holes in his back. He thrusts his hat on the back of his head and will lie down on his horse.

"Much heroism is required of him," said Spratling, when telling of this race for life, "who sits perfectly erect under such painful circumstances."

The foremost of the enemy were within fifty yards when the captain and Spratling sped away on the horses taken from the carriage. Within a mile the fresh steeds added steadily to the distance from their pursuers, but that ridden by the gigantic Spratling bore two hundred and thirty pounds. Its limbs grew weak and Spratling said to the captain that he must soon abandon it. They exchanged horses. The captain weighing only one hundred and sixty-five pounds, the more weary animal again moved rapidly, keeping pace with the other.

They were drawing near the flooded creek when the weaker horse, bearing the captain, faltered and fell. The cavalry were now within two hundred yards and the creek, swollen by recent rains, was about the same distance ahead. The weary horse rose up and making a desperate struggle reached the precipitous bank of the creek. The bridge had disappeared. Neither rider checked his courser. Plunging in over the precipitous bank, they sank, to the riders it seemed an infinite distance, down into the depths of the roaring torrent. When they came to the surface they were rapidly borne down the stream by its angry force. The captain's weary horse, incapable of exertion, could not sustain the weight of the armed rider. The captain dropped into the current, and holding the mane, floated beside the animal, following that bearing Spratling. They had descended the stream perhaps one hundred yards when Spratling guided his horse to a place of possible exit on the eastern bank. Making a desperate effort the powerful animal escaped from the raging torrent. The captain was not so fortunate. His weary steed had not the strength to make the ascent. Struggling desperately, the soft clay of the steep bank yielded and the horse rolled backward, and drowning, was swept away by the angry waves. The captain clambered up, holding to the limbs of trees that grew at the water's edge and swept the water's surface.

If the pursuers, now halting where the bridge had stood, crossed the creek, the scouts were lost. Hurrying to the crossing place and using water-proof cartridges the scouts began firing upon the cavalry.

Spratling and the captain, from behind trees, delivered fatal shots, while volleys fired by the mounted men were harmless. The lieutenant in charge of the squad soon ordered a retreat.

The result of the flight and fight was the death of three or four Union cavalrymen and the wrongful acquisition by the Confederate scouts of an excellent horse.

"Spratling, terrible as had been our exertions and exciting as was the flight and incapable of effort as we were after such a struggle for life, was anxious," the captain said, "to move rapidly towards Starnes' place." He proposed to walk, surrendering the powerful horse wholly to the captain. The latter objected. "Then," said Spratling, "I will have a horse of my own."

At a little farmhouse, hard by, Spratling called. The owner came affrightedly to the door. Spratling said to him:

"My name is Spratling. I am a Confederate scout. I never told a lie, that I know of, in my life. I want a horse. I will ride him only ten miles. Then he will be returned unharmed to you."

The farmer was silent.

"Come," said Spratling, "I have no time for words. Bring me a horse within ten minutes and you shall lose nothing. If you fail, or send Yankees or bushwhackers after me I will burn your house and destroy everything. Do as I ask and you will lose nothing."

Spratling, bestriding a good horse, soon joined the captain. The two scouts, within two hours, were near the modest home of Bessie Starnes.

"Bushwhackers will be on our path to-night. That cowardly, silent, surly little fellow from whom you borrowed that horse," said the captain, "will set a squad of murderers on our track. He has summoned them already and that may be the costliest animal a Texan ever bestrode. I know you must see Bessie and tell her how you came to capture her lover, the Yankee lieutenant, and my prospective brother-in-law. You would tell Bessie how sorry you are and that you did it ignorantly and then you will tell her how you and I and the editor and his brother and the schoolmaster are going to spend a a delightful week at the young lieutenant's home. Then Bessie will hardly know whether she loves you or the lieutenant, and you and she will talk and dream and talk again even until sunrise.

"I will rest on the hill-side that looks down on Bessie's home. Bring me bacon, eggs, and bread when you bring your horse to my resting place. I am hungrier than a famished wolf. It is not well that those who may soon follow us should know where I am. The man from whom you borrowed the animal did not see me. I thought it best to remain concealed while you were negotiating for the horse.

If we are pursued the enemy will have only strength enough to assure success in a conflict with you. We are lucky in this," continued the captain, half soliloquizing, as he left Spratling following the dim roadway, while he turned into the woods to ascend the hill beyond and in front of the house.

Spratling was warmly welcomed. Mother and daughter were alike devoted to the honest, fearless Texan. Deeming Bessie the betrothed of the lieutenant, Spratling was much more formal and reserved in his bearing than when last he met the pretty mountain girl. When she asked why he was thus reserved he gave the reasons with refreshing simplicity and perfect truthfulness, and then told Bessie how he came to capture her lover. When he narrated with painstaking, honest minuteness each incident of the event, how he crept to the tree beside which the lieutenant slept, his head resting on its roots, and how he silently and noiselessly grasped the helpless lieutenant's throat, whispering the word "Spratling" in his ear, Bessie grew pale and shuddered.

"Oh! I knew you would hate me for it," exclaimed Spratling, "but I did not know he was your lover. I did not know he was Lieutenant Hughes! How could I help it? You ought to love me that I spared him. It's a wonder I had not killed him. But he knew me, and that resistance was useless, and then he was helpless."

Bessie insisted that she was glad the lieutenant had fallen into the hands of those who served him so well and that she esteemed him none the less that he had captured her lover.

When Spratling, that she might wholly forgive him, added that he would have died rather than wrong or harm the man Bessie loved, and because she loved him, Bessie stared wonderingly into Spratling's great blue eyes. She did not then measure or comprehend the depth, dignity or worth of Spratling's self-sacrificing devotion. But when the earnest soldier frankly said, "I would rather die, Bessie, than harm even a dog that you loved," her bright eyes sank to the floor, and pearly tear drops of gratitude were priceless jewels proffered in exchange for treasures of affection exposed to her vision by the ardent, honest, magnanimous soldier.

Bessie hardly knew whether she loved more the handsome, lithe, graceful, gallant lieutenant or the self-reliant, honest, frank, and fearless scout. She was now endeavoring, in the solitude of her little bed chamber, when Spratling slept soundly in the adjoining room, to solve the vexed problem. She had seen first and first loved the fascinating lieutenant who was passionately fond of her. He had constantly written to her. When he came to Chattanooga he at once sought her presence. He had endeavored to make her confess the charms and comprehend the intellectual and personal virtues of his sister, Mamie, who, he said, was to become Bessie's sister. But in his absence, and when she measured the wealth of the unselfish Texan's affections lavished upon her and confessed the grand simplicity of his character and personal worth, she confessed for him a degree of admiration and gratitude that almost lapsed into love.

The events of the day followed by those of the evening, the long, hard ride, the flight, the passage of the creek, the fight at the wrecked bridge, and protracted interview with Bessie, were exciting incidents, and Spratling, utterly exhausted, slept profoundly.

He was aroused by hearing his name pronounced by some one at the door demanding admittance.

"Who are you?" asked Spratling.

"I've come with friends to get my horse," was the answer.

"I promised to return him in the morning and nobody ever accused Spratling of breaking his word. Leave the house or I will shoot you."

"Come out or we will burn this house as you did Mrs. Shields', and we will suffer none to escape. Come out, like a man, and spare the pretty girl you pretend to love."

The captain was now aroused. On the hill side looking down upon the house, he was impatient for the disappearance of morning mists that partially obstructed vision making it impossible to select victims for his rifle and repeaters. The weary horses were tethered just beyond the brow of the hill and the captain was ready for the impending fray. His enemies little dreamed of danger and only feared that the powerful Texan, by some means might escape in the dim, misty twilight. Spratling, fearing that the captain slept, sought to temporize. He thought that day-dawn would serve the captain well and therefore asked his untimely visitor why he called so early.

"Did I not tell you," asked Spratling, "that I would deliver your horse to-day."

"Yes" was the answer, "but I knew you lied."

The captain, overhearing this reply, said, when telling, afterward, of the event, that he knew that the conference was at an end—that a shot would follow that word.

"I watched and waited," he said, "only a moment. Spratling knew that his interlocutor was not alone. Instead of opening the door he suddenly thrust aside the window-shutter, and, as he anticipated, found four men in the yard silently watching and waiting at the doorway. Spratling fired. By the flash of the pistol I was shown the object of his hate. I fired into the little group. Two at least were fatally wounded, but one, who was unharmed, fired at Spratling, the shot taking effect in the brave fellow's shoulder. It must have paralyzed him for a time. He withdrew from the window and then the fog rolling down the high hill grew so dense that even the house was invisible. I was helpless, and could only await the course of events. I could hear the conversation of the bushwhackers, but distinguish only now and then a word spoken. Their attention had been so riveted upon Spratling's movements that they did not dream that my rifle laid low one of their number. This was the more wonderful since Spratling had not fired simultaneously. The light from the flash of Spratling's pistol had given fatal direction to my bullet. But strangely enough the intent bushwhackers had neither seen the flash of my rifle nor heard its report. They ascribed the sad havoc to Spratling's diabolical pistol. Satisfied, too, that he was alone they were resolved to capture and destroy him. The farmer whose horse Spratling had taken, was heard insisting that the house should be burned."

As Spratling told us afterward, he had lain down without undressing himself, and slept instantly, unconscious even of his own existence, till he heard his name pronounced. When shot, he staggered away from the window. Bessie, meanwhile, was dressed and watching and listening at the doorway leaning from Spratling's into hers and her mother's apartment. She could see Spratling when he fired upon his assailants from the window and when he started back she knew he was wounded. He called her and telling her to be quiet, said:

"I am shot in the shoulder. I am not hurt. I can still raise my arm. Stop the bleeding. Tie it up tightly and quickly. Then let me have another shot at the rascals."

While he was saying this he tore the sheet on which he had slept, in strips, and Bessie and her mother bound them tightly about the armpit, closing the orifices of the wound in front and rear with cotton. The bullet had pierced the flesh and muscles beneath the shoulder joint.

Meanwhile gray mists of morning had disappeared and the captain could see that only three men were left to capture or kill the Texan. At any moment he could reduce the number by one but deemed it prudent to await developments. He supposed that Spratling was not idle and had good reasons for inaction.

The captain saw one of the bushwhackers leave the rest who stood behind trees some distance from the house. They were perfectly exposed to the captain's aim but could hardly be harmed by Spratling. Soon the plans of the bushwhackers were developed. Flames first ascended from a "fodder-stack" in the rear of the house and then from the dairy hard by the residence. Firebrands were thrown upon the adjoining kitchen.

The captain could endure inaction no longer. He fired upon the bushwhackers, wounding one just as he or his comrade had wounded Spratling. The fellow shrieked, "I'm shot!" and fell. The captain rushed shouting down the hill and with his pistol fired at the flying bushwhackers.

Spratling's arm was now cared for. He opened the door, a pistol in each hand, to find inextinguishable flames enveloping the kitchen attached to the wooden residence.

Maddened to a degree never known before, Spratling rushed into the yard. While the captain pursued the bushwhacker Spratling hurried down the road along which the owner of the horse he borrowed was in full flight. Spratling was fleet as he was incomparably strong. He leaped the fence. His strides were of incredible length as he went headlong down the road. The wretched little farmer looked back. He beheld his doom in the giant's coming. He leaned forward, straining every nerve and muscle and finally fell, breathless and helpless. Armed, as he was, he forgot his pistols in his terror.

Spratling ran beyond the helpless wretch. As he turned back fires of infernal hate and vengeance were lighted up in his face by the flames he beheld consuming the home and all the wealth of Bessie Starnes. Spratling beheld in the miserable, cringing wretch only an incendiary and assassin. He had followed as a murderer on Spratling's tracks He had said that Spratling lied, an offence to be punished, in accordance with the code of morals under which Spratling was reared, with death. He had fired the home of Bessie Starnes. In Spratling's eyes the miscreant's deeds were worse than infernal. At the moment, while Bessie and her mother stood in the roadway contemplating the destruction of all their wealth and of their home, Spratling was infuriated—a very fiend. He set his foot upon the fallen coward, and stamped and kicked him. Bones, ribs, and skull were crushed. He thrust his foot beneath the limp, lifeless body and hurled it from the roadway.

The bushwhacker escaped from the captain. When he returned from the pursuit he was conscious, as when Mrs. Shields' house was destroyed, that instant flight was an urgent necessity. Bessie and her mother would find a safer home after these terrible events, south of the Confederate lines, than in the vicinity of Chattanooga. Spratling was made to comprehend the necessity for immediate action. Bessie was to be cared for and her mother made comfortable, and Spratling had no opportunity to indulge in harrowing thoughts and self-accusations.

Household effects saved from the conflagration were deposited in a wagon, the two horses of Mrs. Starnes were attached to the vehicle, the ladies drove the team, Spratling saddened as never before, by the mishaps of an eventful day, rode rapidly away and without an accident, at nightfall, the party reached our camp. An apartment for Mrs. Starnes and Bessie was secured in a neighboring farmhouse, and again stories of adventure were told at night by the camp fire.

Spratling was interrogated and confessed, with every evidence of keenest anguish, that his acts had caused the wreaking of devilish vengeance upon those he loved. He said it became his duty to replace the home of Mrs. Starnes and that at last he had a purpose in living.

From that day forth he became the self-constituted guardian of Bessie. Affectionate, kind, and of matchless generosity, as he was, he seemed to have forgotten that three or four men, within four days, had lost their lives at his hands. He never seemed to doubt for a moment that the miserable wretch whom he killed by crushing his chest beneath his hob-nailed boot, deserved his fate. Spratling's conscience had been educated in the school of war. It was wholly right to kill if the fallen had a fair opportunity to kill. An Indian's methods of ambuscading, if the enemy's superior strength made fighting under cover necessary, were perfectly justifiable. No qualms of conscience would have disturbed Spratling's repose if he had hurled the wretch who had sought his life and burned Bessie's home, over visible battlements of eternal perdition. Spratling's dreams were never disturbed by the crackling of the breaking ribs and skull of his helpless victim. Human life and anguish, in a soldier's as in a practiced surgeon's eyes, has no value. It is only necessary that it be taken or given "in the regular course of trade."

# CHAPTER XXII.

The Captain Pursued as a Horse-Thief.—How he Escaped very Narrowly.—A
Brave Boy.—Deposition of General Joseph E. Johnston.—How he Bade us
Adieu.—Woes of Richmond.—The Famed Cemetery of Virginia's Capital.—
The Poor Child.—Its Burial Place.

The captain was telling Mamie one evening, some time after events
here narrated, of the devotion and courage of a boy, when traversing
the country below Dalton. Gillehan was not fifteen years of age; but his
sinews were toughened by toil and exposure, and piercing bright eyes
significant of pluck and keen intelligence. His home was in Tennessee in 1863–64, but he now lives in Navvarro, Texas. He and the
captain had been making a long journey, and noting the steady movement of the whole Federal army, now slowly advancing, its wings
moving forward more rapidly to outflank General Joe Johnston on
the east and on the west. It threatened to encompass him and cut
off his communication with Atlanta, thus forcing him again and again
to retreat. But Johnston's army was growing daily in numbers and
confidence, and especially in sublime confidence in the adroitness,
seeming omniscience and caution of General Johnston, who never
sacrificed a man if human skill and watchfulness could obviate the
necessity. Therefore was he beloved, as well as trusted, by his soldiers.
They believed he would not fight needlessly and only when victory
was assured. His fighting force, when he assumed command near
Chattanooga, was less than 35,000 men, and, though fighting every
day, it exceeded 50,000 when he reached Atlanta, in July. Desertions became numberless when Johnston was about to occupy the
heights environing Atlanta, and when President Jefferson Davis, impatient and nervous, and tortured by Richmond newspapers, and by
property-holders of Atlanta, and by subordinates of Johnston who had
displaced Bragg, and now yearned for Johnston's position and power,
removed Johnston and substituted Hood.

"I was sleeping on the floor of a little cabin, beside Major-General William B. Bate, near the southern banks of the Chattahoochee river, and within a few miles of Atlanta, at three o'clock on the morning of the 19th of July, I think it was, 1864," interposed the newspaper man, "when a courier came. I was awakened by the clatter of the horse's hoofs. The speed of the animal told of the excitement of the rider. I received the dispatch, lighted a candle, and handed the paper, without saying a word, to General Bate, who had been sleeping soundly. 'My God!' exclaimed Bate, 'have you read this order from Richmond?' I nodded assent. He sat on the blanket on which we had been sleeping on the floor, with his head resting upon his hands and knees. How long I do not remember. But death-like silence, broken by the echoing hoofs of the flying courier's horse, pervaded the resting place of fifty thousand men.

"'I don't know what will be the result,' said General Bate; 'but this order means that we will fight to-day. Hood and battle are convertible terms. Tell the members of my staff, and let the soldiers know what is coming.'

"Within half an hour I heard the hum of fifty thousand voices, sorrowfully, and in the dead hour of the night, discussing aad deploring the substitution of Hood for Johnston. At sunrise we were moving, and moving sadly and silently as a funeral train, towards the battlefield of Peach Tree Creek, five miles north of Atlanta. Of this bloody event, history tells. Therefore, I would only recall an incident of the memorable day, illustrative of the devotion of common soldiers to General Joseph E. Johnston. Our division moved, just after sunrise, along the country road in front of the little farmhouse occupied by him. Soldiers, at the head of the column called for him. He came out bareheaded, and stood on the piazza looking at us. Bate and his staff removed their hats, while rude, rugged, dust-and-sun-embrowned soldiers asserted infinite love and reverence for the gray-bearded, degraded veteran.

"'Good-bye, old Joe; God bless you!' said one.

"'We love you, and will never forget you!' shouted another.

"'This is the darkest day that ever dawned on the Confederacy!' exclaimed a sergeant near me, and then a thousand or more cried out at once, asserting affection and grief.

"Then the masses of men, accumulating in front of the house, broke ranks, thrust the palings of the enclosure aside, and gathered about the general. Those nearest seized his hands, and it was with difficulty that he escaped from the excited multitude. He was wholly unmanned by this demonstration of affection, and tears fell from his eyes, while bronzed, bearded soldiers wept as if they were children. General Bate and staff sat upon their horses, and though, before the sun went down we rode heedlessly over the dead bodies of many then weeping around their displaced leader, we, too, discovered that unconscious, unbidden evidences of deepest sympathy with these soldiers bedewed our faces. General Johnston disappeared in the house.

" ' Fall in, men! Forward !' And then no other words were spoken, and the steady tramp, tramp, tramp of armed legions moving to victory or death, shook the earth. Seventy men from a single brigade of Tennesseeans had already deserted their colors that fatal morning, and, crossing the Chattahoochee, entered the Federal lines. In portions of the army mutiny was threatened, and if Joe Johnston had not been so thorough a soldier, obeying as he exacted obedience, he would have remained at the head of the magnificent army he had created. These soldiers believed it to be invincible, and knew it would be when General Johnston chose to test its heroism. Its gallant deeds, even when beheaded, on Peach-Tree Creek, and two days later, when McPherson fell, and later, at Nashville and Franklin, only serve to show how brilliant would have been its achievements with Joe Johnston demanding an exhibition of its worth and illustrations of its valor.''

But the captain, when the newspaper man interposed, was telling of incidents that occurred four or five months earlier at Dalton. Gillehan, the brave youth and guide whom he had been commending to Mamie Hughes, and the captain were plodding, foot-sore and weary, toward Dalton, then occupied as General Johnston's headquarters. They were to go west about eight miles, and as many north, in order to learn what changes had been made during the week in the position of the Federal army. Gillehan's feet were very sore. He even complained that his sufferings became intolerable. We saw two Confederate cavalrymen tie their horses in front of a farm-house, and leaving them absolutely unguarded, go down the hill behind it to secure accustomed supplies of buttermilk for their commander, General Martin, of Arkansas.

"It can't be helped, Captain," modestly suggested Gillehan, "but we must have these horses or give up this expedition. I can't walk any farther.''

" It can't be helped then,'' I answered, and while two women and half a dozen tow-headed, half-naked children screamed and called for the " buttermilk cavalrymen '' at the spring, Gillehan and I rode rapidly away.

" The children and dogs and the women, the latter with yellow mops in their mouths, pursued us only a short distance. They could only say we were Confederate soldiers. Knowing that we must return to that point during the night, we informed the pickets of the fact, and since we might be pursued by the enemy's scouts, that we did not wish to be shot at. Orders were given accordingly. This provision for our safety proved to be the cause, as will be seen hereafter, of terrible dangers and anxieties.

"General Martin, when he heard that his buttermilk supply train had been ruthlessly deprived of its horses by Confederate scouts, was filled with wrath. He swore that military law should be enforced and the thieves shot. With his staff, he rode along the lines to ascertain at what point we came in. When he found that we had gone out and had not entered, he waxed exceeding wroth. But when he learned from the captain on duty at the outpost that we would soon return and be sent under guard to the provost marshal, General B. J. Hill, Martin left with this captain enveloped charges and specifications, signed by himself and sworn to by his robbed agents. This paper, if it reached army headquarters, would be fatal, as I well knew, to Gillehan and myself.

"After learning that which we sought to know, Gillehan and I returned to the point on our lines, to be sent, of course under guard, to headquarters. The sun was rising when we asked for the guard. We saw that something was wrong when five, instead of two, men were detailed for this service, and I saw the officer on duty give the sergeant in charge of the squad a large sealed envelope addressed to Provost Marshal General Hill. How to get possession of that paper and its contents was the question. The sergeant was a rude, dull soldier. He knew nothing of the purpose of these papers. None knew my name or Gillehan's. I would have committed any act of violence less than murder to prevent the delivery of that envelope.

"General Hill occupied a square, framed house in Dalton, having a veranda in front. A railing was extended across the hall to exclude those not invited to enter; but scouts were ordered to enter instantly and report at any hour of the day or night. I preceded the sergeant to Hill's doorway. I entered. The guard ordered the sergeant to halt. I turned and said to the sergeant, 'Give me the envelope addressed to General Hill, and I will deliver it and get a pass that you may return to your command, and then you can go.' The unthinking soldier gave me the invaluable package. I thrust it beneath my blouse, and entering, greeted Hill's adjutant general, Miller. Miller asked, eying me suspiciously, 'Why is such a strong guard sent with you this morning?' I answered, hesitating just a little, 'O, I don't know, but several of the boys wished to come into Dalton, and this duty of guarding me served as a pretext.'

"Miller wrote and signed the pass, and I was delighted beyond measure when I saw the stupid sergeant and his ragged followers gallop away. General Hill, deeming my statements with reference to the movements of the wings of Sherman's army important, sent me to General Johnston that I might report in person. I left Gillehan at the tavern in Dalton, instructing him to tie the bridle reins to the saddles on the two horses and start them towards Martin's camp. Horses herded together in a battery or cavalry command become as thoroughly identified, in feeling and attachments, with one another as do their riders. Trained horses, after their riders have fallen in fierce conflicts, never desert their colors. I knew that the horses we had appropriated, when set free, would return to their masters.

"The first man I met at General Johnston's headquarters was General Martin. He eyed me suspiciously, but said nothing. He supposed, of course, that the thieving scouts were already incarcerated. But nobody knew my real name at headquarters except General Johnston and Adjutant General Harvey. I recited my story, received my instructions, and when I emerged from General Johnnston's presence, again encountered General Martin. He was telling Colonel E. J. Harris, Colonel Miller, and General Harvey of the 'infernal daring theft of two horses practiced by two scouts.' Miller gave me a most significant glance, but I made no sign. I heard Harvey, General Johnston's adjutant general, say, 'They can't escape. There is a pair of them, you say? and you sent up the charges with the guard?'

" 'O, yes; d——d them!' answered Martin.

" 'Then,' replied Colonel Harvey, 'they can't escape. They will be in the guard-house before night and under the daisies to-morrow morning.'

"Miller looked at me pitifully again. He evidently knew that I had appropriated Martin's horses and stolen the 'indictment.'

"I did not feel comfortably, and silently beckoned Miller to follow me. He and I went to the tavern. I had brought in a few Yankee luxuries, and Miller loved delicious beverages. Gillehan had prepared dinner, and I produced a bottle, and then expounded General Martin's griefs. Miller laughed till he suffered mortal anguish. We drank again, and as he advised, I hurried away to execute tasks imposed by the latest orders of General Johnston.

"Then other scouts came in from different directions during the day. General Martin still lounged about headquarters. He knew his indictment had been sent up and that the scout it accompanied would be arrested. General Harvey so advised him, and so did General Hill. But no arrest was made. Late in the afternoon, Martin hurried out ten miles to see the officer who had sent me in under guard. This officer could only say that a scout had gone forward with a sergeant and five men and that the sergeant had the papers to be delivered at headquarters. Martin hurried back to General Hill, to be informed that three scouts only had reported during the day and that no papers came with either. Then Martin rode back to see the sergeant. He heard the simple story that the papers were delivered to the scout himself at General Hill's door. Again did Martin fly to General Hill's, to find that the bird had flown.

"I was already bending my steps towards East Tennessee to discharge a service requiring an absence of two weeks. General Martin was now advised that, though I was a horse-thief, I had returned the property, temporarily appropriated, and that my recall was impossible. Colonel Miller explained the facts to Generals Johnston and Hill, and I would gladly tender this apologetic statement to General Martin.

"By the way," continued the captain, "I have here a northern newspaper, the Cincinnati *Gazette*. It tells of terrible events that occurred in Texas in 1861. Mankind can never understand it, but it is true that there was a share of justification for most horrible deeds ever done in Kansas, Missouri, and Texas.. A Federal colonel in Missouri, McNeil, caused a dozen or two men to be shot, at Palmyra in that State, in cold blood. When we learn why this was done the crime is so mitigated that many have approved McNeil's deeds. So it was as regards terrible tragedies that marked these first days of dreadful revolution in Texas. It was then a sparsely populated border State. The worst elements of eastern society, fleeing from minions of outraged law in older States, sought refuge in Texas. In many districts few bonds of society or of good government were recognized. Security for life and property depended on each strong arm. Men differing in reference to pending political questions naturally sought proper affinities, and Unionists were organized, as were secessionists, and each dreaded and hated the other class. There was not in Northwestern Texas a more highly esteemed gentleman than William C. Young. He had filled the office of district-attorney with distinguished ability, and was known and beloved everywhere. He and James Bourland, his devoted friend, were riding on horseback from Gainesville, Texas, to Bourland's home. Both were ardent secessionists, and Bourland was deemed the most influential and, perhaps, the best and oldest citizen of Northern Texas. Colonel Young was shot down by an assassin.

"The killing of Young was the beginning of a series of vengeful enormities. Murder and arson were incidents of everyday life. It was ascertained that a plot was concocted involving the destruction of towns and villages, and the taking off of Bourland and of each prominent citizen of the country. Bourland and his friends knew this to be a fact, and the end came after forty-one of the conspirators were hanged to the great elm tree at Gainsville. Thirteen were hanged, after a fair trial, before a Judge-Lynch tribunal, in Hopkins County; and three, I have been told, under the same circumstances, and after full proof of the criminal purposes of the accused, at Austin. When Federal generals came into power in Texas, after inquiring into the facts affecting these wholesale executions by mob law, they deemed it proper to ignore offenses of Bourland, and of others like him, and punishment, after peace, was never inflicted for terrible deeds, justified perhaps by dangers that begat them. If the editor of the *Gazette* had lived at the time in Texas, he would surely forgive, if he could not forget. The people were not so bad; but the times were sadly out of joint and extraordinary dangers demanded, in frontier communities, extraordinary securities."

The newspaper man said that Bourland did not hang forty-one men to the elm tree at Gainesville because these were Unionists, but simply because internecine war demanded the extirpation of one or the other local party to the conflict. The Federal general, Curtis, was coming down from the Indian Territory, it was thought, into Texas, and conspirators at Gainesville, in Hopkins County, and at Austin, had concerted plans to be executed when Federal armies appeared, involving the extirpation of secessionists. The discovery of plots of this character impelled Bourland and others to adopt desperate remedies for dreadful evils.

"When I was in Richmond, not long ago," said the journalist, "and was clerk of a congressional committee, I ascertained that quite forty thousand Federal soldiers had gone out of East Tennessee, and, from states south of the Ohio, not less than two hundred thousand men had entered the Federal service. Suppose you deduct two hundred thousand from Grant's and Sherman's armies and add two hundred thousand to those of Jefferson Davis. There is instituted an equivalent of four hundred thousand men added to Confederate strength. With this we would surely defeat the North and have on this continent that 'double-barreled' Union for which Davis and Yancey pray. For office-holders, I confess, it would be well, but I don't see in what the people are to be gainers. Duplication of governments signifies quadruplication of taxes; and governments are only taxing, plundering schemes of law-administration; and that which is cheapest, and governs least, is commonly best."

Mamie and Bessie were intent listeners, and Spratling gazed abstractedly into the fire-place when the newspaper man continued:

"Our stories have been drawn mainly from Tennessee and the Gulf States. While I am dreaming of the results of this fearful war I would tell Bessie and Mamie of a little episode in the history of progressive, grand events which they will never forget. I had been some days in Richmond, nearly a year ago, when the starving and half-clad women at the market—most of them widows of soldiers in Lee's army—finding that the money supplied would no longer give them bread, moved in a body to the Capitol. They proposed to appeal for relief to Governor Letcher. It was an unique and dangerous mob of three or four thousand reckless, desperate, hungry, poorly clad women.

"Hearing the shrieks and screams of the multitude, I ran from my room to the Capitol. When I entered the building the women were swarming into the open space between Clay's statue and the monuments reared in honor of Jefferson and Henry, and Governor Letcher's red head was visible amid the throng rapidly gathering upon the portico of the state-house. I heard his friends ask, 'What can we do with them?'

"'Soldiers are helpless and useless,' said the governor, 'we can't fire into that mob, and the women know it.'

"I said to the Governor that 'a steam fire-engine, guarded by a military company would put the poor creatures to flight.'

"But the governor relied upon fluency of speech and gentle persuasiveness and perhaps upon his good looks. The uglier a red-haired, red-visaged man, the handsomer he esteems himself. His Excellency's graces of person and manner and genuine eloquence availed nothing.

"There was a gigantic, red-haired woman—she looked like another Letcher, in a homespun frock—who led the vociferous, shrieking throng. She shouted:

"'We want bread, not words! Let us help ourselves! Follow me!'

"She went rapidly, throwing her hands wildly above her head, and shouting words of encouragement and exasperation to her lean, lank, meanly-clad, reckless, starving followers. They entered Main Street and desolated it. Storehouses were ransacked. They burdened themselves with every description of trumpery with which poverty-stricken trades-people filled wretched shelves. They moved to the quarter-master's depository of army supplies, and expelling clerks and guards, freighted themselves with bridles, saddles, and wagon covers. I saw a dozen women emerge from the building with saddles on their backs. When, at length, they discovered the commissariat, they threw aside everything they had appropriated at other places, and gathering up their outer skirts, filled their laps with flour and sugar. Each sought to take away, in this manner, the largest possible quantity, and when each had freighted her uplifted dress with all she could carry, she started, bare-legged, for her home. The spectacle became as ludicrous as it was pitiful. Merchants and soldiers followed in the train of this army of hungry women gathering up their scattered wares and public and private property. No great losses were sustained, and the incident only led to the adoption of measures by the public authorities designed to prevent the recurrence of such dangers. Food was issued to the poor wives and widows of soldiers themselves. But the rich and those in authority in Richmond never knew or measured the woes and miseries of the poor. I am sure an illustration will interest Bessie and Mamie.

"One Sunday, while in Richmond, a few days before the battle of Chancellorsville, I went to Hollywood, the famed cemetery of Richmond. Time, when peace is restored, will make it an attractive spot. Though the site is admirably chosen, and many of the monuments costly and tasteful, yet the grave-stones are all of recent date. I never cared to wander through a grave-yard in which there are no old tomb-stones. Men just buried are too nearly allied to the living. The gulf that separates us is neither deep nor wide enough to excite those strangely sad emotions experienced when we decipher time-worn epitaphs, ascribing to ashes beneath all the virtues of our race. Two ex-presidents sleep in Hollywood ; and not far away there are countless graves of soldiers of the South, the victims of insatiate revolution. Monumental marble will designate the resting places of statesmen who achieved all the ends of human ambition, but the graves of soldiers who gave their lives, as they believed, for their country's emancipation, have no marks to distinguish burial places in which truest representatives of unselfish patriotism have returned to dust. When war no longer desolates the land, when prosperity reigns, and a grateful people would honor the illustrious dead, there will not be wanting a mausoleum to tell posterity that Hollywood is consecrated in a nation's heart. There they lie, beneath those little hillocks, with rude boards as head-stones, the gallant men who fell in all the battles around Richmond. There, too, are those whose lives went away from bodies racked with pain in Richmond hospitals. Mothers and wives and sisters shall visit Hollywood through many coming years, from all the Southern States, that they may view the spot where the loved and lost repose in undistinguished graves.

"I stood upon holy ground.

"The funeral train of poverty came in at the gateway as I was going out. A market wagon contained a little coffin of rough boards. A gray-haired negro was the driver, and three women, an old man, and half a dozen thinly-clad little girls and boys followed very slowly— all with measured steps and sad faces. As I was going out a little girl, eight or nine years old, poorly clad, was closing the gate. Her face was pretty, and her large lustrous eyes grew bright when I asked the name of the occupant of the coffin. She seemed to think that everybody should know that 'Mary' was dead.

" 'It is strange you did not know Mary. I thought almost everybody knew her. She was so good, and gentle, and kind, and she was her mother's only child. I went to school with Mary.'

"The simplicity and earnestness of the child interested me. I wished to know more of Mary and of that poor, heart-broken woman, so meanly attired, who was following with unsteady steps her only child to the grave, I cannot, of course, give the language of the little girl, but she said:

" 'When I used to look at Mary I wondered how people could ever call her homely; there were so many shades of color in her eyes when I was talking to her, and the blood would come and go in her pale cheeks. She used to help the little children across the muddy streets and give away her scanty meal to some poor child who was hungry at school. She would teach me, too, the hard, long words in my geography. When the other girls made fun of my dress because it had holes in it, and my mother there, who is poor, like Mary's, could not buy me another, Mary used to put her arms around me to conceal the rents. I used to think there was a pretty light around Mary's sweet face, like that which mother showed me in the picture of our Savior. Those who did not know Mary well, did not think she was so beautiful, but we little children did. She was kindest and gentlest to the poorest of us.'

"I had never listened to an eulogium upon the dead more touching than this which fell from the tremulous lips and tearful eyes of Mary's friend.

"She is not homely now. The bright sun when it goes down again upon the little childish group who come tripping out of the old schoolhouse shall not add luster to the changeful eyes and pale cheeks of Mary; her seat in school is vacant; her satchel lies idly on the shelf. The spider will weave his busy web upon the wall in Mary's garret, but there are no lustrous loving eyes to watch him. The heart-broken mother shall often dream that she hears, and listen in vain for the soft, sweet accents of little Mary's voice; she shall see Mary, not here, and many like her of whom the earth was not worthy.

"How coldly and rudely the clods that struck Mary's coffin fell upon that mother's heart! A piercing shriek escaped her lips. Then all was still again, except the falling of the dull, heavy earth with which the old man filled the shallow grave. When all were leaving the place, I asked the school-child friend of Mary how she came to die.

" 'I don't know,' she answered ; ' Mother said that the war took bread from the poor in Richmond, and Mary's mother is very, very poor.'

"I never think of these facts or of the miseries and vices of our race precipitated by this wicked, needless, fratricidal war that I do not involuntarily ask whether they who deem themselves statesmen, and as such inaugurated this conflict or made it unavoidable, will not be consigned to deeper depths of perdition by an outraged God of goodness than that which must be fathomed by common soldiers like ourselves. William L. Yancy, Jefferson Davis, A. G. Brown, Toombs, Wigfall, and the many like them, who followed in Yancy's wake, constituted the dragon of the Apocalypse with seven heads and ten horns whose tail drew after it 'the stars of heaven and did cast them to earth.' I do not question their honesty or patriotism, mark you ; but only ask whether they have not outrivaled a De Golyer in paving hell with good intentions."

11

# CHAPTER XXIII.

Woes of the People.—How Endured.—An Ancient Georgia Village.—Curious Story
about Governor Gilmer and William H. Crawford.—Slave Life Fifty Years Ago.
—Joseph Henry Lumpkin.—How African Slavery became African Servitude.
—Providential Preparation for Freedom.

The very day that the captain and Spratling returned to camp,
Tunnel Hill and Dalton were evacuated by the Confederates and our
way was open to the home of Mamie Hughes. There Bessie and her
mother were gladly welcomed. Their purpose was to remain only a
day and then go further south to their old home in Oglethorpe
County.

Mamie said, when she and Bessie met, "that the invitation, sent
long before, had been accepted most unexpectedly. I am glad," she
continued, "that you are here, but deplore the calamity that sent you
to our home."

Bessie's father had gone to Oglethorpe and could not return because
of the intervention of our army. It was necessary to communicate
with him, and Mrs. Starnes was persuaded to remain with her newly-
made friends until she could advise her husband of misfortunes that
overwhelmed her.

Such calamities were too numberless to excite sympathy, and, of
every-day occurrence, were borne as complacently by the immediate
sufferers as by their friends. People soon forgot the fallen when each
day's list of the dead was countless. Death, in war, has no terrors,
save for the dying. Hunger and suffering are laughed at because
death, the gate-way of escape, is so accessible. Courage, in such an
age, is the only virtue worth the having; and he who shuddered
when wealth became indigence, was the veriest of cowards.

"When the Confederacy rises in the ruins of Lincoln's empire," said Mrs. Starnes, "I will still own the farm, and Mr. Spratling says he will reconstruct my modest dwelling."

Spratling, now an unwilling *quasi*-invalid, was confined to the house by the imperious edicts of Bessie and Mamie. His neglected wound was painful, the shoulder swollen, and left arm useless. Wholesome food and women's watchful care wrought a speedy change, and when dancing at night and hunting by day and stories of army life during the long evenings were indulged, delicious odors of pine and cedar wood fires perfuming the commodious country house, Spratling rapidly regained his wonted vigor.

The captain could not abandon Spratling; the editor and schoolmaster were free to depart or remain; the editor's brother, like the Federal lieutenant, Hughes, had a month's furlough.

A trusted negro servant was dispatched for Mr. Starnes, to Lexington, in Oglethorpe County, the most venerable in its apparent antiquity of all the towns of Georgia. Green moss, on great boulders along white sandy roadways leading into the ancient town, is growing gray. Myriads of pebbles in the long-used streets are worn perfectly round by gliding feet of successive generations, and Sunday-school "scholars" are relieved of the necessity of buying marbles. Bob Toombs and Chief Justice Joseph Henry Lumpkin used to live in Lexington; but when the antique metropolis of Oglethorpe, fifty years ago, was finished and fenced in, they were left outside and migrated. They grew great; Lexington stood still. The venerable village could not contain them. In years long agone, William H. Crawford—deemed by the great Napoleon the greatest of Americans— had his home at Lexington.

"There," said the newspaper man, "I saw this grand old man in extreme old age after he had been almost President of the United States, having competed for the office with Jackson, Clay, and Adams— I saw this gigantic old civilian, in my childhood, sitting on the circuit bench and determining a criminal prosecution in which Joseph Henry Lumpkin appeared for the defendant, an aged man, accused of stealing a sheep. He was palpably guilty; but Lumpkin's matchless eloquence won an acquittal, when Crawford, chiding the jury for its tears and weakness, set aside the verdict and ordered a new trial.

"This William H. Crawford was the only American, perhaps, who knew the great Napoleon, personally and intimately. Among his private papers there were found, after his death, kindliest letters, I am told, from the great emperor. Napoleon could afford to deal with the great American as an equal and as a friend when state policy would not suffer him to unbend in the presence of a subject.

"The other great man of Lexington, Joseph Henry Lumpkin, was the unrivaled barrister till he became the matchless judge. His learning, genius, and logical acumen compelled his professional elevation. He was a native-born abolitionist. When at college, at Princeton or Yale, he adopted and expressed opinions on the subject of negro servitude that enabled his pro-slavery rivals to defeat his honorable aspirations. But such were his unapproachable forensic abilities that the lawyers of Georgia were forced to remove him from their sphere of action. No sentence of death could be pronounced if Joseph Henry Lumpkin appealed to the jury, and, therefore, the orator was merged into the judge. His opinions, as Chief Justice of Georgia, are as admirable specimens of rhetorical logic as the finest that ever fell from the lips of the greatest Lord Chancellor.

"But I may be impelled to speak by the prejudices of my youth," continued the editor. "I was not four years old when I saw the aged William H. Crawford sleeping on the wool-sack in Lexington, while Joseph Henry Lumpkin flooded the court-room with tears because a gray-haired country bumpkin was forced by pangs of poverty to steal a sheep.

"George R. Gilmer, when I was a boy, still lived in Lexington. He, too, was then very old. In another place I have written of his archæological tastes and pursuits, and of the care and toil and money he devoted to the collection of antique and other curiosities of taste and learning. He had been governor and served in both branches of the United States Congress. He was the kindliest, most generous of men. I would never have violated a mound-builder's tomb or traced De Soto's devious path across the Gulf States if I had not heard Governor Gilmer descant upon dim outlines of giant figures that peopled realms of his fancy with splendid visions of war, peace, homes, and cities of extinct races."

The schoolmaster had been listening intently while the newspaper man was reviving phantom figures of departed greatness and when the fire burned low and kettle lid rattled and escaping steam sang a lullaby that begat silence and somnolency, the pedagogue said that, in 1832, then a very young man, he taught a country school near Carter's Hill, in Montgomery County, Alabama.

"Ingrams, Carters, Floyds, Barnets, Lees, Wares, Mooneys, Gilmers, Merriwethers, and Du Pres were household names and words in the modest log-cabin in which I flogged limited learning into tow-headed urchins. I am induced to refer to these facts because I remember that one of my 'patrons' was induced by another to convey a letter enclosing a one thousand dollar United States bank-note to Governor Gilmer. Mr. D. delivered the letter to Governor Gilmer, telling him of its contents, and he remembered that the governor threw it carlessly into a desk. Two years elapsed. Governor Gilmer demanded payment by letter. The debtor wrote that he had sent the money by Mr. D., his neighbor, an honest man. The governor answered that he had never received it. Mr. D. mounted his horse—there were no railways in those days—and went to Lexington, more than three hundred miles. Governor Gilmer, when his old friend came, had no recollection of the letter; but Mr. D. had forgotten nothing. He went to the room in which the governor was sitting when he delivered the bank-note two years before; he caused the desk to be opened and there found the letter, its waxen seal unbroken, containing the money. Governor Gilmer's chagrin was painful and lasting, so my friend, the Alabamian, informed me. Whenever, afterward, the Alabamian visited his kindred about Lexington, he was always entertained at a festival given by Governor Gilmer.''

The newspaper man left his seat and stood facing the schoolmaster.

"Do you know," said the writer for the press, "that he was my father who bore that letter to Governor Gilmer? I was not old enough to go to school when you taught near Carter's Hill, but I knew afterward, all the people you have named. I remember when the Creek Indians burned the houses and slaughtered the people of the neighborhood. I remember how they slew eight of nine passengers on the stage coach just after it left Montgomery.''

Of course the pedagogue had forgotten nothing of facts to which the journalist adverted. He confessed a fresh bond of union between himself and friend and said that "churches, newspapers, and schoolmasters had done a great work in Alabama in a brief period. Red men have disappeared, there are free schools and free churches and people everywhere, and railways and steamers and the highest progressive intelligence and civilization. Less than thirty years have passed, within which all this has been achieved. Montgomery, the wretched little village of one hundred cabins when I first saw it, has fifteen thousand inhabitants.

'' But they were a rude people when I wielded the birchen rod in the log cabin near Carter's Hill, ten or twelve miles from Montgomery. I saw a farmer sell his good-looking wife, a pretty white woman she was, for a thousand dollars to a richer neighbor; I saw Kin Mooney playing poker with a friend, at five dollars a game, in the log church, which was also the schoolhouse, on Sunday, while the good Baptist brother, Jack Robinson, expounded the scriptures in this sanctuary. I saw a savage overseer tie a negro slave, Patrick by name, to a log and draw a wild black cat, by the tail, down the negro's naked back, from his shoulders to his heels. The infernal process was thrice repeated. Patrick shrieked and swooned. A strong solution of salt and vinegar was then poured over the senseless negro's back. When he recovered his senses he was gagged. He wore the gag, constantly moving it to one side, till it carved a slit in the corner of his mouth. The hapless negro could talk a little and drink a little, still wearing the gag. It was made of iron, having hinges, and was locked behind his neck. A flat piece of iron, projecting inwardly, from the rim, entered the mouth. I describe it because, having lived always in the South, it was the only 'gag' I ever saw. When Patrick could talk, eat and drink, wearing the gag, the overseer belled him. An iron belt about the body and another around the neck sustained an iron rod extending along the spine, three feet above Patrick's head. To the end of this rod a bell was attached; and, wearing all this machinery of iron, Patrick was forced by the fiend incarnate to pick cotton. The incentive to this cruelty was jealousy of Patrick's influence with his master, then absent.  When he came home, Patrick, of course, was liberated, given a gun, and instructed to settle with the overseer.  He, hearing of the course of events, fled to Texas.

"'There was African *slavery* in those days.  It is African *servitude* now.  The relations of the races, as seen in the conduct of those about us, even now listening to what I say, and shuddering while I tell of the woes of Patrick, show that African *slavery*, even if party leaders had never organized war in organizing secession, was no more.  African 'slavery' does not exist, and only African 'servitude.'  Within these brief thirty years the institution has been wholly changed with the relations of the two races.  Providence, it seems, prepared whites and blacks, by slow, inscrutable processes, for the social conditions and facts of to-day.  On the statute-books of states, slave codes remain unrepealed; but they are obsolete, and have been for years.  Politicians rave and roar, and abuse one another, and excite infinite sectional prejudices.

"'Fearing they may be reviled as abolitionists, our party leaders dare not reform barbarous slave codes, and these have slowly lapsed, unrepealed, into desuetude.  The law inhibits books and yet negroes are everywhere taught to read and write.  Preachers are hired everywhere to preach especially in negro churches, and the story I tell of Patrick's woes, which I witnessed, could gain credence on no southern plantation of to-day.'"

# CAHAPER XXIV.

How thoroughly a soldier becomes part and parcel of a great mass, losing consciousness of individuality, we have seen, and how, therefore, *esprit de corps* supplants personal heroism, and how one strong man, of any race or latitude, becomes as valuable as any other of equal strength, was often asserted and illustrated when Major-General Pat Cleburne and many others of the best and wisest soldiers and statesmen of the South, in 1863-64, urged the enlistment as soldiers, and liberation as men, of the negroes of the South. Destiny and Jefferson Davis interposed and Africa was freed by the North and not by the South. Thus the negro, an inseperable adjunct of southern industry, civilization, and government, loves, obeys, and serves the North, and always, in affairs of government, involving freedom and slavery, obeys the injunctions of northern party leaders.

At Mamie's home there were more than three hundred slaves. Until Lieutenant Hughes and his friends came, the helpless household had no other guardians than these negroes and none could have given more perfect security. They were devoted to the persons and interests of their white owners, and never was a suspicion entertained, even when detatchments of Federal cavalry traversed the country in all directions, and these negroes knew how thoroughly "the shell of the hollow Confederacy was broken," that negroes plotted against the security of the whites.

It happened, at the period of which these pages tell, that the Confederate forces were slowly and constantly retreating. Even while the captain and his friends were guests of Lieutenant Hughes, and while pretty Bessie Starnes, half crazed by her affection for the Lieutenant and admiration and love of Spratling, the Confederate army was slowly and sullenly moving south toward Resaca and Adairsville, leaving this summer residence of the Hughes family within the Federal lines.

Of the retrogression of the Confederate forces, inmates of the Hughes household were first advised by the appearance at the place of four mounted men in blue overcoats. A breathless, excited negro, entering the breakfast room, where the family were seated at table, announced:

"Missis, de Yanks is acummin' down dar in de road. Dere won't be nary chicken left on de place!" and Jack rubbed his hands together, and amazed by the excitement he begat, set his back against the wall, and grinned and twisted his body and looked from right to left, and when asked again and again, "How many Yanks are there?" he only stared vacantly in the faces of his inquisitors.

Spratling forgot his wound, and with the rest, armed himself, and went out. The prowling cavalrymen did not propose to encounter a number of men greater than their own, and at once retired. No shots were fired, but the Confederates knew that these four would be fifty Federal soldiers when next a descent was made upon the plantation of Mrs. Hughes.

"Three or four days hence," said the captain, "these scouts will have returned to camp and told of our presence here. A force will be sent to capture such stragglers as we are and to gather in deserters voluntarily remaining at points recently occupied by Confederates. We must move at an early day.

"Lieutenant," he continued, addressing Mr. Hughes, "I don't know whether I will regret more the termination of this delightful visit or the necessity which requires you to accompany us. If I can, when I return to General Cleburne's head-quarters, I will make some arrangement by which you may not be sent to a prison-pen. No exchanges are made; the Confederacy is starving; its soldiers are often half fed; and the condition of prisoners of war must be horrible. Soldiers are worth more to us than to you, and you can not afford to exchange, when your resources are infinite as humanity and ours are restricted to sparse populations of the Gulf States. It is a great pity that the cartel is suspended; and I must confess that, while we are delighted as your guests, we are grieved that you are our prisoner. By remaining, we can not serve you or those dear to you. Our presence will only invite attack. If we won at first, we would surely be overwhelmed at last. This might involve the safety of women and destruction of your delightful home.

"We must soon march."

This was said in the presence of the household gathered in the hallway. Mrs. Hughes gazed tenderly in the face of her son. She deplored his fate from which there was seemingly no escape, He was paroled and could not fly, even if an opportunity were presented. If captured by Federal soldiers, he could save himself and guard his home, with those he loved. He was silent and helpless as the mother.

Neither Bessie nor Mamie lifted their eyes from the floor. Bessie knew that Spratling and the lieutenant were studying her face, and Mamie could only listen, while the color fled from her cheeks, as measured words fell slowly from the captain's lips, announcing her separation from him and from her brother.

"In times like these, when we part, we can never hope to meet again," said the tearful Mrs. Hughes. "Some one or more may return, but all of you, never! never! It is dreadful to think, but when I see you strong men going out of my door, I see you stepping down into your graves. I am grateful because you have been so generous to my son, and it is no fault of yours that he must leave me. My prayers and blessings will follow you."

Death-like pallor swept over the faces of Bessie and Mamie. The facts of the moment were too painful for their contemplation. Mamie caught Bessie's hand and drawing her to her side, both, with bowed heads, hurried silently away. Mrs. Hughes followed, and the sad convocation was slowly dissolved.

When we sat, that cool winter evening, about the broad, blazing hearth, the schoolmaster said "he had been studying the character and conduct of negroes all his life. While they do no violent deeds and share, as a race, in none of the toils or dangers incident to their own deliverance, they rarely fail to show, when the test is applied, that they prefer freedom to servitude.

"They have uniformly forgotten personal attachments, such as subsist between your servants, Lieutenant, and yourself, to show that they prefer freedom to slavery. They uniformly betray the Confederates and however earnest in assertions of personal devotion to their owners, are privately and really loyal to the Union. I have found, to the extent that their intelligence may make them trustworthy, that they are useful and efficient spies. They never fail to disclose places of concealment of persons and property, and evince, always, to the extent that they deem it safe, unmixed loyalty to the 'Stars and Stripes.' I tell you this because I have seen how this family is disposed to trust, implicitly, the asserted fidelity of these negroes. I tell you, Lieutenant, your mother will be betrayed by them. She will lose every valuable article she conceals if these 'devoted household servants' suspect the place of concealment. The poor negro thinks to aid and thus win favor in the eyes of blue-coated patriotism by betraying these confidences. The blue-coat never shares the spoils with the negro. The negro does not ask it. His impulses are higher and nobler than those of the white man. He would only serve the cause this white man espouses. The white man—the camp-follower and not the soldier—is content if he may fill his purse.

"Did it ever occur to you that you may direct any genuine bullet-headed African to do any three acts, and that he will obey, but never discharging the three tasks in the order in which you name them? His head is too thick for him to think consecutively. He never recks of the morrow. He is always perfectly blest in the abundance of to-day. Is not this race-peculiarity to be ascribed to race-habits, the outgrowth of countless centuries of slavery? They have never been subjected to the necessity of providing for present or future wants. Their own needs have never shaped their actions; and, therefore, their boundless unselfishness, and their heedlessness and incapacity to think for the future. Their round, thick skulls and brain-forces are conformed to facts and necessities of centuries.

"It is true that in wide districts of the Gulf States, denuded by conscription of arms-bearing whites, negroes outnumbering whites as ten and twenty to one, there has occurred no negro outbreak. There is no negro criminality, and perfect order, peace, security, and industry are maintained. Confederate armies are fed and clothed and kept in the field by negro industry; but let me assure you that each negro, the old and the young, seeks freedom, and prefers it even to this serfdom or peonage subsisting on this estate, or ranche, as termed in Mexico. Wherever liberated they have never consented to re-enslavement, and it is most fortunate that they have been gradually elevated by 'slavery,' which has become 'servitude,' and then serfdom, while local statutes remained unchanged and unenforced. The frightful quarrel between the abolitionists and secessionists made local statutory law irrepealable, but the negro code, like the fact of original African slavery, fell of its own bloody, barbarous weight into desuetude. The age of preparation is passed, and that of realization, perhaps, is come. Who can fathom the mysteries of God's providence in His dealings with races and nations?

"Wherever liberated, as I have seen in Tennessee and Kentucky, these creatures have wandered away at once from their homes. They can not otherwise realize the fact of absolute freedom. They could not otherwise enjoy it to their full bent. The 'old massa's' presence and supreme authority was still confessed in the old cabin occupied through a lifetime of servitude, and they could only divest themselves of its influence by going into exile. But, wherever freed, they have sought supposed delights incident to freedom, which never come. They are still slaves; not of the white man, but of hunger and thirst and cold.

"The forty acres and a mule have never descended, as did the beasts of the fields in a curtain suspended before St. Peter, from the opened heavens, upon the hapless African. After a time these liberated blacks will realize exactions imposed by nature's laws, and there is not on God's footstool a better laboring population, or one more simple and kindly, more contented or law-abiding. As we see them in the rich cotton and sugar producing districts to-day, where they are still slaves, so will they be when freedom strikes shackles from their souls. Such masters as you, Lieutenant, can lose nothing by the extinction of the *law* of slavery; the practical fact, if it be a fact here to-day, will still subsist."

"Yes," interposed Spratling, who had been listening drowsily to this soliloquy of the pedagogue, while the captain on one side of the room with Mamie, and Bessie and the lieutenant on the other, spoke at intervals, in subdued tones,—"Yes," said Spratling, "I asked that black rascal who pretended to be so badly scared this morning when the Yankee scouts came, what he proposed to do when he was set free.

" 'I dunno, massa,' he answered, 'but I'z gwine to sleep in de sunshine, ropped up in pancakes, en yaller-gal angels, dey'll pore lasses ober me.' "

"There's a heavenly picture of perfect negro beatitude, and its realization is coming," said the schoolmaster.

# CHAPTER XXV.

"I am sure that people in future years and centuries will be amazed by accounts of our present modes of living. We journalists," said the editor, "have been reduced to the utmost straits. I printed two issues of my *Register* on pretty wall-paper, using only one side of each sheet. It happened, possibly, because the Confederate Government was getting out a new issue of notes and bonds and monopolized the service of the paper-mills. My only resource was wall-paper owned by a cheerful Hebrew, and the reading matter of the striped sheets was confined to one side of each. It was a queer show when the people, having supplied themselves with accounts of the latest battle, sat along the curbstones and in their doorways holding up the ugly striped, red, white, blue, black, and figured sheets before their eager faces. I was employed, when its editor, John B. Dumble, an Ohio Democrat, was sick, to conduct, for a short time, a daily paper in Atlanta. Sam C. Reid and Dr. I. E. Nagle, two army correspondents of my own newspaper, were in Atlanta at the time. It happened that a blockade-runner had entered Wilmington and supplied us abundantly with Jamaica rum. I paid eighty dollars a gallon and was not aware of the fact that each newspaper of the place, and there were four dalies then published in Atlanta, was in like manner conciliated by the generous importer. There was a famous restaurateur in Atlanta. He drew his supplies of early vegetables and fruits from Florida and commonly spread, though he paid forty cents per pound for salt, a very attractive table. He had no wine, and only the white country whiskey of the period. I discovered my opportunity in the possession of the Jamaica rum, and therefore ordered dinner for eight newspaper men. What was my astonisment when I went to dinner, that I encountered no members of the 'press-gang' except Ried and Nagle. The absentees did not even deign to send apologies for the non-acceptance of my invitation. Nagle and Reid had each seen, during the morning, two of the noble profession, and we inferred, from the condition of these two, that all the rest, as fortunate as I had been, had received a gallon, or even more, of the delicious product of Jamaician distilleries. We three sat down to drink the rum and dispatch the viands before us.

"It was finally proposed and agreed that each of us, and each absent journalist, should contribute a 'rousing dinner-table speech to the delights of the rum occasion.' We sat to work, and each furnished, within three or four hours, two columns of matter for my friend's and my own newspaper. We wrote and published our own and supposed speeches, as genuine, of all the invited editors. We made the ancient and venerated McClanahan pronounce a heartfelt eulogium upon Andrew Jackson Democracy. We reproduced, as Watterson's harangue, the substance of his unique and inimitable delineation of Parson Brownlow's character. It was believed that the parson had died a few days before. Dumble's incisive logic characterized his dinner-table talk. Dill was made to utter a few sentences laudatory of the women of the time, and the whole of these speeches appeared next morning. Readers of the *Appeal* and of the *Register* supposed that the dinner was enjoyed by many guests, and that the speeches were welcomed with loud applause. This was natural enough; but Nagle, Reid, and I were especially dumfounded when we met, three days later, to find that each editor, but one, supposed his published speech genuine; that he had made it as stated, and that his obliviousness of the incidents of the occasion was wholly due to the overpowering influence of Jamaica rum. I congratulated McClanahan next morning after the supposed festival, on his eloquent tribute to the rock-ribbed secession Democracy. He looked at me doubtingly. I said:

"'Mack, you were a little intoxicated, you remember, but you had your wits about you, and your talking tackle was never in better condition.'

"I produced a copy of McClanahan's own paper and pointed out passages in his speech which I especially approved.

"Still wearing a puzzled look, and rubbing his eyes, McClanahan at last concluded that he had been unconsciously 'the orator of the occasion.' When soon afterward congratulated by Nagle, Mack never hesitated a moment, but replied:

"'Yes, Doctor, I had been taking a little rum, but made a —— —— good speech; didn't I?'

"Congressmen print speeches, written but never delivered, and distribute them among their innocent constituencies, and Congressmen have speeches written for them that are delivered as their own; but here we see that editors not only have speeches written, but delivered and printed as their own, of which they never heard or dreamed. But the editors deserved the more praise and less censure in this, that each honestly supposed he made the speech ascribed to him, and each earnestly congratulated the other because of his triumph, and the innocent people were not sought by the journalists to be humbugged."

# CHAPTER XXVI.

Lieutenant Hughes was not loquacious. His position as host and as our prisoner, and, possibly, his doubtful acceptance as a professed suitor of Bessie Starnes, silenced him. His conduct toward her while she was beneath his roof was, necessarily, in his eyes, most guarded. She was his sister's friend, and, as such, his guest. He was, as we beheld his action, studiously formal. He seemed no more desirous of amusing and entertaining Bessie than others of his guests. He said, with abstracted manner, one evening, that stories we had been telling recalled an incident that befell him when, detailed on special service, he went to a little town, New Madrid, in Missouri.

"With one hundred men, I was sent eight or ten miles southwest of the place to capture or destroy a guerrilla camp. A bright, good-natured, grinning negro, very black, came to our headquarters on the low plain, in the rear of New Madrid, to tell me that one Captain H. E. Clark, a rude, energetic rebel, who had been capturing our scouts and cutting off foraging parties, might be easily taken prisoner or destroyed. The negro said that Clark had done him some grievous wrong, and that he proposed to avenge it. I applied to the commanding officer of the post, to whom this 'contraband' recited his story as he had to me. I must confess that now and then I had doubts of the negro's veracity, and vague apprehensions of betrayal were suggested ; but negroes had been found faithful always, and I could not well see how one would have the courage to attempt treason to truth, and to himself, and the cause of his own freedom.

"In any event, I was instructed to take one hundred chosen men and capture or destroy Clark and his freebooters.

"It is a wonderful country just west of New Madrid. The streams occupy deep channels, or crevices, carved out by the earthquake of 1811–12. The water flows through densest weeds and cresses. Brightest flowers bloom and blossom above the surface, and these strange, deep creeks, emptying into the murky Mississippi, are of pellucid clearness. When crossing these streams, we could see fish disporting themselves ten feet below the surface. The country had been lifted up by the eathquake shocks of 1811–12 so that artificial drains, said to have connected the Mississippi with the St. Francis and White, lateral and tributary streams, were broken by this upheaval of the land, and the superabundant water of the great river was left to follow the river's main channel, and submerge farms and houses along its resistless course. States have constructed mighty earthen walls to confine it to its deep and tortuous course; but it defies every obstruction, and carves out its path along the highest ridge between the parallel highlands, fifty miles apart, extending from Cairo almost to the sea. When the water first leaves the overcharged main channel, it holds most mud in suspension, and then, too, this water moves most slothfully, and, of course, at that moment it deposits most mud and most rapidly. Therefore, the banks are highest at the river's edge, and therefore you hear people say they descend the Mississippi in steamers and look down upon the tops of planters' residences and mills hard by the uplifted 'inland sea.' Therefore, the terrors of a crevasse and frightful force of the pent-up flood-tide when a crayfish, or malicious person, or the slow abrasion of the soil has given vent to the accumulated waters. I saw the levee break one morning late in May, a year ago. Houses and fences disappeared as if swallowed by a maelstrom. The people fled as from 'the wrath to come;' and when the resistless torrent reached the forest, one hundred yards distant, mightiest trees, the growth of centuries, went down as did the reeds of the canebrake. The roaring of the rushing flood, and crashing and breaking of falling cypresses, two and three hundred feet high, shook the earth, and no tempest's roar was ever comparable with this echoing thunder of the drunken mighty 'father of floods.' Here it carves out for itself a new channel and slowly renews the process of upbuilding its own banks. In this it is only aided by the construction of levees, those frail earthen walls designed to hedge it in. It rises with successive floods, higher and higher above the marshland plain, until accident or resistless inertia of heaped up floods breaks down all barriers, and pretty homes and redundant crops are again overwhelmed. But standing at any time or place on the shore of the Mississippi, and listening to the sullen roar of its tawny waters, one always confesses the sublime majesty of the mighty river. There is no such impressive embodiment of the ideal of the River of Death, forever sweeping countless myriads into the ocean of eternal rest, as this, which chants forever a sonorous melancholy requiem over graves of nations and cities, and of unknown, forgotten races, that once dwelt along its shores. There is infinite sadness in sombre forests of impenetrable gloom and density lining the low, flat shores, and shutting out the sun's rays. It trends away to one or the other side of its earthen prison walls, and, leaning lazily against it, groans and roars as if its sluggish movements of measureless force were painful to the monstrous river. When weary of resting against the eastern, it slowly moves to the western side of its ever-changeful channel. Its wayward lawlessness is as marvelous as memories of pilots who watch, beneath moon and stars and mocking dancing shadows of the night, its ever-varying courses and measure by miniature whirlpools on its surface, the depth of boiling billows.

"But I was going to tell you of a negro's treason to the Union. It is a single confessed instance, and I was its victim. Of course the black rascal was my guide to the guerrilla Clark's hiding place. My force was compelled to follow a narrow path across the swamp. Any deviation from the track, only wide enough for one horseman, was almost certain death. Quagmires were bottomless. I became interested, as we were going out of New Madrid, in a description a raw recruit from Tennessee, named Tillman, was giving me of Reelfoot Lake, and of its strange origin on the eastern side of the river, and made the intelligent youth promise to recite the whole story as soon as we had leisure, by the camp fire.

"Meanwhile, it occurred to me that we had traveled ten or fifteen, when the negro had said we need only go eight miles. I caused the command to halt. The negro was brought into my presence. I stated to him that his integrity was questioned, and that if he did not lead us at once to Clark's den I would have him shot. I ordered a trustworthy sergeant to ride beside or near the negro, and shoot him if, within the next half hour, we were not at Clark's hiding place. Within twenty minutes I heard the report of a pistol, and riding rapidly forward I encountered a corporal, who said that the negro had taken advantage of his perfect knowledge of the paths through the swamp, and of the different appearances of the miry and of hard ground, and had separated himself and the sergeant from the main body of my command, and that the 'black rascal had shot the sergeant dead and disappeared.'

"Fortunately, it seemed, we could see an 'opening,' as woodsmen term a 'clearing,' half a mile ahead, and moved rapidly toward it. Instead of a barn, we found a 'gin-house.' Its body rested on pillars—great trees hewn square—twelve feet high. Within the building, above these pillars, was the gin that separates the seed from the cotton, and below, on the ground and inside the pillars, was the great cogged wheel and its lever, to which mules are attached, that the gin may be driven to do its office. Here we camped for the night.

"Knowing Clark's strength, I was not apprehensive of an assault; but I posted a strong picket force, and taking with me the youthful Tennesseean recruit who had interested me during the day, I ordered my men to destroy no property, but make themselves comfortable under and about the gin-house. In compliance with an invitation from the widowed owner of the estate, I went to the 'big house,' as designated by the negro who had brought the note of invitation. The widow first appeared. After tendering me the hospitalities of her delightful home, she introduced her daughter, a pretty maiden, blushing into perfect womanhood. I was charmed by the confiding kindliness of the widow, and fascinated by the bright eyes and dewy lips and winsome smiles of the pretty daughter. The widow devoted herself to the youthful Tennesseean, while the daughter was evidently most willing that I should be well pleased.''

It may be proper to add, parenthetically, that Bessie Starnes was silently listening to this recital as made by Lieutenant Hughes, and I could not help watching the color come and go in her changeful, telltale face. Her eyes were fixed upon the blazing logs in the broad, deep fire-place, while she listened intently to the story, and whether the more because of dangers that threatened the lieutenant at the hands of armed men, or of a woman, bending every energy to achieve a perfect conquest, I could not divine.

The lieutenant said that he was hungry, and that it occurred to him that the meal which he had been invited to share was unaccountably delayed.

''I looked at my watch,'' said the lieutenant, ''and found it was nine o'clock. I did not see the reason for this tardiness, and became a little restive. My camp was half a mile away, and I said to the mistress of the house that I would walk down the road a short distance and learn that everything was quiet at the gin-house. The Tennesseean accompanied me. Going out, I observed a spur, freshly worn, lying on the ground. I said to the Tennesseean:

'' 'Some one left hurriedly when we came, losing this spur. Perhaps he was a courier sent to Clark's hiding place to advise him of our presence here. Perhaps supper is delayed that we may be detained till Clark may come and capture us. He spares no prisoners, I am told. He is a lawless fellow, and his followers are yellow-faced dwellers in these malarial swamps. Ignorant and murderous as they are, I am not willing to fall into their hands. Do you ride back to our camp, taking my horse with you, and return instantly with thirty men, stationing them in the verge of this grove, within fifty yards of the house. Send no pickets to the edge of the swamp. Let Clark come. Tell Lieutenant Bradly, my second in·command, to be watchful, and do you let none of Clark's gang escape. I will come to the door occasionally, only to listen, of course, and thus know that everything is quiet at the gin-house. When I am sure danger is imminent, a white handkerchief will be shown by me, and you must advance.'

''I was quite sure that the widow had instituted signals by which she advised Clark's men when to approach the house, and I instructed the Tennesseean to ascertain whether the widow placed a light in any window that could be seen from the swamp.

''I re-entered the house, and telling mother and daughter that everything was quiet at my encampment, I stated, carelessly, that the night was beautiful, and moon and stars shone brilliantly. I then added that since everything betokened a night of perfect repose, I had discharged my orderly and sent my horse to the gin-house. The ladies smiled approvingly, while I was only fearful that Clark's gang might make a descent upon the house before my orders could be executed. In fact I began to suspect that the house would be surrounded by my enemies while I was at supper, and therefore the delay in inviting me to the table. I was certainly very hungry, but was never less anxious to appease hunger. I supposed that half an hour would elapse before my men would occupy the grove in front and west of the residence, while I believed that Clark would approach stealthily from the swamp, east of the farm and half a mile distant. My anxiety was two-fold. I feared I might be captured, and then that I would fail to capture Clark, whose force I was ordered to 'capture or destroy.' But the widow and daughter still exerted themselves, nervously, as I imagined, to entertain me, and still no allusion was made to the meal I had been invited to share. I was morally certain, as the spur at the doorway indicated, that when I was invited to occupy an apartment in the house, a mounted messenger had been dispatched to Clark.

"Anxious and watchful as I was, I became profoundly interested in the good dame's intelligent account of her sojourn in New Madrid. She said :

" 'This is a wonderful country, with a wonderful history. These deep streams, enclosed within precipitous banks, all appeared in one night. My father told me that when he went to bed one night in his cabin, that stood fifty yards from this spot, in the winter of 1812-13, there was no running stream between this farm and the prosperous trading village of New Madrid. The whole country, of an area fifty miles square, had been conveyed by the United States Government to General Morgan for his services in the old revolutionary war. He never parted with the title, except that he gave many farms and town lots to his friends. The rest is simply held by that right, as I am told, which possession gives. But the town prospered till the country, as my neighbors say, "tuk the ager," and sulphurous flames issued from the earth, and heaps of stone, coal, and sand were forced to the surface, and the whole country west of us for one hundred miles was lifted up eight or ten, and in some places, twenty feet. Transverse streams, said to have been artificial, that used to connect the Mississippi with the head waters of the White and St. Francis Rivers, preventing the submergence of the intervening land by the Mississippi's greatest floods, were upheaved and broken. Great lakes, said to be fathomless, were formed. One I have visited on the other side of the river is ten or fifteen miles long ; and, looking down into its transparent depths, I could see the tops of trees standing erect far below the surface, that had once towered two and even three hundred feet above the lowlands. The country went down and pellucid water came up. It is only the visible portion of a great underground sea into which the underground rivers of Mammoth and other Kentucky and Tennessee caverns discharge themselves. I have slept in Union City, not far east from the Mississippi and near this Reelfoot Lake. When railway trains come by at night, I have fancied, when the earth was shaken until the candle fell from the mantel, and when I could hear the hollow, cavernous roar seemingly far beneath my feet—I have fancied that Union City rested above a mightier than Reelfoot Lake and deeper than Mammoth Cave, and that I might awake some bright morning afloat in a newly discovered Mediterranean as fathomless as Reelfoot Lake. On the fatal night of which I was telling, when New Madrid was destroyed, the Mississippi lost its reckoning. The current of the river was turned backward, and Neil B. Holt, who now lives in Memphis, then descending the river in a flat-boat, was brought backward towards Cairo, forty miles. The mighty drain of the continent absolutely changed its course. It must have discharged itself, when this whole region was upheaved during that convulsive night, into these underground seas and lakes, and thus the covering of Reelfoot Lake was lifted up by superabundant water; and when the river resumed its course towards the gulf and the surcharged lake was relieved, the lid fell in, and this famed resort of fishermen, with its pellucid water, wholly unlike that of the Mississippi, for the first time mirrored dense forests and sun, moon, and stars in its transparent bosom. But the Mississippi is always going east, while the great rivers of Europe, that run north and south, move their channels toward the west. Why this difference, I cannot tell; but the Mississippi may yet enter and discharge itself into these seas underlying portions of Tennessee and Kentucky, and I hope to live long enough to see the result. I am sure they have to-day no connection with the majestic, visible drain of the continent. Suppose the Mississippi find its way into Reelfoot Lake, and disappear forever?

" ' But I was going to tell of ludicrous and terrible incidents I witnessed when Bishop General Polk landed here, late in the summer of 1861, with five or six thousand men. He came on all sorts of steamboats and on flats towed by steamers. I went to the river bank to witness the landing of this mighty army. Living always in these solitudes, I had never dreamed that there were as many men on the face of the earth as came from these living, floating hives. There was moored in the midst of the fleet, and just at my feet, a little steamer, which I was told contained all the gunpowder and ordnance-stores for this mighty army.

" ' The army had disembarked and lined the shore. There were not more than twenty or thirty persons on each of twenty or more steamers moored side by side. This vessel, which was freighted with gunpowder and fixed ammunition, was discovered to be on fire in the rear of its wheelhouse. I never witnessed such an exhibition of terror. The army recognized, as I did not, the hazards of the moment. I saw everybody running. Boats half secured at the shore were left to drift down the current. They began to collide with one another. I saw Dr. McDowell, a very tall, slender, white-haired man, flying for life down the main street of the town. When I asked, " For God's sake,

Doctor, what's the matter?" he exclaimed, "New Madrid will be in hell, in less than a minute!" and he fled far beyond the confines of the devoted town to the encampment of Bankhead's battery. Everybody followed in the wake of the elongated, flying doctor, and the devoted place was wholly evacuated. Meanwhile two of the bravest men on God's footstool—the one, Frank Cheatham; the other, Oliver Greenlaw—while I was looking at them, went on board that burning steamer, and with buckets, and before my eyes, drawing up water from the river, extinguished the flames. The planks on the rear of the wheelhouse were torn off by Greenlaw and he and Cheatham triumphed. I had learned, when they ran on board the little steamer, what frightened the multitude, but was so fascinated by the conduct of these daring men—one, Greenlaw, a private citizen; and the other, then a Brigadier-General—that I was wholly unconscious of my own, while contemplating frightful dangers they despised.

" ' I was standing at the bow of the boat when the two men came ashore. I knew them both well. Both were pale and thoroughly exhausted as if they had discharged Herculean tasks. But it was only the superhuman effort of will that broke them down. I ran to a house hard-by and returning, gave them an invigorating draught, and they rested pale and weak upon the bank in perfect solitude, till fugitives began slowly, one by one to return, each giving some ludicrous account of manifestations of terror by some friend or acquaintance. Dr. McDowell's fright and flight became historical because he was a famed lecturer, inculcating theories, and in this instance, the practice, of immediate, violent "secession." '

"I don't know," continued the lieutenant, "when the good dame would have been silenced, but the daughter, who had gone into the dining room, returned, and with a significant glance at her mother, announced that supper was ready. The hostess asked me to accompany her. I said, 'In a moment, madam.' She watched me nervously when I went out. In the hall I replaced my pistols in my belt, and standing in the doorway, raised my handkerchief above my head. I was morally certain that Clark's guerrillas were at hand and that my loquacious hostess knew it.

"We sat at table and I was in the act of sipping coffee, when, glancing at the window, I beheld, distinctly outlined and pressed against a pane of glass, the black face of the traitorous negro guide who had proposed to deliver Clark's marauding guerrillas into our hands. He was surveying the interior of the dining hall, and withdrawing instantly, I suppose was satisfied that he had 'bagged his game.' Of course I made no sign; but, saying to mine hostess that I heard the clatter of horses' hoofs and feared that some mishap had befallen my command, and that I would stand in the doorway and listen, I went out.

"It is needless to say that I walked rapidly. I actually leaped from the front door, and drawing and cocking an army repeater with my right hand, threw up the white handkerchief with my left. I reached the yard gate, twenty steps from the house, and was flying for life, when a bullet from that rascally negro's pistol whistled by my head. He was in advance of the squad sent by Clark, and guided by the good widow's son, to kill or make me a prisoner. The widow and daughter were to fascinate and detain and the daring, devilish black-amoor to assassinate or capture me.

"But the youthful Tennesseean, Tillman, had failed in nothing. I heard him, at the very instant the pistol was fired, exclaim, 'Charge them, boys!'

"To escape shots coming from both directions, I fell upon my face. When Tillman was dashing by, I rose up and said, 'Kill or catch the black traitor and spy who escaped from us to-day.'

"My assailants had left their horses a hundred yards away. Before they could recover them and get into their saddles, we had killed or wounded four, and captured the rest, of the guerrillas, except the twelfth man, the daring negro, who ran as fleetly as a grayhound. Tillman was riding my horse and resolved to execute my orders. Two men followed him closely. The negro made no effort to secure his own steed, but fled towards the nearest woods. Twice he turned and fired at Tillman, who was lying flat on his face, while my spirited animal rushed forward as if he comprehended his rider's purposes and shared his fearlessness. Luckily for Tillman, when he came up with the negro, his comrades were close at hand. Both fired at the fugitive and his right arm was broken. He came sullenly into my presence, and when I said that he deserved death and would be hanged as a spy, he looked vengefully in my face, and grinding his teeth together, said, 'And I'll die weeping because I didn't shoot you at the supper-table; but I was chicken-hearted, and didn't want to scare two women.'

"I never saw such a negro as this reckless dare-devil. His name was Charley Dicks. He had been liberated many years because of his fidelity to his master; and though the code of Tennessee prohibited the immigration of free negroes, the law was never enforced, and Charley was not only a citizen of Tennessee, but a slaveholder. He loved money, and therefore hated the Abolitionists. His slaves were his wealth. Thus he became a fierce secessionist. Prior to this, he had been employed by Bishop General Polk as a spy in Cairo. There he shaved General Grant in a Cairo barber-shop, and that night, crossing the Mississippi in a dug-out, he sent to the Bishop General, a full report of his interview with the kindly brigadier of that early period in the progress of inter-state hostilities.*

"But it is growing late, and my story, perhaps, tedious. I'll tell at another time how Charley escaped from us, and how we punished the bad faith of the bright, buxom widow and of her pretty daughter."

Then we bade one another good night.

---

*Charley still lives and still wields the razor in a prosperous southern city.

# CHAPTER XXVII.

The latest hours of the evening were made delightful by stories recited by Lieutenant Hughes, who said he reproduced them as originally given by Tennesseeans captured near Fort Pillow, above Memphis on the Mississippi, and brought to New Madrid while he was stationed there. These prisoners insisted that the Mississippi itself was waging war against the Confederacy. "It seems to concur in purpose with General Grant, who said, just after the battle of Belmont, in November, 1861, when exchanging wounded prisoners with the Confederate General McCown, on the old steamer *Ingomar*, that he had originally started out simply to open the Mississippi from Cairo to the sea. I heard him say this while he and McCown, at a table decorated with sundry glasses, revived memories of by-gone days, when they served under the same flag in the old army on western plains. They had been classmates at West Point, and were devoted personal friends. Grant insisted that the river was an indivisible unit, and that McCown, as a representative of the Confederacy, had no right to dam it up at Columbus or Cairo. 'It belongs,' said Grant, 'to the Northwest as wholly and thoroughly as to the Gulf States. You have been firing into our steamers at Vicksburg, and General Pillow, I am told, has absolutely stretched a great iron cable across the river at Memphis that free navigation of this stream, which your prophet, Calhoun, pronounced an inland sea, may be divided between the North and South. It is simply absurd,' continued Brigadier-General Grant, "and I am now on my way to New Orleans, and I will never stop till I get there. I used to be a Democrat, Mack, as you know. I didn't care or think much about parties or politics, but I was a Democrat. Let me tell you that I have changed my mind about it. I can't go with a party whose leading thinkers and theorists have undertaken to destroy the Union and dam up the Mississippi. That absurd Kansas squatter-sovereignty abstraction does not concern me. Party leaders used it down South to delude innocent country bumpkins and divide and destroy Democracy in the South that Lincoln might be elected and secession accomplished. It signifies nothing now that war is inaugurated, and I think you are wholly wrong. I am *en route* to New Orleans.''

"McCown was no talker, but devoted to Grant personally. I heard him say afterward that Grant's hard horse-sense was always unanswerable and always victorious.

" But I was telling you," continued the lieutenant, "that the Mississippi made war on the Confederacy. Every fortification on its banks erected by the rebels was speedily swept away. The navy-yard at Memphis, the heights at Randolph, at Fort Pillow, and at Columbus, and works at Island Ten have been removed by the resistless forces of the mighty drain of the continent. Within a very brief period there will be no vestige of an earthwork reared along the river to shut out northern commerce from the South. The Mississippi itself will not tolerate them. Like the Rio Grande, this great arm of the sea, is constantly moving bodily toward the Atlantic. It carves away the hills forever along its eastern shore. When De Soto died, three hundred and twenty-two years ago, as the newspaper man was telling us, the river ran along the base of lofty bluffs, just below Helena, in Arkansas. To-day the river touches no highlands on its western side from Cairo to the Gulf. Neither the unity of the river nor its ownership was designed by Nature to be disrupted. Pillow's mighty chain was broken again and again by the forces of the resistless current, and the Mississippi can no more be fettered by manacles or confined within prison-walls by levees than free people and states along its shores. When Xerxes attempted to close the Hellespont with cables of iron, these, his bridges, and ships were destroyed by the rebellious waters. The freedom of rivers and seas should never be violated. Yazoo Pass, making Vicksburg accessible from the east, was closed by a mighty earthen wall. Grant cut it and the Mississippi thrust out a great arm, bearing Grant and his gunboats and army even to the rear of Vicksburg.

"The Confederates devised a costly vessel, so ingeniously and strongly built that it was indestructible by shot and shell. It swept every Federal gunboat from the river, and was going confidently and victoriously to New Orleans to destroy the northern navy that had entered the Mississippi. There was never a more terrible engine of war than this ram, the *Arkansas*. At its sharp bow or prora there was a rostrum or beak of iron, like those of Roman and Carthaginian war-vessels, weighing forty thousand pounds. Its strength was such that the toughest, strongest ships were crushed by its blows. A long steel rod was projected over and beyond this. To its end was attached a shell to be fired by an electrical battery from within when in contact with an enemy's boat. The *Arkansas* was roofed with railroad iron. Over this was a layer of solidly-compressed cotton-bales, and over these another of heavy railroad iron, which could only be stricken by a ball impinging against it at an angle of forty-five degrees. The *Arkansas* was simply the masterpiece of gunboat builders. Commanded by the most skillful of seamen and bravest of officers, it reached Baton Rouge, after many frightful and destructive conflicts with ships and gunboats, unharmed. Victorious again and again, its officers confident of the extirpation of the fleet at New Orleans, it became the prey of the mighty river. Mud was injected, with the water on which it floated, into the machinery of its life. It became unmanageable and helpless, and was at last blown up by orders of its own commander, and when Vicksburg fell, Grant's way to the sea was unobstructed. But the strongest and stanchest vessel that ever floated on the Mississippi, or elsewhere in the world, my rebel friends insisted,'' continued the lieutenant, " was this dreadful ram, the *Arkansas*, built by John T. Shirley, at Memphis.

" I was told of a most ludicrous mishap which befell a learned and able lawyer of Memphis. This distinguished jurist bore the honored name, Bickerstaff. He was wonderfully tall and slender, and must have encountered Washington Irving at some period in his earlier years, or the matchless story-teller never could have drawn·with such precision and clearness, outlines of that ever-memorable picture of Ichabod Crane, which, never painted save in words, stands out before our eyes as sharply and distinctly defined as the strong, solemn face of Washington, or honest, earnest, ubiquitous physiognomy of U. S. Grant.

Bickerstaff, a most logical reasoner and perfect master of his profession, was singularly careful in his dress, as in the preparation of his speeches. He was an Indianian by birth, and by early training as a pedagogue. Of course he was an inflexible, but silent, Unionist. He was conscious of his physical peculiarities, and, though an attorney, and rich ·withal, was never known to speak to a woman. Still, he dressed himself with painstaking care, always obeying the injunction, ' Let thy dress be costly as thy purse can buy.' His nose was of extraordinary height and length and thinness, and like a dromedary of two humps. His face was thin, sallow, and long; his eyes bright, keen, and penetrating. His neck was of extraordinary longitude, and therefore he always wore a standing shirt-collar. Bickerstaff, six feet three and a half inches high, rarely rode on horseback. His long, slender legs did not present a seemly aspect, while his big feet dangled out into the stirrups from loose, baggy breeches legs. Therefore he went from Memphis, nine miles, to Raleigh, to attend county court in a vehicle drawn by a beautiful and valuable horse. Returning about noon, on the coldest day, perhaps, ever known this century in this latitude, the first of January last, he encountered a dozen rebel guerrillas. He was recognized, of course. No citizen of the country was more widely known or esteemed as a man and as a lawyer; but guerrillas are no respecters of persons. One of them walked deliberately around the buggy with an axe, breaking the spokes in the wheels until the body of the vehicle rested on the ground. The horse, of course, was appropriated by the highwaymen, and Bickerstaff's clothes were thoroughly searched. The horse was assigned by the captain of the thieves to one of his men, who bestrode a hideously ugly, long-haired, emaciated mule. The captain remarked, 'That mule, Mr. Bickerstaff, drew a dray twenty years in Memphis. We stole him at night, when we couldn't see. He will go back rapidly.' Bickerstaff was about to set off on the mule, congratulating himself that be had escaped so fortunately, when the little, short, round thief who now held Bickerstaff's horse, said that he 'must have the great lawyer's clothes. You won't have time to freeze in mine. That old mule has been trying to go towards Memphis all day. You'll travel when you start; but I must swap clothes with you. My coat and breeches are nearly worn out. Git down and shuck yourself; I can roll up your sleeves and trowsers and have a perfect fit.'

"The captain of the squad interposed. 'Dismount,' he said; ' you have only five miles to ride, and will go a-Gilpin, I think. Swap with that young man; I want to see how you two will look when you've exchanged drygoods.'

"The freebooters were half drunk. Bickerstaff hesitated; but the captain was relentless, and there on the dreary roadside, shivering in the cold wind, the dignified and learned lawyer thrust his long legs through the short, rusty breeches, and his interminable arms through the contracted sleeves of the round little rebel's ragged roundabout.

" 'Here's your mule, mount him and go,' said the captain of the squad to Bickerstaff. ' 'Go! I tell you. We wish to see you start. Oh! you are a beauty ! The fit of your clothes and your shape are charming. You will be sending out a cavalry force to recover your property as soon as you get into Memphis, and we must march; but I would first see how fascinating you are. If I'm caught, don't forget that you are my lawyer. They'll hang me if they can. Remember, Judge, that I've given you that mule and them pretty clothes as a retainer.'

"Bickerstaff, with most sorrowful visage, rode away. The robbers could not restrain themselves. Cold as they were, and miserable as was poor, shivering Bickerstaff, they laughed till his nose, blown like a weathercock to the right or left by the pitiless winds, and the jogging mule, whose bones rattled as he trotted away, were no longer visible. Bickerstaff felt badly. One yard of each leg was covered by socks and drawers only. There was a vacant space, overspread by white linen alone, of almost a yard, between the lower hem of the rusty, ragged roundabout and the upper rim or waistband of the greasy, copperas homespun breeches. That he might not freeze, Bickerstaff kicked vigorously and threw his arms violently about his head, and jogged along rapidly. He drew his fur cap tightly down to conceal his nose and face, and went, bent forward, kicking, and cursing his luck, into the city. The few wayfarers on the street stared at him in unutterable wonder. He only pulled down his cap and kicked the mule's ribs and bent forward till his shirt, no longer reaching his pants, fluttered in the icy breath of January 1, 1864. He entered Pinch, the densely populated Irish district. Ireland loves fun. Even the women turned out. Bar-rooms were emptied, and hot whiskey was forgotten. A great mob, from a quarter of the city which produces annually three thousand Democratic votes, and in which there was little sympathy with the woes of the Whig and Unionist, Bickerstaff, was soon gathered about the woe-begone mule and its luckless rider.

" 'Isn't he a beauty, Bridget?'

" 'Oh! the swate crayther; its the mon I mane, and not the dirthy baste.'

" 'An' the tailor that made thim coat and britches, wasn't he sparin' of the cloth? Me old mon is hard-up and it will give him a job.' And yells and shouts of laughter rent the air. The mob grew apace, and while the chagrined, maddened Bickerstaff kicked and cuffed the ancient, bony mule, the hooting, roaring throng accompanied him in grand triumphal procession to his office in the centre of the city. He escaped at last, his friends, in a body, moving to his relief, and bearing him in a swoon of horror and cold from the mule into his private apartments.

" 'Poor Bickerstaff,' said the prisoner who told me this story, 'never recovered from the effects of exposure, chagrin, and shame resulting from this pitiful adventure. He did not long survive it. A numberless, tearful procession of friends and admirers followed his elongated coffin to the grave. The endless throng, as it moved slowly and solemnly to the famed and beautiful cemetery of Elmwood, about which the newspaper man once wrote a book, talked of the kindly Bickerstaff in soft, low, pitying undertones. Genial smiles at first shed sunshine over the multitude; but as coincident facts were recalled and recited, the mirthfulness of the procession grew in force, It was the more violent because of the necessity for its repression. The very sadness and solemnity of the occasion gave force to ridiculous stories then reproduced, and the absurdest and jolliest procession that ever entered a graveyard, these Tennesseeans said, went roaring with laughter, when poor Bickerstaff was entombed, into Elmwood.' "

# CHAPTER XXVIII.

An Extraordinary Escape.—We Take Water.—A Voice in the Wilderness.—Was it a Spirit?—A True Man and Heroic Wife.

"You know," the captain said to Mrs. Hughes, while we were seated the next evening about her broad fire-place, "the farmer, Willingham, who lives perhaps five miles north of your upper plantation? I had information that induced Mr. Spratling and myself to call to see him at his modest home. He has a good face, and, after a brief interview, I said to Spratling that I was almost unwilling to arrest such a man charged with so heinous an offence. That he had deserted his colors, we knew to be a fact, but when I saw his bright, busy little wife spinning cotton threads inside the cabin door, while three pretty children rolled about in the yard, I could not help thinking that such a man, with such ties, and such duties imposed by God's laws, should not be put to death for desertion of a cause, which, even if defensible in law and morals, is rapidly and palpably becoming almost hopeless.

"But my duty was plain and its exactions inexorable. I ordered Willingham to leave his plow in the unfinished furrow and presenting handcuffs said that he must accompany us to the quarters of the Provost Marshal General. The poor fellow shrank back aghast. His face was of ashen hue. His limbs shook. He sank, at last, helplessly upon the ground. But his cowardice was redeemed by generous, unselfish devotion to his pretty, little, unsuspecting wife who had told us where to find him. His first low, half-sobbed exclamation was:

"'And what will become of my helpless wife and children? And then that I should bring down upon them this inexpressible sorrow and disgrace!'

"I confess I was almost unmanned by the anguish of the hapless wretch, and it occurred to me to devise a pretext for his possible

escape.    I had forty dollars in gold, given me by General B. J. Hill,
the Provost Marshal General, that I might obtain articles, greatly
needed, from Federal stores in Cleveland.    I said to Willingham that
he had taken the 'iron-clad oath,' and that his loyalty to the 'old
flag' was not questioned, and that if he would go to Cleveland that
night and the next day, and meet me at the great oak that had fallen
across the main road at the mill on Coahuila Creek, bringing with
him the articles wanted by General Hill, that he, Willingham, should
be liberated and unharmed by the Confederate authorities.

"Willingham assented, received the forty dollars, and Spratling and
I, as you remember, returned to this place.    I never doubted Willingham's integrity of purpose.    But *l'homme propose, et Dieu dispose.*    Two
cunning bushwhackers had traced Spratling and myself to Willingham's house and witnessed, at a safe distance, our interview with him.
We were hardly out of sight, as we learned only yesterday evening
from the wife, when these two men, by threatening to declare at the
nearest Federal outpost that Willingham had been seen in close con-
sultation with two most murderous and daring Confederate scouts,
compelled the frightened Willingham to divulge all that had been
said and agreed upon.    The bushwhackers at once forced Willingham
to accompany them.    He was only given time to enter his house,
change his apparel and make his little wife cognizant of his agreement
with us.    He instructed her, in case he did not return in time, to
meet us at the fallen oak, and warn us of possible danger and tell of
his own capture and helplessness.    Of course we knew nothing of all
this till yesterday evening.

"When the day came for the meeting with Willingham, as you
remember, Spratling and I left here about three o'clock.    There was
ample time in which to reach, at sunset, the place of rendezvous.
We trudged along leisurely enough, and were passing through a dense
wood two miles or more from the great fallen tree beside the field at
which we were to meet Willingham.

"I am not superstitious.    I never encountered a ghost, though I
once thought differently, when, as I was telling some time ago, the
unhappy woman rose up out of the newly-made grave at the little
church not far from Mrs. Shields'.    But as Spratling and I moved
along quietly towards the rendezvous, two miles distant, I heard, with
perfect distinctness, a clear, soft voice, telling me, 'Don't go, oh !
don't go !'    I stopped and asked Spratling, 'Didn't you hear that
woman's voice?    It reminds me of the low, sweet, childish tones in
which Willingham's little wife told us where to find her husband.'
But Spratling heard nothing.    My senses were wonderfully acute.
Some inscrutable inspiration was telling me, at every step, that we
should not go further.    A somber melancholy was shed over the dense
woods by the sun's pale rays, hardly penetrating mists of the wintry
afternoon, and diffused like gold dust over the yellow leaves of the
lowly-moaning trees.

"Again I heard the soft, low wailing of a woman's voice, clear and distinct, but seemingly a long, long way off.    It only repeated the words, 'Don't go, oh! don't go!'

"I could not shake off the effect of the unaccountable supplication. I repeated it again and again to Spratling, insisting that I heard in the remote distance the wail of sorrow of poor Willingham's wife. She was surely begging us not to meet her husband at the fallen oak. 'Of course,' I said musingly, 'it is impossible; but the words do come with perfect distinctness, and I was not dreaming, when I first heard them, of the woman or of any probable danger.'

"When the mysterious warning was again repeated, I said to Spratling, 'I wish to go back; let us respect this strange invocation.   I'll tell you that the spirit of the good little woman who asked us to eat at her table, and brought us so cheerily that great gourd full of refreshing spring-water, and directed us so smilingly to her husband in the field—I'll tell you that she or her wraith is somewhere in these woods to save us from some great peril.'

"Spratling answered me that if I had not talked about ghosts and strange voices in the air, he might have been persuaded to turn back; but to be cowards, and cowards for such a reason, because we thought we heard a woman crying, who was certainly five or six miles away, was a proposition too ridiculous to be entertained.   'We would be laughed out of the army about it.'

"I could only assent; and yet faintly, more faintly, dying away at last among the gentle sounds made by the pale leaves, that rattled softly when the trees were swayed by the cold breath of the silent afternoon, did I hear the woman's clear, low, distinct words, 'Don't go, oh! don't go!'

"We were now within a few hundred yards, as we thought, of the rendezvous, and, of course, moving very slowly and watchfully.   The sun's slanting rays only touched the treetops, and the shadows of a misty February evening were gathering slowly about us.   We were not sure of our precise distance from the fallen oak, where Willingham was to meet us, or deposit the articles bought for us in Cleveland. My senses were wrought up to the highest tension, and again did I tell Spratling, in a low whisper, 'Listen; don't you hear the tender, earnest wailing of that little woman?   It is far away, but seems borne along the ground and clasps my feet.'   I stood still, and a cold tremor ran over me.   My senses were never so acute.   'Stop,' I said; 'see there!'   And yet Spratling saw nothing and heard nothing.   But I did; I saw the pale light of that cold, silent afternoon flash from a gilded button in the dense thicket, a hundred yards away on our right.   At the same instant, as I believed, I beheld the sudden movement of a woman's ghostly apparel in the same dense woods.   I grasped Spratling's arm, and both stood still, while I whispered of what I heard and saw.

"We crossed an open space, and were, perhaps, a quarter of a mile from a fence on our left, enclosing a long, narrow field beyond it, two hundred yards wide.   Far away on our right was the dense thicket.

" 'Look,' I whispered to Spratling, 'don't you see men lying on their faces along the verge of the thicket?'

" He answered, 'I see nothing; you have surely gone mad.'

" Just then a dismounted cavalryman rose up. In sonorous accents he ordered us to 'Halt, there!' Twenty figures sprang from the weeds and grass and low bushes along the road, and mounted men were visible ahead of us. Time for reflection was brief, and questions of policy few. If we surrendered, we would be shot or hanged on the spot. If we fled, by bare possibility, we might escape. Of course, flight was instantaneous. We did not run directly from our pursuers, but diagonally across the open space towards the field. Men using rifles or pistols know how certainly they kill a bird flying directly from them, and how certainly they fail when the bird flies diagonally across the line of the shot. Spratling and I ran so that our backs were not exposed to the shots of pursuers. A bullet passed through my cap, and left its hot breath on the crown of my head. Spratling's baggy breeches were pierced, a bullet leaving its mark on his knee-cap. We heard bullets sing merrily while we ran furiously towards the fence. We climbed or leaped it. It was no obstruction in this maddening race. We had crossed half the width of the field when a bullet, piercing the dense folds of my blanket, which was rolled and wrapped over one shoulder and under the other, cut the string confining its ends. It fell and I left it. We were still unharmed and nearing the woods, when, through the growing shadows of the evening, we saw that mounted men had passed round the little field to intercept us. Our struggles were now superhuman. We had outstripped those on foot and knew, at a glance, that if the horsemen met no obstruction, we could hardly precede them in entering the woods. Spratling and I kept far enough apart to prevent the death of both by one bullet. There is as much skill, courage, and coolness illustrated in flight as in attack.

" A little creek ran across the field into a larger stream, the Coahuila. The cavalrymen, seeking to intercept us, were retarded by this obstruction. They fired at us, but, their horses at full speed, of course, harmlessly. We crossed the fence and entered the dense woods, in the verge of which ran the larger stream.

"'What was our horror, reaching the creek, to find the further shore a precipitous height, which we could not ascend. The cavalrymen were hard by. Entangled among vines and dense undergrowth, they swore vigorously. We heard the shouts of our other pursuers at the fence we had last surmounted.

" 'Caught at last,' I said in a low tone to Spratling, as we stood in the dim twilight and dense shade of the forest on the banks of the mountain torrent. A tree had fallen into the creek, lying low along the water's surface, and partly submerged.

" 'There is no help for it,' I whispered, 'we must enter the water and get beneath that tree.' After such a race, the water seemed of icy coldness. The tree's body was slightly curved, and upheld along its length by its great branches. There was a space, at one point, of four or five inches between it and the water's surface. We immersed ourselves, and stood half erect in the stream beneath the fallen tree. The cavalrymen rode up and down the creek, seeking in vain for a crossing-place. They uttered horrible imprecations. They had recognized my *fidus Achates*, Spratling, and supposed at last that he had climbed the precipice, carrying me upon his back.

"When men on foot reached the spot, two crossed the creek on the log beneath which we shivered in unutterable iciness. Men never suffered more in moments that seemed an age of anguish. But when these weary soldiers went back and forth above our heads, we were resting securely veiled beneath the first deep shadows of nightfall. The last soldier who stood above, and within two feet of my head, muttered maledictions, leveled at Spratling and myself.

"Motionless awhile, and looking up and down the precipice, evidently wondering how we climbed it, he pronounced a few homely oaths, significant of disappointment, and went slowly away. How slowly, none can imagine save Spratling and I, almost dying in this intolerably cold bath.

"Never doubting that we had crossed the creek, and were far beyond it, the Yankee captain of the squad soon gathered his men in the field. They were weary and hungry, and when we, half dead and shivering, reached the enclosure, we heard the order, 'Fall in, men;' and then, finding that none were missing, came the words, to us most grateful, 'Forward, march!' We entered the field and found my dry blanket on the yellow grass. We cut it in two and substituted it about our freezing bodies for wet clothing. Then we set out for this place.

"But the memory of those strange words, 'Don't go, oh! don't go!' made me hesitate. I reminded Spratling of what I had surely heard. 'No impression made by events of to-day will last as long,' I said, 'as that wrought by the mysterious, womanly voice to which I listened late this afternoon. I cannot leave this place till satisfied that Willingham's little wife is not here.'

" 'How absurd,' insisted Spratling, 'that you should have heard her, when we have never been within half a mile of the fallen oak, where we were to have seen her husband. She surely did not accompany him; on the contrary, he betrayed us, and neither he nor his wife are here.'

" 'I can't help it,' I answered; 'you may leave me, if you like, but, suffering as I am, I must go to the fallen oak.'

"We turned towards it. It lay at the end of the field near the creek, and more than half a mile from the point at which the pursuit and flight had been begun.

"At the root of the tree, sure enough, on the cold ground, lay the brave little woman. She was moaning in her seemingly broken sleep. We could catch no words. The side of her face was swollen and black. We read at a glance, even by the light of the stars, what had befallen her. I was never so enraged, but was silenced by Spratling's imprecations. Cold as we had been, we had not exhausted a capacious flask of brandy which always accompanied us. I raised the almost lifeless body very tenderly while Spratling, from the little cup that covered the stopple, administered the brandy. A tremor ran over her frame; and at last she opened her eyes, and looking up into our faces, closed them, evidently to shut out visions of a supposed dream. She drank again, and then asked who we were and 'Where am I?' and 'How did I get here?' We slowly reassured her. At length she stood up, and then she began to recall and recount the events of the terrible day.

"As we bore her in a hammock made of Spratling's blanket, I holding one and he the other end, to her home, she recited the story of her adventures. Her husband was imprisoned at Cleveland, and she came to the fallen oak to warn us of danger. She had brought the forty dollars in gold to return it to us, and even then had it concealed on her person. She went near the fallen oak, and finding soldiers already there, wandered about the woods, in growing anxiety and alarm, as night was coming on, till she was insane with terror. She said, 'I remember begging you not to go to the fallen oak, and that while I was saying, "Don't go! oh, don't go!"' I was silenced by a great, rude soldier who came suddenly out of the bushes and knocked me down. He thought he had killed me; for I saw him no more, and only remember saying in the dreams that afterward came, "Don't go! oh, don't go!" I thought I was talking to you two soldiers who had been good to my poor husband.' "

The fire was burning low when Spratling said :

" We bore the little woman safely to her cabin and made her retain the gold fairly lost by the Provost Marshal-General, as he will confess when we tell him of our adventures of yesterday."

" Meanwhile," interposed the captain, " I would gladly have Mrs. Hughes and Mrs. Starnes, or the philosophic Mr. Wade and the newspaper man, tell me how I heard, through the woods and in the air and creeping along the earth, the strangely muttered words and prayers of the earnest, brave little woman when she warned me, 'Don't go! oh, don't go!' She was probably two miles from us when I first caught the sounds, and most distinctly, 'Don't go! oh, don't go!' We found her cold and senseless, more than half a mile from the path we trod. Does that odic and phrenic force through which one brain is said to communicate with another, like two distant telegraphic stations, also reach the external senses? I know I heard the very words and listened to the low, sweet voice of the brave little women when she was two miles distant, and I know that Spratling thinks that God is in it."

The fire had burned very low and ashes covered the living coals and dead fagots had fallen over the andirons when we bade one another good night.

13

# CHAPTER XXIX.

The Hughes Farmhouse assailed by Federal Soldiers.—Heroism of Bessie Starnes.—Conclusion.

> In memory's garden long I sought
> To cull the fairest flowers of thought,
> A worthier tribute to have brought;
> But these winged flowers, by zephyrs blown,
> Soared upward to the great white throne,
> For there the " Unknown" all are known.
> *Emily Thornton Charles.*

The sun was rising when the faithful, watchful negro, Jack, made watchful because he discovered that either Spratling, the Captain, or the Mississippi cavalryman was pacing back and forth in the front yard through the night, was heard at the door:

"Mistiss! mistiss! De Yanks is cummin! Deas a eben duzzen. Dis nigga counted 'em dis time."

There was wildest confusion in the residence and among the negroes. The Captain, Spratling, and the Mississippian, trained soldiers, and accustomed to war's alarms and surprises, were cooly intent on preparations for defence.

" See," said the Captain to Spratling, "that the schoolmaster and Lieutenant Hughes remain in their room. They cannot share in this fight. We need only knock three or four of those gay fellows out of their saddles and the rest will run away. They are not crazy to fight, and only want plate, gold, jewels, and pictures. Four of us can make it impossible for them to come near enough to apply a torch and burn us out; that is the only danger."

A gaily dressed subordinate officer was in command of the assailants. Spratling, watching from a window the approach of the enemy, said :

"I don't like the signs out there ; I never saw a vain fellow, tricked out in gold lace and feathers as gaudily as that young ape, who would not fight desperately. Vanity stimulates and makes his courage drunken. That fellow will give us trouble."

Doors were barred and bolted, and windows closed in apartments below, occupied by Mrs. Hughes and other inmates of the household, and everything was ready for action.

"Didn't you hear the Captain order my brother and Mr. Wade to remain in their room ? It is just over ours," said Mamie. "Let us join them ; I would die here of mortal anxiety, seeing nothing, and hearing firearms and quick, sharp words of command, and not knowing who has fallen."

"Of course," answered Bessie ; "we will disobey orders. I am skillful as yourself in the use of a pistol. Mr. Spratling gave me a beautiful weapon and taught me how to use it. The good schoolmaster told us how you learned to handle guns and pistols in East Tennessee."

Spratling was looking from the window in the front room when the two girls, unseen, entered the apartment at the head of the stairway, occupied by Mr. Wade and Lieutenant Hughes. The mothers of the girls followed, more frightened than Mamie, and infinitely more than fearless Bessie Starnes, whose constant contact with soldiers, through months, and even years; whose modes of life, such as are led by the people in the wild country about Chattanooga, and whose habits of thinking, induced by stories told by Spratling, and countless men who frequented the country in which she lived, had inculcated lessons not without value at a time like this. Bessie knew little of books, but everything of country life, and everything of which soldiers talked.

She told the lieutenant to assume his uniform. "You can't fight, and if we are whipped, you can save us. But there is no use in our being whipped. Mother and I have kept drunken soldiers out of our house when they threatened to plunder and destroy it. To be shot from behind a brick wall like this, and by a woman, at that, isn't comfortable. These wandering Yankee soldiers may be the bravest of the brave ; but there is no need to show heroism here, where nobody sees it, and where nobody will know of it if they run. They only want Mrs. Hughes' silver and jewels. These Mr. Spratling has concealed, and he will fight for their safety with ten-fold the pluck of men who only wish to rob him. Our danger," added Bessie, who sought to reassure Mrs. Hughes, "would be much greater if these soldiers coming up the avenue knew that two pretty girls were looking at them. They wont fight after they have learned that it is Spratling and the captain they have hemmed in. All these scouts have heard of Spratling ; but they don't know him as well as I do. They never saw but one side of him. There isn't a Yankee scout in the Yankee service who hasn't heard how Spratling killed the bushwhacker by stamping him into the earth at our house, and not one who hasn't heard how he held a powerful horse, struggling to go forward, still as death in the road with one hand, grasping the hindmost axle of the wagon, while he, protected by the wagon-body, fired and killed two out of three assailants. They all know how terrible he is; but they don't know how good, and gentle, and truthful, or what a big heart he has."

Bessie had forgotten herself, or had only become her real self, and talked freely, when excitement and dangers of the moment rendered others silent and incapable. She glanced at the lieutenant, and expressions of admiration for Spratling's conduct and character were instantly silenced. The listening lieutenant's face was flushed, and when his eyes met Bessie's they were suddenly averted. She was not sure that he suspected her fidelity to himself or her devotion to Spratling, then almost confessed. She imagined at the moment that he did doubt her honesty, and that questioning glance, never forgotten, was reproduced before Bessie's eyes whenever the face and form of her affianced lover, in after years, rose up from the dreamland of memory.

The Yankee marauders approached the residence very warily. A negro had informed them that Spratling was shot through the shoulder and that the four Confederates held two prisoners in the building. Spratling's supposed helplessness, and the fact that there were, as they understood the facts, only three fighting men within, and that one of these was required to watch the two prisoners of war, induced the marauders to make the assault. The Captain and newspaper man occupied a window each in the room on the right, and Spratling and the cavalryman on the left, of the building. The assailants advanced slowly. five of them going, when within one hundred yards of the house, on the right of it, and five to the left. They seemed to think that the inmates would seek safety in flight.

"Oh, the rascals!" said Spratling. "What fools and cowards they think us? Why suspect us of the purpose to run? What's to be made by it? It is time enough to run when we can no longer fight, and when we run we must fight at last, and then, unguarded by these strong walls; and then, after fighting, I think there will be fewer to pursue us, and of these a few will be lame. Of course we will fight."

The Captain need not have said it, but he ordered us to take good aim. "Make ready," he said at length, as if we were duelists; and then came the word, "Fire!"

The enemy were within sixty yards. Three saddles were emptied, and the leader's horse fell, the rider seemingly unharmed. He was a gallant little fellow. His gorgeous gold lace glittered when he rose up and called to his men, "Follow me!" He ran to the porch, one story in height, and was secure beneath its roof. His men followed at full speed. How they escaped, we could not tell; but only one was unhorsed by our bullets, though others were wounded. Horses were turned loose. The door was broken from its fastenings, and the hallway below occupied by men who evidently knew how and intended to fight.

Lieutenant Hughes and the schoolmaster, confined in an apartment with women, were most restive. Accustomed to danger, and wholly fearless, they were most impatient of this restraint. Their sympathies, of course, were with the defenders of the residence. As Davy Crockett, shut up in the Alamo, when accustomed to fight beneath the open sky and in the open woods, begged to be led into the open plain to encounter the overwhelming force of Mexicans, so the schoolmaster and youthful Union soldier were impelled to violate orders. When the great door gave way in the hall below, and the marauding assailants rushed in, the lieutenant could not restrain himself. He and Mr. Wade, armed with pistols, rushed to the head of the stairs. The lieutenant leaned over the railing, and looking down, was instantly shot. The bullet pierced his body. He was borne bleeding into the apartment he had just left.

"Perhaps he is dying," whispered the schoolmaster to Bessie. "I must avenge this. See the anguish and dismay written in the eyes and pale faces of the mother and sister? I am a rebel now."

He placed the dying youth upon the bed, the mother and sister and Bessie looking on, horror-struck and helpless.

All of us, with Mr. Wade, leaving the lieutenant to the care of the women, were now at the head of the stairs. Spratling came last. He held uplifted, forgetful of his wound, a long, heavy marble slab, taken from a bureau.

"Stand back!" he exclaimed; "this will protect me and destroy them. Stand back! I will crush them. Let them start up the stairway!"

The gallant little Yankee popinjay was heard to say, "We have killed one of them; I hear women's wailing. There are only two fighting men left. There are six of us almost unharmed. We must kill or capture that wounded giant, Spratling, and his cunning captain.

"Follow, boys!" he exclaimed.

They started up the broad stairway. Spratling stood still. They were on the staircase, when he suddenly leaned forward, pitching the ponderous stone edgewise and endwise, with tremendous force, down the stairs. Bullets came up from pistols below, only to strike the lower surface of the descending stone. The leader and three others of the assailants fell beneath the shock and weight of the marble slab. The rest withdrew to the front door. While they looked after their captain, with his broken skull, and others killed and wounded, we learned from Bessie, whose courage never faltered, that the lieutenant, she thought, must die.

"He is bleeding internally," said Bessie. "He told me so, and bade his mother and sister stand aside, that he might tell me this and other facts he did not wish them to hear. I will tell you some day," said Bessie to the schoolmaster, "but not now;" and she turned towards Spratling, whose arm was bleeding afresh. She ran to his side, and looking up sadly but lovingly into his face, made him sit down, while she bound a handkerchief tightly about his shoulder.

The Captain's fitness for his position consisted not more in his courage, endurance and cunning, than in rapidity of thought and action. He went to the window and called for the man in charge of the Union scouts.

"See here," said he, "this place and this house which you propose to set on fire, in order to expel us, is the home and property of a Union officer. He is here our prisoner. Accidentally you have shot him. He will die if you do not have a surgeon sent to his relief. It may go hard with you. Ask the negroes there in that cabin; they will tell that all I say of Lieutenant Hughes, of Colonel Cliff's regiment, is true. There are four of us rebels. We will never be taken alive, as you have reason to know; but these people have been kind to us, and served one of our number who was wounded some time ago. We have no business here and no desire to remain. Your Captain, who is not dead, as well as Lieutenant Hughes, needs a surgeon. If you will agree that this family shall be protected as it must be when you know that Lieutenant Hughes is its head, we four rebels will leave. Go out of the house. We will not fire upon you, but propose to leave in twenty minutes. If you consent to these terms, start one of your men at once for a surgeon. Send the negro, Jack, for the country doctor whose office is three miles distant."

"All right," a voice from below soon responded, and the Federal scouts went out. We counted them from the window. Four seemed unharmed. Two others were bleeding, and another had a broken arm. The rest of the twelve were dead or helpless.

"It's a pretty good day's work," said Spratling. "I would be well pleased if it wasn't for the poor lieutenant lying there, his young life going away so slowly but so surely that while he suffers not at all, he feels the blood, he says, gradually filling his body. The mother and sister are dazed by the shock. The only one of us who, as we thought, could incur no danger and was perfectly safe, has fallen, and—poor Bessie! poor Bessie!" And then Spratling drew his hand across his eyes, and after a moody silence, added very slowly, "What is to become of Bessie?"

His eyes were fixed on vacuity.

The Captain went to the Lieutenant's bedside. Neither uttered a word.

"I never saw the Captain," said Spratling, telling the story in after years, "so cast down. Mamie was at the foot of the bed, gazing into the pale face of her dying brother. The mother and Mrs. Starnes knelt side by side. Unconsciously I had taken Bessie's hand and was drawn to the Captain by a force of sympathy I could not resist.

"While tears, the first I ever saw the Captain shed, streamed down his face—it was Mamie's presence and grief that unmanned him—he took the cold hand of the lieutenant and kissed it. He turned and was going away, when Mamie ran to him saying, 'You must not go. We cannot spare you.'

"'Yes,' he answered; 'if I and my men do not leave, re-enforcements will come to these intruders below, and the house will be burned and there will be no help for your brother. The surgeon will come. I have sent for him. I will return. In the presence of your dying brother,' he whispered, 'I pledge you deathless fidelity.'

"He drew her outside the doorway, and while tears streamed down their faces, kissed her."

We bade adieu to the good and brave schoolmaster, instructing him to communicate with us through General Cleburne. Spratling said good-bye to Bessie, telling her that he was her guardian; that he would meet her in Lexington; and that the schoolmaster would bring him her letters, telling her how to address him. She followed Spratling to the door leading into the yard and kissed him as confidingly and affectionately as if he had been her father. He was thrilled by it. Her face was flushed when she detected it and turned away, with tearful eyes, to re-enter the chamber of death.

Of the fortunes of the Captain and of Mamie Hughes, who is rearing a family in Arkansas, her home in Georgia having been destroyed and property swept away, the writer of these pages may tell hereafter.

Spratling's love of adventure grew inversely with his devotion to pretty, blithesome, winning Bessie Starnes. He prized Bessie's life so extravagantly that he began to set a higher value upon his own. He was surrendered with the wreck of General Joe Johnston's army in North Carolina; and when last heard from, was reciting, beside the hearthstone of his modest ranch in Callahan County, Texas, the very stories here recorded. Bessie, the heroine, save when a baby cries, is the intentest listener.

THE END.

# ERRATA.

On page 49 the word "Chickamauga" should be substituted for "Chattanooga," and on page 181 a paragraph from "Fern Leaves" should be quoted.

www.ingramcontent.com/pod-product-compliance
Lightning Source LLC
Chambersburg PA
CBHW030545040726
47497CB00008B/2591